The Song of Sangr

By: Gustavo Bondoni

Three Ravens Publishing

Chickamauga, Ga USA

Credits:

The Song of Sangr was written by Gustavo Bondoni

Cover art by J.F. Posthumus

The Song of Sangr by: Gustavo Bondoni /Three Ravens Publishing – 1st edition, 2022

Trade Paperback ISBN: 978-1-951768-49-2

Dedication

To Val and Fede, the world's greatest beta readers, who've invested their own time to read and comment on (and thereby improve) this and so many other stories.

Northern Sea
Northern Wastes
FIRE MOUNTAIN
Banshee Plateau
LABYRINTH CITY
SANGRIS' VILLAGE
The Ju
The Plains
SUMMERLAND
KRENN
PSLL'S BANE MOUNTAINS
Endless Sea
JUNGLE KINGDOM
Sea of Tears
Southern Jungle
Southern Sea
Connie Santilli

Iced

Night was the time of death. No predators, human or otherwise, were responsible for this as any who braved the night would soon be as dead as their intended victims. The air itself, the biting cold strong enough to freeze a large bucket of water in minutes, would make certain of it. Shocks of pain radiated outward from the few patches of skin exposed to the night, around his eyes.

While it was never wise to be caught outside one's own dwelling at night, Sangr knew that, in this particular case, no harm would come of it. Lunk's forge was warm, despite having been banked for the night. The chamber was carved into a stony outcrop, since the ice would not have lasted long under its heat, had it had been built there. Lunk was one of the few people in the village who could work all night – the heat from his forge acting as a comfortable counterpoint to the killing wind. Sangr often joined him—the warm forge was a good place to hone his skills with the village's only sword—an ancient rapier that had washed up with a shipwreck.

The Song of Sangr

Sangr knew that Lunk would never allow him to wander drunkenly away, so he could safely down as many flagons of seaweed ale as he liked.

What the blacksmith lacked in sharpness of wit, he more than made up for with sensible level-headedness, and what he lacked in agility he made up for in sheer muscular bulk. Sangr had seen him consume prodigious amounts of drink and not even get tipsy. Tonight's taste of ale wouldn't affect him at all.

Sangr, on the other hand, was at that mellow point where all dreams become possible. "I tell you, old friend, there must be something more, something beyond our tiny village. Somewhere a man can do something more with his life than just survive it for their allotted years."

"Of course, there is, Sangr. You know there are other villages," Lunk said, re-sealing the cask and putting it away with a solid thunk, his expression making it clear that Sangr wasn't going to get any more. "You've been to Roskent to the north, and just last year I bought an anvil in Trenge."

"Bah," Sangr spat, "fishing villages just like ours! What can I do there? Get a wife?"

Lunk thought this over. "I hear that there are four unmarried girls in Trenge. One of us is going to have to go outside the village for a woman. Why not you?

You're the smartest person in the village. You could talk the best of the women into your arms even if you needed to. But you won't, because that hairy trader, Wigger, probably told everyone how you caught the boy who stole his pendant."

Impatience flashed briefly in Sangr's eyes, but a lifetime spent growing up alongside this man allowed him to control it, despite his slightly inebriated condition. Getting angry at Lunk never changed anything, and if he got angry at you, it could get painful.

"I mean something more important. We know there are people living to the West, across the Stormbound Sea." The wreckage of large, strangely painted ships occasionally found its way to the place where the eternal glacier flowed into the sea. Sometimes the bodies of sailors who'd died of the cold before drowning were brought up in the fishing nets. "The people of the west must have cities. And I've heard that there is also a great city carved into the ice to the east. A city of four thousand souls, built with the ancient magic of the ice mages!"

"And you'll cross the Banshee Plateau to get there, I suppose," Lunk made the warding gesture against magic and then laughed a deep rolling sound that echoed off the stone walls. He looked at Sangr fondly and his expression changed. "Well, I suppose there's no penalty for dreaming."

Lunk would not tell him anything until he had it completely worked out in his mind, no amount of cajoling would convince him otherwise, and Sangr was not in any state to try subtle verbal maneuvering.

He simply wrapped himself in his sealskin cloak and drifted off, wondering about his friend's big secret and dreaming about a crystal city carved deep into a mountainside glacier.

A bright, uncomfortable light, reflected on the endless snowfields and entered through the uncovered doorway, which forced Sangr to turn around, but it was no use. The combination of the light and the infernal clang of metal on metal as Lunk created some masterpiece or another in his forge eventually convinced him to sit up and open his eyes, which he soon put to good use, glaring at the blacksmith.

"My head," he said.

Lunk just laughed at him. "Can't hold your ale, can you? Drink your tea and stop whining."

The tea was made of seaweed too, but of a darker kind, with a more medicinal taste. It was about as awful as could be expected but soothing. By the time he'd drunk half his cup, Sangr was feeling human again. He was even charitable enough to recognize that the day had dawned beautifully; not a cloud marred the sky, and the sun made the temperature seem almost above freezing. No wind broke the reigning stillness.

Off in the distance, a shout broke through the night, right between two of Lunk's strikes bringing Sangr to his feet.

"Lunk," he began, but his friend had also heard it and was standing beside him looking out onto the ice.

The shout came again, allowing both men to identify the source: it came from the docks.

They moved instantly. A problem with the boats was never a good sign. They were the lifeblood of the village, but, at the same time, they were a constant source of dread. Any man who fell into the water was almost certainly lost to the icy fingers of the water spirits or the even colder wind on the surface after he was pulled out. This was not a calm, peaceful sea.

They slid recklessly down the path to the docks, a thin staircase carved into the glacier towards the waterfront. The steps were regularly covered in sand, but treacherous all the same. Sangr, rapier-thin and athletic, reached the docks well before his corpulent friend and froze at the sight that met him as he rounded the corner in the trench dug out of the ice.

Ahead of them, on the open stretch of ocean warmed by the strong current from the south, all four of the village's fishing boats were present, sails furled and tied to their moorings – simple iron rings embedded into the ice near the staircase. The crews stood on the decks, obviously unsure what to do next. They greeted Lunk and Sangr's arrival with shouts and pointing.

There was no need to point, however. Sangr immediately saw what they were excited about: among them, and towering over them, floated an unfamiliar vessel, a ship similar to those whose wreckage sometimes washed up on their shores.

The foreign ship had once had two masts, but the mainmast, with a trunk twice as wide as Sangr's torso, had broken off about ten feet above the deck. The paint on the hull was peeled, faded, and in some areas, charred by some long-extinguished fire. To Sangr's eye, the vessel was afloat only by the slimmest of margins.

A group of eight strangers huddled on the deck, mainly women and older children, the oldest was maybe fourteen years of age. A single grown man, short and thin with long blond hair and a bushy beard, stood before the group with sword drawn, eyeing the fishermen with distrust.

Sangr immediately grasped the nature of the situation. The fishing boats had evidently run into this wreck drifting out at sea and towed it in. Even if the wreck had been empty, the wood alone was an incalculable treasure for the village, representing a year's supply at the usual, frugal rate of consumption. The people had probably been waiting in ambush below decks in case they were boarded. They'd been smart enough to realize that it might be their best chance of ever seeing land again, so they'd hidden and waited.

Now that they were safely back on dry land, however, they saw no choice but to come up and find out what was happening. The shouting Sangr and Lunk had heard had been produced by the fishermen realizing that they weren't alone and calling for backup.

"Hello," Sangr called out to the stranger.

The blond man turned to look at him. So did the fishermen, who, concentrating on their unexpected guests, hadn't seen him coming. They looked relieved that someone was taking the matter out of their hands. Despite Sangr's youth, the whole village respected his practical and sometimes ruthless intelligence.

The man on the ship said nothing.

"My name is Sangr. Welcome to Nev." It occurred to him that these people might not speak the same language, but there was nothing he could do about that if it were indeed the case. He kept talking. "We mean you no harm. Come, don't be afraid."

Still, the man said nothing. Sangr had, by that time, reached the fishing boat nearest the stranger's ship. With Lunk's help, he picked up a boarding plank and placed it on the edge of the larger ship, making a bridge between the two. Sangr walked calmly up the incline.

The blond man met him at the side, curved sword at the ready, his expression wary.

Sangr stopped about an arm's length from the man and held out his hand, palm upwards, in a gesture as unthreatening as possible.

"My name is Sangr," he repeated.

The man's eyes flashed for an instant, causing Sangr to think that he would strike, but he seemed to make a decision. With his free hand, he quickly grasped Sangr's arm.

"I am called Shtarel," he said.

He pulled Sangr aboard.

That night, the whole village came together in the Roundhouse to celebrate the coming of the strangers. Sangr and Lunk were pretty tired by the time the festivities got underway: they'd spent the afternoon lugging water from their warm cave where fires burned eternally to melt snow to the Roundhouse itself.

After Chief Emnius finished introducing their visitors, the evening was enlivened by the exotic food from the ship, strange salted meats, and spiced wines, along with a roasted seal that one of the fishing boats had trapped. All told, between villagers and newcomers, forty people were present.

Sangr was seated with Lunk on his left and the other man of marrying age, Breed, on his right. Breed was the apprentice Ale-Maker, a soft job that involved little or no work in Sangr's opinion. But that might have been influenced by his dislike for the man who, with his shoulder-length, dark, greasy hair and darting eyes, seemed to have some of the rat in him.

They were celebrating the fact that the strangers had agreed to settle in the village. Their ship would be salvaged for its wood and the supplies distributed among all the villagers. While celebrating the disaster suffered by others might seem heartless in the extreme, there was little room for sentimentality on the ice. At least the people who'd lost their ship had survived the ordeal. Most didn't.

The seal course was complete when Shtarel rose to speak. He was immediately rewarded with silence as thunderous as the previous merrymaking had been. Even Sangr, who had already heard the man's tale, gave him his undivided attention. This was the most interesting event to happen in his lifetime, and the first time that a surprise turned out to be a good thing.

"People of Nev," Shtarel began in his deep voice. His speech was slightly accented, with rolled r's, but easily understood. "I would like to begin by thanking the brave men of the fishing fleet for saving our lives. We had been drifting for weeks on the northbound current, headed for certain death in the icy wastelands. We wouldn't have survived many more nights. Quite a few of us didn't survive the nights that came before." He raised his cup towards the fishermen, and everyone cheered, raising their own flagons in salute.

Shtarel began to tell of their voyage. They had once been part of a noble house in a kingdom far to the southwest, across the vast expanse of the Stormbound Sea. Treachery had forced them to retreat from the enraged Duke's army. Shtarel's father and brothers had been killed in battle outside their last bastion, the tiny walled seaside town of Mulsanne. And, finally, they bid a painful goodbye to their nation, boarding the ship with his surviving sisters and a few loyal retainers, most untrained in the skills of seamanship.

Sangr allowed his mind to wander. He entertained himself by observing the reaction of his fellow villagers. Most of them sat rapt, clinging to every word. Their icebound existence had no room for glorious battles, tragic escapes, or heinous betrayal. They were too busy trying to scratch out an existence, caught between the implacable ice and the bountiful but cruel sea.

They often dreamed of escape but knew it for what it was: an impossible dream.

At the very front of the audience, no doubt placed there by her mother, sat Rita. Rita was the most eligible of the unmarried women in the village. Not only was she the chief's daughter, but she was also stunningly beautiful. Her dark skin and straight black hair were offset by sparkling blue eyes. It was common knowledge in the village that Breed had already proposed to her on several occasions and had been turned down each time. The excuse given was her age, but most people believed she was waiting for the interest of one of the two other bachelors: the brilliant, unpredictable Sangr or the solid, dependable Lunk.

Even so, common wisdom saw her eventually marrying Breed. They expected Sangr to die in some misguided attempt to explore beyond the neighboring villages. And Lunk – well, who knew what Lunk felt? Getting him to talk about his feelings was like trying to get a wall, or a door, to open its heart.

But the arrival of this new, dashing addition to the village had changed everything, and one look at her told Sangr that Breed's was a lost cause. She sat with a longing expression, eyes fixed on Shtarel, and gasped loudly at each dramatic or suspenseful moment in his tale.

Shatrel couldn't help but notice. Very soon, he began to look directly at her whenever he related a daring maneuver or harrowing escape. He began to exaggerate his own part in the action before finally beginning to summarize in order to finish quickly and talk about himself.

"The reason we were betrayed, the reason our neighbors were jealous," Shtarel announced, "is that our family is composed of sorcerers. We all have the gift. Some of us could control earth magic, others wind. I can call upon an unquenchable fire."

This was met by silence, his audience torn between awed fear and complete disbelief.

"Bollocks!" Tristana's voice, obviously inebriated, reached them from the depths of the roundhouse.

"Show us!" called Grave.

Shtarel looked them over gravely. "Very well." He pulled the sleeve of his shirt back, exposing his arm to the elbow, and closed his eyes. Gradually, a glow developed around his outstretched fingers, eventually surrounding the entire exposed portion of flesh. Finally, the glow became a crackling flame, and he waved his arm, showing the crowd that the fire wouldn't go out.

The crowd acknowledged this with a roar of approval. Rita laughed nervously and clapped her hands.

"I can create the fire along my whole body, but to demonstrate, I would have to disrobe, which I prefer not to do right now. There are ladies present, and some of them are very beautiful." He looked straight at Rita as he said this, causing her to laugh and blush.

"This also means that only people I choose to tolerate can touch my person," he concluded. "I would like to thank you for listening to our sad tale, and for your generous hospitality. We shall remain here for as long as you will have us."

The crowd stood, roared, applauded, and stamped its feet. But Sangr, who was watching Breed, noticed hate-filled eyes, a clenched jaw, and an early exit before the applause had died down.

For this reason, Sangr was not surprised when Shtarel's murdered body was discovered the following morning.

The body was kept in a cave while Breed, the obvious suspect, was being held in his own house; a small, round bachelor's hut built on the ice at the foot of the rocky outcroppings that were the village's only protection against the murderous winds.

The elders had already looked at the body, as was their prerogative. They had then discussed the murder, trying to explain how it had been done. There was no doubt in their minds that Breed *had* to be the killer because the elders were always careful to keep abreast of the latest gossip. After knowing your peers for forty years, the gossip of the young was the only thing likely to bring up any interesting news.

Had the man been murdered with a knife in the back, they wouldn't have hesitated. Breed would have been summoned, tried, and summarily exiled on the spot.

But there was a problem. Breed had taken one look at the body and had said, "How in the world am I supposed to have done *that* without touching him?"

The elders had been understandably stumped. They couldn't really convict him unless they explained what had happened. Chief Emnius ordered that Sangr be called in to investigate.

As always, when the elders or the chief summoned him to help, he was supervised closely. Two of the six grey-haired elders accompanied him: Tiana the fishwife and Keller, the chief's equally grizzled brother. Any progress he made would be claimed by the council.

If he failed, of course, he was on his own.

"Let me look at the body," he told them.

Keller nodded and led him towards the cave, actually a shallow cleft in the ice with a bend about ten feet in that hid the contents from anyone looking in from the village common.

The reason for the concealment became apparent as soon as the corpse came into view. Shtarel's body was encased in a rough block of ice, with only the face and part of the upper body clearly visible near the outer border. His clothes were tattered and charred, revealing the pale, dead flesh beneath in many spots. A hollow wooden tube protruded from his mouth and reached all the way out of the ice. Shtarel's hands were frozen in place at his side, red marks clearly visible around each wrist. His blue eyes were wide open, even in death.

Besides the body itself, there were other items frozen into the block. A dozen metal rods protruded from the front of the block, surrounding Shtarel's form but not touching it. Sangr touched his finger to the exposed side of one rod. The metal was numbingly cold, and he quickly pulled his hand away.

He looked at Tiana and Keller.

"Where did you find him?"

"In the old trough Lunk uses to temper his swords. Someone had filled it with water and dumped him inside. We had Lunk pull the body out, ice and all."

"But what killed him?"

Keller looked unhappy. "What do you mean?"

"There doesn't seem to be a single mark on him, other than the wrists and all that water would have taken at least an hour to freeze, so he must have been dead when he went in. What killed him?"

"We don't know."

Typical. They wanted *him* to find out.

"All right. The first thing we have to do is get the body out. Maybe his neck was broken, and we'll see it once we get him free. Maybe he was poisoned, and his tongue will be black and swollen." Sangr felt that anything of the sort would be much too lucky for it to happen to him, but he was an optimist by nature.

"How do you propose to do that?" Tiana asked, raising an eyebrow.

"We'll melt the ice. Just leaving it next to Lunk's forge for a few hours should do the trick."

Tiana nodded, signaling that Keller should take care of it, and looked back at Sangr as if expecting him to do something else, and not necessarily something pleasant. Sangr endured the look for a few moments, trying to solve the crime in one blow. But the facts he had so far pointed him in a direction that he preferred not to explore for the moment.

He sighed. "Take me to where Breed is being held."

Breed was being watched over by two of the elders, Banid and Fornr. How anyone expected the toothless white-haired men to hold him if he decided to make a run for it was anybody's guess. Most likely, they wouldn't even try, secretly hoping that the man would escape, thereby proving his guilt and saving everyone a great deal of hassle.

But Breed, true to form, had refused to cooperate even in this. He just sat there, occasionally exchanging a few words with one guard or the other until Sangr arrived to question him.

A sneer greeted his entrance. "So, now they're bringing you in to make up a story about me. I should have known."

"Nobody is going to make up any stories. We just want to find out what happened."

"I don't *know* what happened," Breed spat. "I went home after the feast. I left early, and I know you saw me. You were watching me every minute. The last thing I wanted was to see that bastard anymore."

"I think what everyone believes is that you left early to lay the groundwork for your ambush. To get the water from the cave."

"Yeah, right. Not only am I a superhuman who can attack a man who can set himself on fire with his bare hands, but now I'm a ghost, too. I thought he'd walk back with the chief and the women," his face contorted as he said this. "What was I supposed to gain by killing him in front of half the village?"

That was something that had been bothering Sangr quite a lot. What had Shtarel been doing out on his own in the middle of the night? Might there be someone else who'd seen what happened? Maybe one of the strangers, who, having seen their last protector brutally cut down, was too afraid to come forward?

Then another thought struck him, and he turned to face Breed.

"So, you were asleep the whole night?" he asked the rat-faced man.

"Not asleep. I was too angry to be asleep. But I didn't leave my house."

Sangr turned to Tiana, who'd accompanied him to the interrogation. "Let him go," he told her. "There's no use in keeping him confined. If he was going to run, he'd just be saving us the effort, and if not, well, why waste other people's time with him?"

Breed looked surprised, almost grateful. He tried to hide it since he knew that Sangr didn't like him, but it showed through. "So, you can tell I didn't do it?"

"If it had been a knife in the back, nobody would have doubted it for a second."

Breed snickered mirthlessly. "And you'd probably have been right, too."

"But there's no way you could have managed this one. Not on your own, at least."

Sangr walked out of the hut with a rather unhappy Tiana on his heels. "So, who did it?" she asked.

"I need to think about it," he replied. "Could you give me a couple of hours? I'll find you as soon as I have an answer."

As a matter of fact, Sangr had no intention of going off to a secluded spot and giving the thing a good think-through. He wanted the time to speak to a couple of people in private, without the council's meddling.

He needed to talk to Rita, so, making certain that Tiana had gone the other way, he walked in that direction. The walk from Breed's hut to the larger house occupied by Rita's mother and the two sisters was not long and led him past the house where the strangers were being housed. He almost stopped to speak to them but held up when he considered their likely state. They would be frightened, mourning, and probably desperate to escape this strange, forbidding place. No, if his suspicions did not pan out, he would speak to them later.

He also passed the forge and waved at Lunk, who was beating something energetically with a large hammer. His friend smiled and gestured with the hammer at something on the floor, which Sangr quickly recognized as the block containing Shtarel's corpse. It had shrunk considerably since he'd last seen it, but there was still some melting to be done before the body could be examined.

Rita was speaking to her six-year-old sister outside the house. Sangr asked if he might be allowed a word with her, and she nodded. One look at her red-rimmed eyes told him that here was a person who, having been shown a brighter future, had had it snatched away forever.

"Rita, I'm really sorry," he said, taking her hands in his. Despite the fact that he had no interest in marrying her, they'd been friends since childhood, and he wanted to help her if he could.

But he suspected that he wouldn't and that his questions would only make her sad. He suspected that the resolution of the matter would most likely make her even more unhappy and generate more questions than it answered.

The worst part of the whole thing was that he really only had one question for her.

"Did he come see you last night?" he asked her.

Tears welled in her eyes again and Sangr immediately knew that he'd just discovered the key to the whole affair. Probably only Rita and her mother knew of this, and they would not have said anything.

"We talked for about two hours, inside the house. My mother was good enough to let us use the main room and watched us only occasionally. He is," she sobbed and Sangr held her as she got herself together. "He was a wonderful man. Brave, dashing, articulate. And then he walked back, and that must have been when…"

She broke down completely, so Sangr ushered her inside, where her mother took hold of her in her arms and thanked him with a look. He walked back out infinitely sadder than he'd ever been, but also somewhat relieved to have had the choice he'd been postponing for so long taken from his hands. He stood outside Rita's house, knowing he would need a few minutes to gather his wits and to push down the emotions before moving into the final phase of his investigation.

Once composed, he walked back to the forge, stepping over the rapidly melting block of ice, and stood in front of his friend.

"So," he said, "you were working late last night, I gather."

Lunk shrugged, not taking his eyes from the red-hot piece of iron he was beating, "Malo and Dink asked me to make them some new grappling hooks, since they'd broken a few trying to secure the stranger's ship. They needed them by morning."

Sangr said nothing, listening to the clanging of hammer on metal, and, in the ringing silence between blows, the dripping of water as the ice melted from Shtarel's icy coffin.

"Are you going to ask her to marry you?" Sangr said, finally.

Lunk looked at him, straight in the eyes. "That depends on what you tell them, doesn't it?"

Sangr looked around, eyes falling briefly on his enormous friend, big enough to hold an ox with one arm, on the assorted tongs that could be used to hold large pieces of white-hot metal in the coal-fed fire of the forge, and the thick leather apron and gloves that would protect the wearer from accidental contact with his materials.

"There are only two things I don't understand," Sangr said. "Why the tube in his mouth, and why the metal bars?"

Lunk immersed the piece he was working on in a barrel of water and stared at his friend through the steam. "She deserves better than some hopped-up trickster, so I used the tube to make sure the bastard could breathe. I wanted him to *freeze*, not drown. Drowning would have been too quick. And he made the freezing even slower with that damnable fire of his. He managed to keep it on for nearly a minute before the water defeated it. I had to place the metal bars in there to radiate heat out of the water so it would freeze once and for all. Not easy to do while holding him in there with one hand. Fortunately, I'd come prepared." He smiled weakly.

Sangr nodded. "You know, the real giveaway was the fact that there was water in the trough in the middle of the night, and not ice. That's what got me thinking about it. The distance from the forge was short enough that you could have dumped warm water in and waited for him, adding another bucket if it looked like it would freeze," he said. "You wouldn't have needed to go all the way to the water cave."

The silence between them was longer this time. They just stood and looked at one another.

"Goodbye, Lunk," Sangr said after an eternity.

Lunk's head dropped. "So, you're going to tell them?" he asked.

"No. You're going to tell them I came by to say goodbye, and that I was leaving. Forever."

Lunk, understanding, came over and embraced him, crushing his back.

"Thank you," he whispered hoarsely.

"But make her happy," Sangr said.

"I will. It's all I have ever wanted since we were four years old."

Sangr laughed. "You sure have a funny way of showing it." He gave his friend's arm one last squeeze. "Give me half an hour before you tell them," he said.

Walking towards his own bachelor's hut, Sangr planned what he would take with him as he wondered whether anyone would really believe that he'd been the murderer. With no other explanation, they'd just have to accept it.

The only other question was where he would go. He knew of the villages to the north and south, along the sea, and of course, the sea itself made it difficult to go west – he would never endanger the village's survival by stealing a boat.

That really only left him one interesting choice: he would go east.

Into the ice.

The Song of Sangr

Merchandise

Sangr shielded his face with his hand. The midday sun beating on the endless ice created a glare that hurt his eyes, but he wanted to see if there was anything in the distance before putting his goggles back on. He was disappointed.

After three days on the ice, his main concern was to put one foot in front of the other, but he knew that walking in circles would kill him as surely as stopping where he was.

He'd started out so full of confidence. After all, he'd been surrounded by ice his whole life. He knew its ways, welcomed its feel, knew how to live with the cold. Back in the village, he'd always been safe in the knowledge that the sea was not far off, a source of sustenance but, much more importantly, a break in the monotony.

He could never go back, so he forged doggedly forward, the easterly wind hindering his progress towards the center of the continent.

Loyalty to Lunk was only part of it. He could never face the eyes of his people, his lifelong friends who, by now, would be convinced that he was a murderer.

And even if he decided saving his life was more important than saving his honor, he was too far away to turn back.

He knew that he might be marching straight towards his doom. Perhaps all that awaited was death, his limbs frozen into unlikely positions, his body forgotten under a sun that would eternally be too weak to thaw him out.

Faith kept him alive: trust in the fact that the gods would favor him because of the noble sacrifice he'd made. Trust in the belief that somewhere, within or beyond the ice, lay a city of unparalleled beauty and unimaginable riches. Trust in the logic that held that, if the rumor could reach his village, then someone from his village could reach the city. It was a thin strand of hope, but enough for the moment.

He'd spent the three days thinking of what he was doing. Had he chosen correctly in running like a thief in the night from the consequences of solving a crime which had left him with two options: accept the blame himself or ruin the life of one of his lifelong friends. In light of the fact that Sangr had never intended to remain in that tiny village his whole life, the choice had been an easy one.

The afternoon passed and shadows lengthened, allowing him to see without covering his eyes. Night fell quickly in the north, even on the short nights of summer. An outcropping, a rare knife of rock among the whiteness, created a shield against the worst of the wind, but he would still have to stop to dig a cave under the snow. But not yet. He would continue to walk until he was nearly exhausted. Only then would he dig.

Sangr stared into the darkness as the mind-numbing chill descended. The starlight was enough to illuminate the barren plain before him, seemingly to the edge of the world. It reflected off the ice, creating fantastic spire-topped cities and phantom armies in his imagination. Some of these were so lifelike that they'd nearly killed him the first night on the ice. Delighted to find civilization, he'd dropped everything and run joyfully to an ice castle only to spend the better part of a cold hour retracing his steps to find his provisions.

So, he ignored the red glow at first. It was just the universe playing tricks on his eyes. The light from a distant star refracted through a crystal of stained ice. Or something. Blood snow wasn't uncommon near the village… but what had been a joyful diversion in childhood could be a deadly distraction now.

And yet it refused to be ignored. It wasn't his imagination. The light was definitely orange in cast, not the cold white of the stars. He could almost imagine that it was a fire, burning brightly, cheerfully on the plain. A large fire that would keep him warm, truly warm, not like his own tiny blaze which would only stave off death, but could never heat him all the way through.

He began to feel the cold. Soon, it would be time to dig his shelter and light his fire. He stopped, determined to ignore the mirage… And found himself walking along the ice, stumbling on the cracks, making a beeline towards the single yellow light. The howling gale stripped him of strength even as the hidden cracks in the ground attempted to bring him down.

As the light resolved into a fire, he couldn't believe his eyes. There were people there, and some kind of large animal. Even sleds. They would have food, warm blankets.

But the fire was further away than it seemed, and by the time he reached the circle, any thought of human companionship had faded. All he knew was that he had to reach the light before the demons of laughter froze him in his tracks.

Something touched him as he came to within a few paces of the glorious flame. Sangr shrugged it off. He could feel the warmth gently caressing his skin. He knelt at its edge and exulted in it, the crackling calling to him. How nice it would be to let himself be engulfed by the warmth and light, ignoring the pain of the heat when he got too close.

He felt the last of his strength leave him and pitched forward, happy that his end would not be a cold one.

"So, you're awake," a rasping voice said. "We weren't sure you'd make it, and then we'd have looked like right fools, losing two days on the ice just to watch you die. Well, at least you made it interesting. First time I've ever had to use my burn poultice out on the ice. Usually, I only get to snip off frozen toes. You were lucky you only managed to put the back of your hand in the embers."

Sangr opened his eyes. He was lying in a bundle of furs on the ice in some kind of tent while a dark-skinned and wizened old man peered at him through rheumy eyes. Pain radiated from his left hand, and he lifted it to see it bandaged. "Do you even understand what I'm saying? Strange guy like you, all the way out here in the middle of nowhere, prob'ly from some savage Ice People. Prob'ly lookin' ta hunt us and eat us, but ya got lost." The man's accent was strange, but he was certainly speaking Hennic.

"Water," Sangr said, surprised by how difficult it was to get the word out.

"Ach." The old man looked disappointed. "Here you go. Funny how it doesn't matter whether one is frozen or burnt or taken a spear in the chest, they always seem to ask for water. My name is Hugo, by the way."

Sangr gulped greedily. "Sangr."

"Sangr?" The man's eyes brightened again. "That doesn't sound like a plains-dwelling name."

"It's not. I live by the sea. I mean… I was born by the sea."

"Hmm… Perhaps you should save your strength. Carmel asked to be notified as soon as you woke, and she'll want to hear your tale firsthand. No use tellin' it twice in your condition." The old man left through a slit in the side of the strange thin-looking fabric, unlike anything Sangr had seen before. How could anything that flimsy keep the cold out?

But it did. The interior of the tent was warm, heated by a stove with a chimney that emerged through the fabric. Sangr sat up and regretted it immediately as he was assaulted by a wave of dizziness. He discovered that he was dressed only in a nightshirt and cast about for his clothes. They were not inside the tent, which meant that he was at the mercy of his rescuers, for good or ill; he wouldn't last more than a few minutes on the open ice dressed like that.

The tent flap fluttered, and Sangr hunkered into the furs against the cold. The old man entered, followed by a man and a woman who could have been twins. Both were much too tall for the tent, with raven-black hair cut to the shoulders, green eyes, and pale skin. Both were covered in identical black capes. Only the man's massive shoulders and the woman's delicate facial features set them apart.

"Welcome back to the land of the living," the woman said. "My name is Carmel deDubois, and this is my cousin Nereo." Her inflections were less familiar to Sangr's ears than the old man's had been, harder consonants grating strangely. And yet, the diction seemed precise, and her air was unbelievably refined.

"I am Sangr. I believe I have you to thank for my life."

"That might be a little premature. You see, we can't afford to give you provisions, and our path leads us into danger. You might be better off walking in a completely different direction."

"Out on the ice?"

She shrugged. "At least that way you won't have to face the Ice Giants."

Sangr looked at her levelly. "I've never heard of anything but some cities out on this ice. What are the Ice Giants?"

"They're the ones who built the cities," her cousin interjected. "We don't know much about them except that some people say they were human once, back when this Ice was just grass. Now, they're monsters of the worst kind."

"The worst kind?"

"Man-eaters. Every so often, they come into the lowlands and carry away a child or two. The villagers aren't strong enough to stop them, so they called for our help. We lead a volunteer squadron against them whenever we feel that they've grown too strong."

Sangr wondered at that. Neither the man nor his sister looked at all how he imagined the leader of an attack force. They were both too soft, too effete for it. Even the scattered merchants that had passed through his village every few years had had a lean and hard appearance, despite their wealth.

And something in Nereo's eyes made Sangr doubt that he'd volunteered for anything out of love for potentially kidnapped children.

"How far are we from these monsters?" he asked.

"A day and a half, maybe two days march," Carmel said. "Why? Are you thinking of coming with us?" Her eyes, on the other hand, gleamed with excitement, perhaps a little too wildly.

"That depends on how far we are from civilization."

She smiled at him. "A little too far, I'm afraid. At least seven days due south."

"And you won't give me any food?"

"No."

"Not much of a choice."

She shrugged. "I assume you have a pack out there somewhere. I'll have the scouts go find it and you can use your own supplies."

"I don't have seven days' worth." She said nothing and Sangr understood. They wanted him along. "I guess I'm going with you, then."

"It looks that way. Can you use a sword?"

"I'm good enough with the rapier, but I don't have one with me." It was true. The only sword in the village had been a rapier, washed ashore on a wrecked ship. Sangr had spent entire days pretending to be a fierce warrior with that sword in hand.

Her cousin snorted. "Why the rapier? Weren't there any weapons fit for a man? I'll see if we have something for you." He left, giving Sangr the impression that he wasn't entirely happy with his kinswoman's decision.

Carmel stayed a few seconds more, measuring him openly. "I hope you're worth the trouble of saving, and the time we've lost here. And I'm still going to want your whole story when you get your strength back, so you'd better get some rest. You have a long day ahead of you tomorrow."

She left and left him wondering what she was all about. There was something predatory about her, but not necessarily in a good way.

The next two days were as advertised. Long, cold slogs through ice and wind, punctuated by an unexpected snow flurry on the afternoon of the first day. But Sangr wasn't complaining. The strange furry pack animals, four-legged, thick-bodied beasts with long, dark brown hair, were strong enough to drag food and shelter for the entire troop along behind them, something that meant that his survival was no longer uncertain.

Now that it looked as though he would reach the fabled ice cities and not become—as he'd feared over the past day—a frozen corpse lost in the glacier until the world's end, Sangr wondered what he would do next. Obviously, that was subject to surviving the Ice

Giants, but it became an important question for the first time. He'd always assumed that he'd leave the village behind someday, but now that he had actually done so, he had no idea what he wanted to do with his life.

The first night was a huge contrast from anything he'd known before. Not only did the southerners burn more wood for their fire than even the best driftwood season had permitted in his village, but they also ate strange meats. He was certain that the meat must come from some animal that was neither fish nor seal nor bear. Dog, perhaps? But no one would eat a dog, they were too valuable. Even the ale seemed to be made of something other than seaweed, and they called it wine. He drank too much of the sweet, addictive brew and was nowhere near his best when Carmel asked him to tell the tale of his sojourn.

The story came easily enough, but he feared that he might have revealed too much about his village's position, and much too much about Lunk's killing of the foreigner. But he felt, at that moment, that he could take on a legion of hell-sharks, and that the woman's deep, hungry eyes were his alone. He would tell her anything, reveal any secret.

If that night was heaven, the next morning was hell. He dragged himself out of his loaned tent and seriously considered just letting the rest of the group go on without him, but was given no choice. A bright-eyed Nereo found him and slapped him on the back, making the world spin. "So, fisherman, I was right. We do have something for you. Here you go."

The weapon had obviously not been cherished or even particularly well cared for. Rust spots marred its entire length. The blade was anything but sharp, but it did seem solid, and the balance was excellent. One of the good things about being friends with the village blacksmith was that Sangr had learned to recognize fine craftsmanship – and this weapon fit the bill. He hefted it once or twice, tentatively. "Thank you."

"You're welcome." The sneer in Nereo's voice could be heard as far as the coast, but Sangr ignored it. Considering the type of sword the other man carried – a two-handed longsword suitable for very little other than fighting in extremely large and uncluttered areas – it was likely that he didn't even know what he was giving away. Sangr made a mental note to ask Hugo for a whetstone that evening, if the pounding in his head didn't kill him first. "You'd better be as good as you claim, though. I doubt that thing is going to do much damage to an Ice Giant."

The man walked off and the day's cold march began.

"There. The palace of the Ice Giants." On the morning of the third day – the unexpected flurry having pushed back their schedule – Carmel's voice rang with satisfaction and Sangr suddenly realized why they'd all been on edge. Seeing the hulking block of ice atop a long rise made him realize that the forty men they had in the party might not be enough to storm the thing.

Had his guide not pointed it out, he would have missed it altogether. From a distance, it looked like any other piece of glacier, a dirt-streaked bump in the whiteness. Closer inspection revealed openings that could only be entrances and slits that might be windows. And once that connection was made, its scale became apparent.

"We're going to try to storm that?" he asked. It didn't seem like a good idea at all.

"Don't worry," Nereo said. "They aren't particularly bright, and their skin is just as vulnerable to steel as ours." His eyes gleamed evilly. "Besides, I have a plan."

"I'm happy to hear it."

The other man faced him earnestly. "Now is the time. You need to make a decision. Will you join our assault, or will you remain behind with Carmel and Hugo?" The contemptuous look he gave Sangr made it very clear that he expected excuses, and protestations that he was too weak to participate in an attack.

"Well," Sangr replied, ignoring the unspoken insult, "I spent two hours sharpening and polishing this sword last night. It would be a shame to let that go to waste. Count me in."

Nereo's eyes widened slightly, but he gave no other outward sign of surprise. "So be it." He called one of his sergeants, a thin man that seemed to always be around Carmel after sunset, over to them. "You've got a new recruit, Gren. Name of Sangr. He wants to test his theory that a light, maneuverable sword might work against the Giants."

Gren grunted in Sangr's direction, made a barely acceptable bow towards Nereo, and walked back to his men. Sangr, seeing no other option, followed.

About halfway there, the man turned. "So, you're the one who gets to kill me?"

"What?"

"Don't play coy with me. I know what Nereo wants. All I can tell you is that I'm going to keep you beside me wherever I go, and I'll be watching every move you make – so if you try anything, I'll gut you like a fish. I'll have one eye on the Giants and the other on you. He's tried before, you know, and I've killed every one of his murderers."

"I have no idea what you're talking about. I never met any of you before two days ago."

"Yes, I'm well aware of how we 'stumbled' on you. But I think it's just a wee bit suspicious, just running into someone in the middle of the ice. A little too convenient." He turned back. "I've given you fair warning. Do as you see fit."

Sangr shrugged but held his tongue. Nothing he could say would change the other man's mind. He would have to prove his worth in the battle to come.

The rest of Gren's squad greeted him with a marked lack of enthusiasm and more than a little suspicion, making Sangr think that, just maybe, the sergeant wasn't quite as paranoid as he seemed. He also realized that it had been a mistake to spend all his time with the expedition's leaders and with Hugo, completely ignoring the rest of the men.

It was too late to do anything about it; the group was making ready to storm the structure. Gren motioned for Sangr to march along beside him at the front of the line while a second group, with Nereo at its head, headed towards the western side of the palace.

Sangr wondered how Nereo was planning to get into that building with such a small force. Even if the

Ice Giants fought with their bare hands, they had the advantage of knowing where the attackers were coming from. Stealth might have been an option for a handful of men in the night, but even if they caught the enemy unaware, thirty-five soldiers would have a hard time staying hidden very long.

The sergeant's group came to one of the openings on the south side with no indication that they'd been spotted. Gren himself, with Sangr in tow, moved forward to inspect the entrance.

Sangr didn't like what he saw. The opening led into a tunnel perhaps twenty paces long, twice as tall as a man, formed entirely of ice. But while the ice on the slope was pitted and rough, ground into the snowpack by the wind, this was smooth, wet, and slick-looking. Not the surface on which he would have chosen to fight anything described as an 'Ice Giant'. Two round gaps, a pace wide, punctured the roof of the tunnel. Sangr hoped that they were just ventilation shafts, but knew he was being naïve. Those holes were there to make life miserable for anyone doing what they were doing.

Motioning for Sangr to follow and for the rest of his squad to stay where they were, Gren moved into the tunnel, keeping to one side. Sangr held his breath and did the same, breathing again only after they'd cleared the first of the gaps in the roof. The fact that nothing fell from it was the first clear sign that, just perhaps, they might have arrived unseen.

Out of the corner of his eye, Sangr detected a sudden movement behind them and pressed his body against the wall. Something hissed by at knee height and the back end of a crossbow dart sprouted from Gren's calf. The man screamed.

As the tunnel filled with huge white forms, Sangr understood Nereo's plan and the depth of his betrayal. The crossbowman, one of Nereo's troops, gave them a salute and disappeared before the defenders could spot him.

An Ice giant materialized in front of him, looming nearly an arm's length over his head. Human-like eyes stared at him from a face covered in white fur. It growled, and Sangr simply dropped his sword. He would never survive a fight with the strongly muscled creatures – his only hope was that they thought he was harmless. Arms like iron bands took hold of him.

Gren was not so lucky. Maddened by the pain of the bolt he thrust at the nearest defender, opening a huge gash in its stomach. But there were too many of them and the enormous manlike forms, heads nearly scraping the high ceiling, descended on the hapless sergeant. Limbs flew as he was torn to shreds, the blood pooling on the ice in places, while it seeped into the slush in others, forming a pink mush. Mostly, it seemed to land on the long white fur that covered the giants from head to toe.

The defender that Gren had attacked lay unmoving to one side with the sergeant's sword embedded in its chest – probably the product of a final, frantic strike. The others grouped around it and let forth a roaring, keening cry. The one holding Sangr joined the lament and twitched, slamming him into the wall.

Blackness.

Ice-cold water on his face brought Sangr sputtering to his senses. He reached out to attack whichever of the village's practical jokers was behind this outrage, but his attempts to move were crushed. He went still immediately as he remembered where he was, allowing his eyes to come back into focus.

He didn't like what he saw. One of the Ice Giants was inches from his face, strangely human features wrinkled in distaste.

"You have stink of south on you, but it is new stink, not your deep stink. Your own smell is clean. I can tell you come from ice. Not same Ice as our Ice, but Ice all the same"

Sangr reeled. "You can talk?" In such close proximity, he expected the giant to smell like any animal, but he detected nothing.

The Giant looked at him critically, as though inspecting a particularly slow child. It was hard to tell under the fur, but the face seemed female. Or maybe that was just an impression Sangr got from the melodious voice. "Yes, some of us talk. We capture little people, make them teach we."

Sangr's stomach heaved. *So, it was true. They did kidnap village children.* "And then you eat them?"

The Giant's face wrinkled. "No eat. They no taste very good. Smell bad, like smoke and dirt. Not clean like ice."

"Then why do you take them?"

"Take?"

"Why do you go to the cities and steal the children?"

"What is children?"

"Children. Many young humans. Little people."

"We no see young ones. We only see little people." The Ice Giant seemed genuinely puzzled. It placed a huge finger on Sangr's chest. "You little people."

Then he understood. The term 'little' was applied to all humans, even adults. It was logical enough: even the largest human was tiny beside the Ice Giants. "But you take the children. You eat them."

"No."

"Then why would they come all the way out here to defend themselves?"

The Ice Giant seemed to hesitate. It sniffed Sangr again. It grunted rhythmically, and another series of grunts came from behind Sangr, probably from the Giant that was holding his arms. It sniffed him again. "You no come with the other folk."

Sangr knew what the creature wanted to hear. "I am from the ice."

It nodded and gestured. One of Sangr's arms was freed. "Then I show you."

He was herded through cold, wet passages into which light seeped from the top and sides to a place where a small patch of ice had been smoothed out, acting as a window. Through this small transparent piece, Sangr could see two men laboring over the body of an Ice Giant. They were working quickly, looking up frequently to make certain that none of the creatures could sneak up on them, but Sangr had seen seals butchered often enough to recognize the motions. "They're taking the pelt," he whispered to himself. It made sense – logic indicated that the coats would be warm, and the fur was fine and beautiful.

"We not understand," the Ice Giant told him.

"The little people are killing you for your skin. Your hair."

"That is the reason?"

"Yes. They use if for clothes, to be warm in the cold."

"But the south is not cold. We know this."

"It is for us. We do not have fur to protect our bodies." Sangr kept watching the men work, and fury rose inside him. How could the men be so barbaric? "I would like to help you," he told the creature. He was certain of it now: this one was a female, a mother mourning lost family.

"You no can help. Him already dead."

"I can make certain this doesn't happen again."

"How you help?"

"Give me my sword. Lead me to the place where men are."

A warning growl came from the Giant holding Sangr's arm. He was shorter than the other, but broad and pug-nosed.

"No," the first one said.

"I will fight them. We can fight them."

"We no can fight. They have magic teeth. Sword."

"But you are many. They can't kill you all. You'd beat them if you fought."

The Ice Giant shuddered. "No can fight magic teeth."

They were clearly terrified of the southerner's swords. But it was stupid. Why didn't they just use the swords they took from the men they killed? "Where is my sword? The magic tooth I brought."

"It stay where it fall."

They must have learned that the touch of a blade brought pain, not realizing that the swords were merely weapons. "Take me there."

She hesitated. "You no use magic tooth to hurt we?"

"No. I want to help."

They led him through another series of passages back to the tunnel through which he'd entered initially – easy to recognize with Gren's dismembered corpse littering the floor. The grip on his arm released, and Sangr bent to pick up his blade and turned to face them.

The Ice Giants took a step back and growled menacingly. Sangr sheathed the sword. "I am not going to hurt you," he said, holding out his hands. "I want to hurt the southerners. Show me how to reach them."

They seemed extremely reluctant, but finally, the first giant to speak to him walked down a passageway. Two steps in, she turned back, as though expecting him to follow. Sangr hurried after her, slipping on the slick surface.

They came to an opening at the end of an endless maze of ice tunnels. "There," the Ice Giant told him. "I go no farther."

Sangr nodded and pulled the sword. Its light but not insubstantial weight comforted him as he turned the last corner. The two men had finished skinning the carcass and were speaking to Nereo. "…and with this one, we have enough pelts to make the trip profitable. We don't need to go into the tunnels to look for more."

"I say we do," Nereo said. "And I think I know just the person to guide us." He smiled. "Sangr, so good of you to join us. I must admit that I underestimated your swordsmanship. Not everyone can fight their way through a mass of angry Ice Giants."

Sangr shrugged. "I underestimated you as well. When you said you had a plan, I thought you were going to breathe on the palace until it melted."

Nereo smirked. "I probably deserved that. But if you ever want to get back to civilization, lead us to more of these creatures so we can make some money on this trip."

"I suspect that leading you anywhere would probably end with your sword between my ribs. You don't look like the kind to keep his word. That would be my opinion even if I hadn't already seen you betray one of your own men. Some people just smell wrong."

"You're coming dangerously close to being abandoned here when we leave. I am of noble blood – there is only so much you can insult me without consequence."

"Any true man would have drawn his sword already. You seem pretty brave against terrified animals, but not much when the opponent can think for itself. Let me be clear then. I am going to kill you. I'll do it even if you don't pull your sword, but it would be much more satisfying if I can gut you in a fair fight."

Nereo tugged at the sword he wore in a scabbard across his back. The blade was an impressive piece of armory, as long as Sangr's rapier and more than twice as thick. "I am a master swordsman. This is your last chance to repent."

Sangr doubted it – master swordsmen didn't advertise the fact. They just chopped you to bits. All he said was: "And I'm very upset with you."

The two men circled on the ice of the small courtyard, as the others watched in silence. Sangr couldn't tell if they were simply frightened to get in the way of two armed men, or if they hated Nereo and saw this as a good way to get him killed without being blamed for it. Sangr would have preferred to face that monster sword in the corridors, where its weight would have been a disadvantage, but even this situation wasn't hopeless. The important part was to avoid getting in the way of the other man's blade because even deflecting a blow with the rapier would probably do little to slow it, unless he could parry with the very bottom of the blade.

Sangr feinted a pair of times, trying to see what Nereo would do to defend himself. The bigger man refused to be drawn out, all he did was to take a step back, making extremely certain that he was out of the smaller man's range. He held the longsword two-handed, which nullified what little advantage Sangr had due to his own weapon's lighter weight.

And yet Nereo's overall movements were cumbersome. His feet were planted just a little too flat, the speed with which he changed direction to face his opponent a little too slow. He was well aware that he only needed to land one blow for the fight to be over.

The Song of Sangr

Sangr feinted again, and his opponent smiled. "Not ready to commit yourself yet, are you?" It was an attempt at distraction. With the word 'are', Nereo launched a savage attack, pulling the sword over his head on the backswing and cutting diagonally down.

The swing was well-judged, starting while Nereo was out of Sangr's reach, and finishing where his shoulder met his neck – or it would have if Sangr hadn't dived to the right.

Sangr would have been able to dodge easily if he hadn't slipped on the icy surface as he evaded. He received a deep gash in the left arm for his troubles and cried out.

Nereo also misjudged the surface, and overextended, leaving himself open to a counterattack, but Sangr, still sliding on the treacherous floor, was unable to strike.

They got themselves upright once more. "First blood to me, it seems," Nereo said.

"That's not the one that counts," Sangr replied, but he was worried. He hoped the bigger man would attack again quickly; he knew the other had the advantage of being able to block Sangr's strokes, and the only way to do him real damage was to catch him after a strike, where the big sword's inertia could work to his favor. The real risk was that Nereo would stop and think about things, and turn the battle into an exchange of blows, something he would have a decided advantage in. He needed to get the man off guard. "I suppose I shouldn't take this personally. You probably didn't want to have Gren's brats in the family. I guess I was just in the wrong place at the wrong time."

Sangr said that for the benefit of the men listening. He wanted them to be well aware that they could be next, especially if that would keep them from intervening on Nereo's behalf.

"On the contrary," Nereo replied. "Things couldn't have gone better. I was just hoping that Gren would spare me the bother of gutting you myself."

The big man's words were measured, but Sangr could see he'd managed to score a verbal victory. He smiled. "Second blood to me, it seems. Watching the way you looked at Carmel when she spoke to Gren was fun. It would probably have been even more fun to accept her insinuations on that first night by the fire. Cousin Carmel wants everyone but little Nereo, doesn't she?"

Nereo attacked, a sweeping strike that began on Sangr's left and would have disemboweled him in a perfect horizontal arc. But the little man was ready for it. A sideways blow had the advantage that it was difficult to avoid by stepping to one side, but Sangr had spent hours practicing out on the sheet ice beside the forge, matched against the much larger Lunk the blacksmith.

Sangr jumped. A single mighty push sent him straight into the air, and he pulled his feet up beneath him, as far as they would come. He saw Nereo's eyes widen as the sword passed under him. Sangr concentrated on landing as straight as possible – if he slipped, the opportunity would pass.

Nereo kept spinning, the force of the blow rotating him so that his back was to Sangr. He wind-milled his shoulders, sword akimbo, trying to straighten out, but it was much too late.

Sangr pushed forward with the point of his rapier, striking his opponent in the right kidney and driving the sword upward, grating against the ribs, puncturing kidney, lungs, and anything else in his reach. Nereo's feet gave almost immediately, and he collapsed sideways. Sangr followed the big man to the ground. The longsword buried itself in the Ice Giant's half-frozen fluids.

Nereo coughed blood and attempted to lie on his back, but the rapier's wrist-guard made it impossible. Sangr pulled the blade free and helped the defenseless man to turn.

Nereo attempted to smile. "I should have known," he said, voice a soft, bubbling wheeze. "You were just too eager to join us. And too quick to switch sides." He coughed and weakened visibly. "My men will hunt you down, you know. Even if they didn't stay around to help."

Sangr looked around, noticing for the first time that the two men who'd been there before were nowhere to be seen. They must have run away when they saw their leader slain. "I guess they didn't like you much."

"No, but Carmel does. She'll have them feed you to the dogs."

"She'll have to catch me first. But why did you say I was too quick to switch sides?"

Nereo gave him a contemptuous look. "Don't play coy with me." And then he smiled weakly. "But everyone knows the diamond's cursed. Perhaps it would be justice if you found it."

"Diamond?" Sangr asked, immediately interested – he *liked* diamonds, and had once been punished as a child for stealing the only ones in the village, those on an old brooch that had washed up long before he was born. But Nereo was beyond reply, no matter how much he was shaken and cursed at. Soon, approaching footfalls sent Sangr back into the relative safety of the ice corridors, pausing only long enough to pick up Nereo's sword.

Well inside, an arm reached out to stop him. It was his old acquaintance, the Ice-Giant-Mother. "You kill them?"

"I killed one of them, the leader."

"There are many."

"Yes, but I can't do it alone. You have to help."

"We no can fight. They have magic teeth."

"Now you can have magic teeth, too." Sangr held out the longsword he'd taken from the fallen noble, hilt-first. The Ice-Giant recoiled, but Sangr insisted. "Take it. It can't hurt you now. The owner is dead. I have his magic, and this won't hurt you."

The creature hesitated, sniffing Sangr again before reaching out to touch the pommel with a single extended finger. It pulled back quickly, but soon realized it hadn't been hurt and allowed Sangr to take its wrist and show it how to hold the blade.

The Ice Giant soon gained confidence and was brandishing the sword like some kind of palace guard from hell. Sangr would have hated to be the next fur merchant to enter the passages, and he wondered whether he'd done the right thing in breaking their fear of cold steel. These monsters could be a formidable force if they ever decided to avenge the wrongs done to them by the southerners.

He contemplated the huge creature holding the enormous sword – which looked ridiculously small in its grasp – with a ferocious scowl and decided that it was definitely not the right time to ask about diamonds.

Gustavo Bondoni

Qalnoth's Favor

The common room was jumping, which was not a surprise. After all, there were fourteen of them, and they'd gone there specifically to get drunk. It was the only way to be safe inside the town walls.

There was no real need to worry. Giant, mute Erwyn and their new best friend, Crastor, the inn's owner, would watch their backs, making certain that, despite their condition, they would remain unmolested to drink their fill and get to bed. The following day's hangovers would be legendary, but no price was too high when it bought your life.

Sangr knew he was a little behind his comrades in pursuing the night's objective. This was certainly not the place in which he would have chosen to spend either his time or his copper, but the choice had not been his. He couldn't even complain about the moldering straw on the floor or the fact that the pewter mug had probably last been washed when the serving wenches were still virgins and had nothing better to do. Anything out of character could get him killed very, very quickly.

He didn't even want to think about the ale. Lowland ale was always awful – he believed it must have something to do with the polluted water they use because they're too lazy to bring it in from outside the city. But, once again, he had to hold his tongue. His companions already knew that he wasn't from Krenn, but they had no inkling that he wasn't from the plains at all. Sangr preferred to avoid speculation along those lines among m current companions, mainly because they were more useful to him alive.

Still, I'm here for a reason, he thought, *so I might as well get on with it. After all, the sooner I'm drunk, the sooner I'll be indifferent to the taste of the ale.*
And the sooner he'd be safe.

Despite the drunken friendliness, Sangr had met his companions less than a week earlier. Their temporary status as brothers-in-arms arose from an enormous misunderstanding that Sangr had perpetrated in an attempt to save his life.

He'd stumbled on their camp one night while walking towards Krenn. One look had convinced him that they were simply a group of farmers on their way back from the town market: replete with fat (or at least recently filled) purses, and insufficient sense to post a sentry. Any guards they'd posted would have been more than evident.

Sangr quietly pulled his rapier out of its sheath and started towards the nearest sleeping form.

He was caught completely unaware when something heavy – the sentry? – landed on his back and sent him to the dreamworld until dawn of the next day.

The morning sun stabbed through his eyelids, not improving his headache in the least. Once Sangr remembered where he was, he was more than a bit surprised to find himself alive. Although they'd tied him quite solidly to a tree, his captors had shown quite a bit more compassion than he himself would have, had their roles been reversed.

I just hope that they didn't really think that I was going to rob and murder them, he thought.

He was about to speak up, ask for water, beg for mercy, or whatever came to mind, but, out of respect for his throbbing head, he decided to wait a while before speaking.

That decision probably saved his life.

"So, is he one of the Favored?" He heard someone say. They obviously thought he was still asleep. Either that, or they didn't care if he heard them or not.

"I don't think so. We had a Beacon out on the other side of the clearing. Any one of the favored would have gone in that direction and eliminated the obvious sentry before moving into the camp."

It was a woman's voice. Strong and deep, but unmistakable. But, despite not having seen a woman in nearly two weeks, he didn't care. He was preoccupied with other thoughts: hoping that he'd been really tired the previous night. That was the only explanation Sangr wanted to contemplate for the fact that he'd missed not one, but two sentries set out by these rubes. *I'm normally much better than that.*

The second explanation, namely that they weren't just a bunch of farmers, would mean that he'd fallen into the hands of some potentially dangerous people, who might find it expedient to kill him for practical reasons, as opposed to just moral indignation reserved for run-of-the-mill robbers and murderers.

The third possibility, sorcery, he just avoided thinking about altogether. *I'd rather be dead than mixed with the kind of magic I'd seen up north.*

"So, just a thief?"

"Probably a murderer, too. He had his sword out and was headed for the camp, and with no provocation whatsoever."

"We might be able to use him. Anyone on the wrong side of the law has more to fear from the Favored than we do."

The woman laughed. "Nobody has more to fear from the Favored than we do. They're specifically out to get us. And besides, what good would an incompetent thief do us? We need disciplined minds and swords, not bungling petty criminals."

That one hurt, but she was right. The only impression possible after Sangr's less than brilliant invasion of the night before was that he was a complete idiot. They moved away, and the pain from the ropes digging into his sides almost tempted him to call out after them, but he finally decided that he'd be better served to wait a while and fake an awakening in a half-hour or so. It was the only way to keep the farmers from suspecting they'd been overheard.

Before he deemed the time right for his "awakening", however, rough hands shook his shoulder.

"Wake up, scum," a voice said. It was the man he'd overheard earlier.

Sangr opened his eyes.

"You have about two minutes to come up with one good reason for me not to kill you," the owner of the voice said. He was a stocky man with dark hair, a week's growth of stubble and at least a trace of Treni blood in him, visible in the narrow eyes.

"I've done you no harm," Sangr knew it was weak, but wanted to establish that from the beginning.

The guy laughed.

"So, you were just going to wake one of us up and introduce yourself?" he said. "Ask for some soup? Come on, we're not that stupid."

Sangr had already figured that one out, but, sadly, a bit too late. He was seriously worried now and was actually relieved when a girl approached. Although she was probably the one he'd heard earlier, he hoped that, when it came down to it, a woman would be a little more compassionate. She was lithe, lean, and just curvaceous enough to satisfy with delicate features that were highlighted by her short hair. Maybe just a little too boyish in her stance and dress, but she looked like she'd clean up well.

"So, kill him and let's get out of here," she said.

Sangr immediately realized that they weren't going to get along. A jolt of fear coursed through him.

"Just a second, Yella," the man said. He turned back to Sangr. "Last chance." The butcher's knife that had appeared in his hand wasn't a particularly orthodox weapon, and it wasn't elegant, but there was no doubt that it would get the job done.

Sangr gambled it all. "I was trying to find out if you were Favored." He had no idea what Favored actually were except for something he'd heard about them having a big temple in Krenn.

The man moved in, pressing the blade's point into the side of Sangr's neck. "And what," he hissed, "would you have done if we were?"

Sangr looked straight into his eyes and tried to fake desperate bravado. "I'd have killed every last one of you, like the rabid dogs you are."

The knife moved quicker than the eye could see, cutting one of the ropes on the right.

"Get up. You're coming with us. Make one sound other than to answer my questions, and you're dead. You'll get your weapons back if we think you're useful enough to stay with us. Otherwise, we leave you behind at the crossroad. And if you convince me that what you just said is true, we'll even let you keep a few of your belongings."

Not the greatest introduction to the inhabitants of Krenn. But it could have been much, much worse.

Over the next couple of days, Sangr kept his mouth shut and his ears open.

"So why do you hate the Favored?" the man—his name was Hareg—asked.

This was a tricky one. Sangr knew almost nothing about the Favored. But the flip side of that was that these people knew almost nothing about him. He decided to use that.

"They killed my brother."

Hareg looked doubtful. "What was his name?"

"Lunk," he lied. He was probably married and fathering children by this time, but they didn't know that.

The guy grunted, showing no sign of recognition, which was understandable: as far as Sangr knew, Lunk was still freezing up north. "Why'd they kill him?"

"I don't know." Sangr hung his head. "That's one of the things I want to find out. And find the bastard that did it so I can tear out his guts."

"Careful with those thoughts once we get into town," he cautioned. "That kind of thinking is liable to get us all killed."

Sangr had no idea what the guy was talking about, and it must have shown.

"What do you know about the Favored?"

"They killed my brother and they're based in Krenn. If I need to know anything else, I'll ask about it in town."

The man stared; incredulity etched on every feature. Then he laughed. He laughed and laughed and laughed until Sangr was ready to throttle him. Tears streamed out of his eyes.

"You," he said when he'd managed to control himself, "are the luckiest man alive."

Sangr could have argued with him all day: I don't feel particularly lucky. My rope burns don't feel lucky, and I'm still slightly dizzy from the bump the sentry gave my head. But he kept his mouth shut, sensing that he was about to learn something important.

Compassion had replaced mirth in the man's gaze. "I hate to be the one who tells you this, but the most likely reason for the death of your brother is that he had the misfortune to think unkind thoughts about one of the Favored."

There it was again, the insinuation that your thoughts could get you in trouble with the favored. This wasn't shaping up to Sangr's liking at all.

"What do you mean?"

"The priests of Qalnoth can read the unguarded thoughts of all people. The ability to do so is seen as a sign of the god's favor, and that's why they call themselves the Favored. The people who dwell in Krenn have learned to control their thoughts in their presence, but outsiders often fall victim to their own thoughts. Even though we know this, we've been losing people steadily for months."

"But killing someone just for having the wrong type of thoughts?" Sangr didn't have to pretend to be enraged. These guys sounded like they needed someone to teach them some manners.

"Well, they claim that most of the foreigners they execute were plotting to steal the giant diamond out of Qalnoth's altar, but I suspect that they throw some into the flames just because their unguarded thoughts show a lack of sufficient awe for their power and their gift."

"Why don't the people get rid of them? They don't sound like very pleasant neighbors."

"It's hard to overthrow an armed regime that knows what you're planning to do so. The worst part about it is their habit of sending men with the gift out at night to pick up unguarded thoughts that people have when asleep. The original resistance was nearly wiped out that way, since it's difficult to hide your thoughts when asleep. The men and women you see here are all that's left of the coalition to overthrow the hated priesthood."

Just my luck. First the worshippers of the ice troll and now this. Sangr sat silently for a while, trying to suppress his own worst nature.

Nature, however, always wins out. He just couldn't get rid of the image of an enormous diamond – his imagination gave it a slightly pinkish cast – embedded in the altar to a strange god. A god that wasn't his god—to be fair, none was—and to which he owed nothing. A diamond that could be reached by any enterprising soul with the means necessary to distract the guards.

And no matter how much Sangr wished he could think about something else; it was obvious to him that his companions seemed hell-bent on becoming a huge distraction for anyone guarding the stone.

"Sangr, finish your ale. You need at least six more mugs to be completely drunk," Yella said in her characteristic husky voice. She wasn't anywhere near drunk, but Sangr decided not to mention it. Their relationship had gotten no warmer despite the fact that he'd convinced Hareg that he was sincere in his hatred of the Favored and would help them on their quest, whatever it was. As a matter of fact, she'd argued forcibly in favor of leaving him behind at the first crossroads we passed, sans weapons and gold and, ideally, strung up by the neck from the nearest convenient tree.

Seven days later, she still didn't trust him, despite, or perhaps because of, the fact that he'd tried to charm her out of her breeches on the first few nights after his capture. That only stopped when Sangr learned that she'd been the sentry that dropped on his back that night. From then on, pride kept things in check.

Sangr's pride, of course, seemed to concern her not at all, and she was still standing around, contemptuously watching him to make certain that he was drunk enough that his sleeping thoughts would be incoherent to any of the favored that might pass by, and therefore would guarantee that he wouldn't endanger the rest of the group.

"Why don't you go bug the rest of them?"

"I trust the rest of them," Yella replied coolly. And then she smirked, "Besides, they don't seem to need a whole lot of help."

She was right. Except for Erwyn, one of the men who'd been part of the group since the day they captured him, and who was loyal, but too slow to understand what was going on. The rest of the group was already singing an off-key version of a harvest-time tune which had had its lyrics horribly perverted. Young Trein was dandling one of the barmaids on his knee and judging by the position of one of her hands, she didn't really seem to be putting up much of a fight.

Sangr got down to the grim task of swallowing the vile liquid, imagining the ways he would get back at Yella for this.

He would begin by showing Yella that she would have been an unimportant conquest. He decided to do this by taking one of the remaining barmaids along when he retired to the hayloft that had been the only lodgings available by the time his turn to choose where he would sleep – after the rest of them had taken all the comfortable places – had come around.

Looking around the bar, Sangr realized that only one other girl seemed to be present and that he would have to drink a lot before she became a viable proposition.

He swallowed another draught.

The bucket of ice-cold water which woke him was wielded with unerring aim. So precisely, in fact, that the barmaid lying on the crushed hay only two feet away was only hit by a few drops. She complained softly, not waking, and Sangr saw her large, white behind move away slightly, naked as the day she'd been born.

He spluttered and looked through bleary eyes at the figure who'd done the wielding. The blurry outline soon resolved to become Yella, observing him with a condescending smile, and causing him to jump into the air to cover himself and mutter complaints about freezing water, which only made her laugh.

"Get moving Sangr. Everybody else has been up for an hour, and we only let you sleep in deference to your," Yella cleared her throat, "extra activity."

Sangr really couldn't remember if there had even been any extra activity; he'd been that drunk. At least he'd been able to pull off her dress and his clothes, although how or why he'd put his boots back on afterwards was a mystery.

His head was killing him, and the rope burns hadn't gotten any better, just slightly crusty and quick to seep. But even through the physical suffering, Sangr felt a strange sense of dread, of something not being quite right.

Sadly, the most likely answer to what might be wrong seemed to be that his mind was in such terrible shape after the previous evening that a full day's scouting capped by a surgical attack against the most powerful armed force in this valley would likely prove suicidal.

"So, are you going to move, or are you going to stand there contemplating your navel all day?"

Ah, my little ray of sunshine, seemingly always there to make certain that I was on pace with everybody else, he thought. Luckily, Sangr was dressed by that time, or Yella might have put his clothes on forcibly, which was an idea to study in more depth at some other time.

The courtyard beside the stables was full of men and weapons. Hareg greeted him gruffly and handed over a bundle which contained the bulk of his belongings. He was relieved to note that the sheathed blade of a rapier protruded prominently from the beige cloth wrapping. At least they won't be forcing me to join their suicide mission unarmed.

Sangr would have been badly hurt and offended if they hadn't returned the weapons. It would have shown without any shadow of a doubt that they trusted him not at all.

The fact that he had no intention of joining their mission, and that he was planning to skip out as soon as the enemy descended on them like a plague of locusts, leaving the diamond unguarded, made no difference. Sangr would be perfectly trustworthy until that moment, so they had no call to treat him like a common criminal.

Hareg gave Sangr a stern look. "Remember what we discussed," he said. "As soon as we come within a quarter mile of the Palace, you need to start thinking farmer's thoughts. Think about produce, poultry, and how you're going to get the best deal in the marketplace. Don't slip or we're all dead."

It sounded incredibly simple, but that was the core of the plan. The resistance movement, taking enormous risks and losing a lot of people in the process, had found that the Favored could only read the thoughts uppermost in a mind, so avoiding them was simply a question of thinking about something else.

And yet, the resistance, even armed with this knowledge, had been losing members steadily enough that they had finally decided to risk everything in one commando strike against the Favored before they were finally reduced to complete ineffectiveness.

Steadily enough that Sangr suspected that they were probably being betrayed by someone on the inside. And that the strike would be a serious massacre.

Anyway, that night wasn't his problem. Sangr needed to concentrate on the task at hand –

specifically the scouting mission that morning. He also wanted to correct the fact that, unlike his companions, Sangr had no idea what one of the Favored even looked like.

They split into small groups of twos and threes. Unsurprisingly, Sangr got paired up with Yella, whom he suspected had been selected because she wouldn't trust him until he took an arrow for the cause, and would therefore maintain her vigilance throughout.

I guess Hareg doesn't trust me after all. Or maybe it was just his way of having a laugh at my expense. In either case, Hareg ignored the sour look Sangr shot him and continued to organize his troops. They were instructed to walk to the left of the inn in order to enter the marketplace that was installed in the plaza facing the palace from the west.

As they walked, Sangr contemplated Yella for the hundredth time. The boyishness he'd imagined in her stance the first time he saw her had become, in his mind, a sign of confidence instead of androgyny. She seemed to become prettier and prettier every time one looked at her.

Sangr's bad luck, present since the night he'd met Yella, held. Choosing that precise moment to glance his way, she caught him staring at her. Sangr dropped his eyes instinctively, knowing it for a mistake as soon as he did, and tried to cover with some banter.

"So, how did you fall in among the resistance?" It sounded as lame as it felt, but she chose to ignore that fact and dignify it with an answer.

"My father was a miller who tried to cheat some of the Favored into buying bad flour. It was a long time ago, when the Favored had just taken the palace and nobody really knew about their power. They tied my father to his water wheel and forced me to watch him go around and around until he drowned."

"Oh. I'm sorry," he said, now feeling even worse. Even though she'd been making life miserable since they'd met, nobody deserved to have to see that.

She shrugged. Instead of being angry with him for bringing it up, she seemed slightly softer and more vulnerable. But her words, as always, showed no chinks in her armor.

"Don't worry about it. I was six at the time, and I can hardly even remember what happened. The Favored actually took me in as a ward, eventually finding a family for me among the rich merchants. So, I had a much more privileged childhood than I would have with my father."

Something about the way she said it made him think that her childhood might have been full of little trinkets, but had not been a normal, privileged, or happy one. In his mind, an orphaned girl would not be much of a boon to a wealthy family in normal circumstances – and those trinkets probably came at an appalling cost.

Yella looked at him sharply, probably wondering how much he'd been able to deduce, and then continued. "My stepfather was part of the resistance, a distant cousin to our exiled royalty who had lost too many privileges to the new regime. Eventually, of course, the Favored got him, too. But by that time, I was old enough to strike out on my own. I met Hareg when I was serving mead at an inn."

Sangr concentrated on keeping his features blank. She smiled, the first time he'd seen her do it.

"And three years later, here I am. I hope that today, we'll see something beautiful happen."

"Yeah, I was wondering about that. How are we supposed to pull that off? After all, there's a lot of them –"

"More than fifty mind readers and five hundred retainers and servants," Yella interjected.

"And they're all locked inside that castle."

Yella chuckled slightly, but quickly turned serious again. "We know. But you also have to take into account that we've been watching their movements. The Most Favored and his retinue – both regular sycophants and other high-ranking Favored –

go into the market every moonday just before dusk. They know that they will receive gifts of fresh-baked moonbread from frightened stall-keepers. One of the merchants will cause a disturbance, and we'll fall on them from the crowd. In one strike we'll decapitate the bastards."

That seemed highly unlikely, but Sangr kept his thoughts to himself. He was about to ask her a few questions of a more personal nature, maybe something along the lines of, 'You know that you're all going to get killed, so why don't you run off with me instead?' but she held up a hand in warning.

"From here on out, keep farmer's thoughts at the front of your mind. Sheep, wheat, potatoes. If you must, think about how I'd look naked and what you'd do to me." Yella said this without even a hint of humor – deadly serious, that was the little ray of sunshine he'd come to love. "But try to avoid getting us killed with anything else. The trick to fooling their mind-reading is to keep any subversion in the second layer, and always concentrate on keeping the inanities foremost. Since you're the least experienced, and therefore the greatest risk, we'll stay apart from the main group, as backup."

That suited Sangr fine, although the likelihood of him jumping in if they needed backup was so close to zero that it didn't really bear thinking about.

By then, the spires of the palace had come into view, so he tried to think about potatoes. It didn't really catch, possibly since he'd been born on a sheet of ice next to the sea far to the north, where the main crop was seaweed and their diet consisted mostly of fish and seal meat. Unlike peasants on the plains, Sangr found it really hard to get at all enthusiastic regarding dirt and seeds.

Yella, on the other hand, bore contemplation. That a woman could walk around in those leather breeches and not get raped on every corner spoke volumes about her ability to defend herself. He fantasized happily about pulling them off, something he imagined would be difficult even with her cooperation; they were just too tight, and they would probably snag in the most delightful places.

She glanced over at him, a half-smile on her features. *I think she can tell that farming wasn't my thing*, he thought.

Soon enough, the marketplace, a relatively typical example of its kind, appeared. The senses were immediately overwhelmed by colors and smells. Incense battled valiantly against the sharp scent of pigs, while clashing orange and brown awnings made it impossible to look over the square without cringing. A wicker cage full of live chickens squawked and fluttered loudly enough that Sangr could barely hear the voice of the crier's over their din. At least the square was cobbled; stone slick from the excretions of countless goats, chickens, and foot traffic would always be preferable to the more typical churned mud.

Dominating the square itself loomed a huge building which, at first glance, looked like one of the temples of the sea god on the coast: a huge central nave with two spires growing out of the front wall. The main difference lay in the massive, rectangular building behind, evidently living quarters of some kind.

"That's the palace," Yella said unnecessarily.

"An inspiring sight." Sangr was trying to fit into his role as an unsophisticated farmer. The building was big enough that someone less traveled might conceivably be amazed.

"Come, let me show you the world-famous eye of Qalnoth." They were laying it on a bit thick, but nobody seemed to be paying us any attention, so maybe Yella knew what she was doing.

The entrance was built on the same scale as the building. The double wooden doors were twice Sangr's height, guarded by two men in black robes, hook-ended scimitars prominently displayed on their hips. Impressive, but mostly for show; the doors were thick enough that, if closed, it would take a battering ram to open them.

Sangr realized that he must have let that last thought slip through his veil of innocent tourist's musings because both the guards suddenly turned their heads and studied him sharply. He grinned at the nearest and said, "Everything's so big here." And thought furiously about the height of the door and the beauty of the exterior decorations. They relaxed slightly and made no move to stop them.

The public area of the palace was obviously a temple, presumably to the glory of Qalnoth, a deity he'd become extremely familiar with over the last three days, but one which he was happy never to have heard of before. One of those father/world creator types, but with the huge difference that those in positions of trust in his church were granted special powers – in this case, the power of telepathy. These were the guys who'd been making life miserable for his adoptive brothers in arms.

"Wow," he said to Yella, happy that he could stop faking. It wasn't necessary to dissemble in order to show awe at this church. Gold was evident everywhere. On the altar, the cups, candlesticks, vessels. Arcane symbols shaped like all-seeing eyes were hung on every available surface.

It was extremely obvious that this Qalnoth had been doing quite well for himself – the townsfolk must have found it hard to hide riches from acolytes who could read their minds.

And then he saw it. On the wall behind the altar, held in place by a simple-looking iron clasp was the largest diamond Sangr had ever laid eyes on, the size of both of his fists held side by side and, he noted with delight, it actually was slightly pinkish in color. And it was right there where anybody could see it. The Eye of Qalnoth.

Nevertheless, it wouldn't be easy to take. Eight visible men, complete with robes and sharp objects stood at various strategic points around the nave. Two of them lurked at the foot of the stairs leading to the altar, effectively blocking any ascent.

Sangr caught his thoughts straying towards methods by which he could take the stone. Knowing that *those* sorts of thoughts could easily be lethal, he simplified them. *Pretty diamond, pretty diamond, pretty diamond.*

It must have worked because, after he tired of just looking at the thing, they were allowed to leave the Church of Qalnoth in one piece.

The fact that the plan called for Sangr and Yella to remain on the sidelines unless sorely needed, along with the need for the different groups never to cross paths or words, dictated that the afternoon passed in relative tranquility. They took a late lunch at the inn on the square, a dark stone affair which compensated for its interior gloom by putting tables out in the sun. Despite the marketplace smells, Sangr decided that it was a pleasant spot to spend a few hours in the company of a pretty girl.

They watched the world go by, criticized the inhabitants' dress sense, the ball-kicking technique of the urchins among the stalls. They talked about the sunny weather and how beautiful Krenn could be in the spring. Basically, they talked about everything except (for obvious reasons) the expected early evening entertainments and (less obviously) details of her life and his own.

Whether Yella was only playing at being friendly in order to avoid having him think things that would get her, and her friends killed, or she was actually warming up to him, it was an enjoyable afternoon, and the sun soon began to cast long shadows from the vendor's stalls over the flagstones of the plaza. He'd had no time to even begin planning the removal of the stone from the altar, which, considering the attitude of the locals towards people who move against their interests was probably just as well.

Just before dusk, the guards at the palace's side entrance were changed again. This time, the two ceremonial soldiers with halberds were replaced by eight men who looked like they knew exactly what to do with the swords hanging from their belts. The lack of jeweled scabbards made Sangr pretty nervous.

"It seems that they're expecting trouble," he said, nodding towards the men. They were about a hundred yards to the right, on the street that formed one of the sides of the square, and which also ran beside the palace. Sangr's face must have shown the strain of talking about enemy positions while thinking about corn; he definitely felt it scrunch up most unnaturally.

"No. That's about the same number of men they always use to guard the Most Favored. They have no illusions regarding the love that the people actually have for them – the only reason they haven't killed everyone is that they wouldn't have anyone to grow their crops for them."

"Are you really thinking of attacking those guys? They look like they could cut Hareg's men to ribbons without even breaking a sweat." He thought hard about corn. *Corn, Corn, Corn.*

"Our men are tougher than you think, and these guys will be distracted by the diversion. We'll get them this time."

Sangr grunted. He wasn't at all sure of that.

The Favored themselves began to emerge only minutes later. Well-fed men in black robes surrounded by hangers-on and lavishly dressed women were easily identifiable as the ruling class in a town where most wore coarse homespun and leather.

They set out towards the square with no ceremony and the air of a group of people going about their accustomed routine. They walked into the marketplace unconcernedly, and some of his foreboding lessened. *Corn. Chickens.*

Once the Favored were completely lost to sight behind the tents, Yella signaled that Sangr should accompany her. They took position on the steps of the Palace temple entrance, from where the tops of some heads among the stalls, but not much more, could be seen.

Suddenly, flames burst out among the tents and shouts sounded from the square. The cries of alarm turned to anger as the unmistakable ring of sword on sword emerged from the confusion.

So, Sangr thought, shaking his head, *the ambush actually worked.*

But this was premature. Nearly forty men, armed to the teeth and dressed in the black of the Favored ran out of the alley and hit the marketplace, swords drawn. Yella started and ran towards the battle, pulling out of his grasp despite his best efforts to stop her.

Sangr almost ran after her, enchanted by her charm of the afternoon, but caught himself after five steps. He didn't really owe them anything, and Yella… well, he comforted himself with the thought that she was uninterested in him, anyway.

He suspected that the ambushers had been betrayed, and that none of them would live to tell the tale. It was wiser simply to try to gain what he could from this and make a run for it. But it was hard to give up on them.

He turned and sprinted up the steps, taking them three at a time. The massive door to the Temple was slightly ajar, and Sangr hit it with his shoulder. The single guardsman inside, just a few paces from the door only managed a slight squeak and an asinine look before Sangr ran up to him and drove the point of his rapier through his neck. He died in a thrashing heap; the blood unable to darken the already black front of his robes.

Jumping back from the body, Sangr scanned the gloom for the rest of the guards, ready to go head-to-head with up to three of them or run like hell from any number greater than that. But the temple was deserted. Evidently, the Favored had decided that cleaning up the resistance required all the manpower they could lay their hands on. The guard on the floor had been deemed sufficient, probably because he had forty friends just a few yards away in the square.

It would prove to be an expensive mistake.

Four heartbeats later he was at the altar. After a few more of using the rapier as a crowbar had the stone loose. And one after that saw his fingers close around the diamond. Sangr was delighted to see that it was too big for his hand.

He ran back to the door, pulled it open, and stopped. The noise that hit him from the battle in the plaza was like nothing he'd ever heard before, as if the legions of hell were all whispering together, but louder than the horns of Arien.

He put his hands to his head. He couldn't clear his thoughts, and the only idea he could push through was that one side had called in some kind of vile sorcery. The worst part about it was that, visually, nothing seemed amiss. A large group of Favored seemed to have surrounded a small warehouse on the far end of the market and were trying to fight their way through the door.

The Song of Sangr

Sangr charted a diagonal course down the stairs towards the street on the side of the square, wanting nothing more than to leave the whole thing behind. He ducked into a crossing alley, waiting to see if there was any pursuit, but nobody came in after him. Not trusting himself to the dark, muddy cross-street, he continued down the paved main road, trying to appear casual to passers-by, desperately trying to avoid thinking of the stone he was carrying.

There was no need to worry. The streets were completely deserted, and he couldn't blame them. A pitched battle was going on in the town square – a sorcerous battle which, even here, could be felt. Every once in a while, one of those deathly whispers could still be heard, and here on the fringes, he could even make out the words.

…how will we pay for… seemed to hit him from an open window.

…such a beautiful evening to… came up with the breeze when he crossed a wide street.

Sangr ran, and the whispers ran behind him, beside him, within him. Snippets of some unholy thought, each sounding as different from the rest as one voice is from another.

He kept going until he left the town, left the voices. He stopped about a hundred yards from the nearest house, hands on his knees, panting.

You should always look behind you.

Sangr jumped and turned, sword ready. Had it been a human voice or a sorcerous whisper? It seemed familiar.

Yella stood about ten yards away, laughing.

"You just couldn't resist touching it, could you?" she said.

Sangr just looked at her. *I'd thought she was dead.*

"No," she giggled, "I'm fine. You didn't really think I'd jump in and get myself disarmed, captured, and raped to death by that bunch, did you?"

It took Sangr a moment to realize that he hadn't said anything, and yet she'd answered.

"You!" Sangr exclaimed, pointing at her with the rapier. "It was you all the time. You're one of them! You betrayed Hareg and the rest."

She just smiled.

"But why?"

"My stepfather probably deserved it. And Hareg's bunch?" She shrugged. "The Favored's gold was good enough to overcome any qualms I might have had. When I turned in the merchant, they kept their promise and made me one of them, so I knew I could trust them to pay up this time. Everyone understood that I would be much more effective in hunting down subversives if nobody knew about it, so here I am."

"You won't capture me," Sangr said. She'd surprised him once, and now he knew why. She wouldn't beat him in a fair sword fight.

She smirked. "Are you so sure?" she asked. "Anyway, I don't want to fight you. I want to run away with you. Don't think the Favored won't be able to convince anyone of the power of their god now that they've lost the jewel, mind readers or not. I predict that they'll start turning up dead with alarming frequency."

"Yeah, that's just what I need – a woman who can read my thoughts and who enjoys getting her friends killed for a little money. Go away and maybe I won't kill you."

She actually looked hurt. "You don't need to worry about me. I won't be able to hide anything from you."

"Yeah, right," he laughed. "You keep forgetting that you're the Favored here, not me."

I've got some bad news for you, she didn't say.

Sangr knew she didn't say it, because her lips didn't move. He was watching, and yet, he heard it.

He sat down, hard, on the packed dirt road.

She smirked. "You shouldn't have touched the diamond."

"What?"

"The diamond. It's ensorcelled, and once you touch it, you become telepathic."

"So, it wasn't the god?"

She laughed again, the pretty tinkling of snowmelt into spring pools. It contrasted beautifully with her deep voice. Sangr didn't care; he could have cheerfully strangled her.

"Don't be silly. The head priest of the favored was just a guy who happened to rob the right corpse after a magical battle. That and a good story created what you saw today."

"So how do I get rid of it?"

The tinkle again, and this time Sangr's murderous intentions must have been foremost in his mind because she said, "If you kill me, you'll never find out if you could have gone through with your fantasies. By the way, you've got a really sick imagination." She actually had the gall to leer? "Oh, and you can't get rid of it, so you might as well learn to use it. I can help you with that."

As his world tumbled around him, knowing he could never have a moment of peace as long as people were anywhere nearby, that he was a freak and a monster, and that he would never be fit for human society again, Sangr dimly noticed that Yella was dragging him to his feet and to the side of the road, where she'd hidden a couple of horses.

She mounted and looked down. "You don't really want to get caught, do you?"

Sangr must not have, because he got on the horse. But he swore this was definitely the last time he'd ever steal a magical diamond from a mysterious temple.

Yes, I know that's what I said last time, he thought, before remembering that thoughts were no longer private.

Favored Methods

"**D**id you just think that?" Sangr said.

"Think what?" Yella replied.

The exasperation she was feeling, as well as a couple of thoughts along the line of 'I probably shouldn't have let him have the power to read minds' came through, louder and clearer than what he'd felt before.

"Never mind. It wasn't you. This thought… tasted… different."

Yella nodded in satisfaction. "I'm glad you're starting to get the hang of it. You've been driving me nuts. I told you: relax. You'll learn how to tell people's thoughts apart just like you can tell who's talking by the sound of their voice. You just need to give it time." She took another swallow of her beer. That woman could drink. "Besides, it's bad enough having to hear you think things. When you blurt them out as well, it's just annoying."

"Well, I just caught an interesting thought."

"Was it about flaying a couple of prisoners before feeding them to the fire spirits?"

"Yes."

"It came from over there." Yella nodded in the direction of a table halfway across the common room where a big man with a long black beard and dark robes was laughing with a woman.

"Yeah, he looks the part."

"Not him, her."

Sangr focused on the woman. About thirty, dressed in a perfectly normal brown and blue riding outfit. He'd dismissed her as a noblewoman who enjoyed being seen with magicians. She had a round face, blond hair, and big, innocent blue eyes. Very pretty, but not particularly sinister looking. "Really?"

"You'd better believe it. And judging by what she's thinking now, she is the very woman we want. We'll have to follow her."

His disbelief faded when the lady got up and strode towards the door, big man in tow. The crowd parted for her like she was an armored troll. The big guy didn't seem to notice. He was watching her body through her riding breeches. Sangr caught some of the things he was thinking of doing to her.

Yella's smirk told him that the man was likely to be out of luck.

As soon as the door closed behind them, Sangr left a couple of coins on the rough wood of the table, and they followed the pair outside. After the hot, dense atmosphere of the inn, the crisp night air—

even tinged as it was with the distinct smell of the town's sewage—felt glorious.

A carriage could be heard disappearing into the night.

"No need to get horses," Yella said. "I don't think they're going very far."

They followed along, using the driver's thoughts—and Yella's experience with the gift given to them by the accursed diamond—to track them effortlessly on foot. They walked unhurriedly.

About an hour later, a lump in the darkness beside the road brought them to a halt. Flies buzzed around something sweet-smelling. Sangr lit a small taper.

"By all the gods!" he exclaimed and turned away. The few moments of light had been enough to show them a flayed piece of dead meat the size and approximate shape of the man with the beard.

"She didn't waste much time." Yella studied the body. "She must pay her coachman really well."

"Or keep him constantly under threat."

"Perhaps, but she can't watch him all the time. On these plains he could run in any direction. She'd take ages to find him again. The way to keep this kind of employee is by paying good wages."

"I wish the guys following us would take ages to scour the plains."

"The Favored need their diamond back. Without it, they're as good as dead. And besides, they can read minds. No one who saw us can conceal our whereabouts. But that's not our main concern right now. We need to reach this woman before she goes to bed. I don't want to wake her."

"Yeah, we might catch her in a bad mood and who knows what she'd do then."

"Relax. We'll be fine. Remember: we'll know what she's planning as soon as she thinks it."

"Yeah. The question is whether we'll be able to prevent her doing it once we know what she's going to try."

"Stop complaining," Yella said. "I know where they're going."

"Do we really want to go after her."

"If you want to get a good price for that diamond… yes. We don't have any other choice."

They trudged along the dark dirt highway until they reached a tall, forbidding wall. It wasn't much of an obstacle for Sangr. He'd made his living and his reputation getting into complexes like this one, most of which didn't have walls that were this easy to climb. Once atop it, he let a line down, allowing Yella to join him.

The woman's house was set in huge, wooded grounds, and they arrived just as the doorman was about to close the main door for the night.

"This is where we announce ourselves," Yella said. They'd discussed it. Sangr had wanted to ambush the sorceress in her room, but he'd been outvoted by one vote to one.

Before they had a chance to address the lackey with the huge ring of keys, however, a voice sounded from within. "Tell them to come in, Isstvan."

The two adventurers exchanged a look and a shrug, then walked into the entrance hall. The woman was seated in the next room, a roaring fire casting a warm yellow glow over everything. "Just when I thought I was going to get to turn you guys into cinders, you decided to act civilized and come to the front door. I'm a bit disappointed. I don't get many unwanted visitors I can practice my really nasty spells on."

See? I told you. Yella's thought reached him as if she'd spoken in his ear. He shrugged mentally; certain she could sense his thoughts.

The woman eyed them expectantly. "So, are you going to tell me what you want, or should I just kill you and get it over with?"

Sangr stepped forward. He wasn't going to lose a sale over something as banal as a death threat. "Look at this," he said, unwrapping a stone the size of both of his fists. It had a slightly pinkish cast and sparkled spectacularly in the firelight.

The sorceress' scowl disappeared, replaced by a look of avarice. "That is a pretty rock."

"It's a diamond."

"Ah," the sorceress replied. "*That* rock. I assume you've both touched it."

"Yes."

"Interesting."

So, the woman knew about the Eye of Qalnoth and the power it conferred to those who laid hands on it. She knew that every thought going through her mind was an open book to the two interlopers standing in her midst. Interesting was an understatement.

"You're thinking that you could just do away with us and pry the diamond from our corpses. But Sangr is very fast with that rapier. Are you sure you can get it done in time?"

The ghost of a smile played along the corners of the woman's mouth. "As I said, interesting. Do you know who I am? Or did you choose me because my house looked like someone rich lived in it?"

"Your reputation precedes you, Ki."

Sangr did a double-take. With the way people had been taking about the bloodthirsty, implacable

Ki, he'd imagined that she would be a scarred, evil necromancer of about three hundred years of age, each unnatural second of it squeezed from the life-force of an unwilling victim. Instead, she was an attractive woman not much older than he was. Then he remembered how quickly the formidable-looking man in the inn had been reduced to a wet red mess and his mind returned to the task at hand.

Yella was still speaking. "You are the only magic user whose use for a stone like this happily intersects with the availability of funds to buy it. And, equally important, you have the ability to keep possession of it once it's in your power."

"You actually want me to pay you for the privilege of keeping the Favored tied up while you make a run for it?" Seeing Yella's shocked expression, Ki laughed. "One doesn't have to be a mind reader to understand how petty thieves think. If you bite off more than you can chew, it is expedient to pass the problem to someone with stronger jaws."

"Then you won't buy it?"

"I never said that. But you'll have to knock the irritation off the price. I'll give you two hundred for it, in gold."

"Two hundred? Kragler will give us five hundred without even having to haggle."

"Ah, but can you reach him before the Favored catch up to you? I hear they're very hard to shake. And I also assume they're very annoyed with you for walking off with the source of their power."

"We'll figure it out. We've stayed ahead of them so far, after all."

"Unfortunately, you don't have time."

"We—" Whatever Yella had been about to say was drowned out with the sound of shattering glass as three men entered the room through the window. Unwrapping their heads, which they'd covered against being cut by the glass, they began to go for their swords. A gesture from Ki froze them in their tracks.

"Hello, gentlemen," the sorceress said. "We've been expecting you."

The leader strained against the magical bonds holding him and snarled. "Who are you?" The woman just smiled, and the man blanched. "I'm sorry for the intrusion, Mistress Ki. Abjectly so. This has nothing to do with you at all. We are just trying to bring two thieves to justice."

"And yet you had no qualms about destroying my window."

"We didn't know it was yours. We will pay for all damage plus some extra for disturbing you. Just give us these two fugitives and you will not have to concern yourself with trifles."

"Ah, but I'm already concerned. You see, these two are in possession of something that interests me. I'll give them back to you if I can keep the stone."

"What? Impossible!"

"I thought you might feel that way. Too bad, really. It would have saved you all a lot of bother. If that's the way you feel about it, then… how about we play a little game. If the thieves win, I'll buy the diamond for three hundred in gold. If you win, you can buy it back from me for a thousand in gold."

"And what about the thieves?"

"If you win, they will already have been dealt with."

That didn't make Sangr particularly happy.

"And what do we have to do?"

"Ah, no. That would be telling." Ki snapped her fingers, and the world went dark.

Sangr had absolutely no forewarning.

"Yella? Yella? Are you there? I can hear you thinking, but I can't see you. Are you all right? Ah, yes. I caught that thought perfectly. I see you're fine and as pleasant as always."

"Will you be quiet? Just think what you need to say. I'll get it."

He kept from answering verbally, but it was an effort. The clammy, humid darkness put his nerves on edge.

And so will the Favored, he thought.

I don't feel them here.

Why is it dark? Did she do something to us?

I don't think so. It's just dark. Come towards me.

Guided by her thoughts he groped around in the darkness, trying to keep from falling on his face over the uneven floor. He reached down to feel the ground and realized that it was paved with cobbles, but that they were torn and jumbled, not the smooth surface of market town squares.

He reached out ahead of him, trying to avoid slamming into something when he moved, and his hand touched something. Yella's thigh. He caught the indignant mental yelp and smiled to himself, allowing a couple of very dirty images to escape.

Keep dreaming.

That's not what you said the night we took the diamond.

I was drunk.

Not that drunk.

All right. I was happy. I'm not happy now, and you won't be either if we die here.

They advanced slowly, hand in hand, towards a slight easing of the pitch darkness off to the right.

Their eyes hadn't deceived them. As they made their way into the more illuminated area, they slowly gained the ability to see shapes around them. Mounds of some sort loomed to all sides. The cobbles wound between them.

"What is this place?"

The sound of Yella's voice startled him. It echoed back towards them from a thousand different directions.

He peered at a pile. "Just junk. Old wooden fittings. A metal grate of some kind. Old pots. It almost looks like Ki just transported us to the deepest cellar where her servants piled everything they didn't want anymore."

"Perhaps… but why?"

"To see whether we could beat the Favored back up?" Sangr ventured.

"I doubt it. She was very clear that if we didn't win, we would be dead. I think that, wherever we are, we'll soon be running into considerably deadlier things than old kitchen parts."

Sangr shrugged. "We still don't have much choice. Either we risk it, or we rot here."

"I don't think we'll rot," Yella replied. "Listen."

In the darkness behind them, a noise could be heard: a scratching sound reminiscent of insects in a cupboard but, somehow, giving the impression of much larger in size. A metallic clang, probably a displaced fitting falling from one of the piles echoed through the chamber.

Without a word, they turned and ran towards the light area, helping each other up as they stumbled over unseen obstacles. Sangr managed to give himself a sharp knock on the shin, but Yella took the biggest spill when she hit a short staircase lost in the gloom. He pulled her back to her feet, and they ascended the steps.

The light got better as they rose. A doorway came into view, tall and thin, at the top of the stairs. They ran towards it.

"Locked!" Sangr spat. He kicked at the door jamb with all his strength, but it held. Fortunately, one of the first skills he'd learned when he came down off the ice was how to get through locked doors. "I'll have to pick this."

Yella looked back towards the room and spoke. "Well, you'd better get it unlocked quickly. Concentrate on the door." He heard her pulling her sword from the scabbard.

"I should…"

"Can you get it unlocked or not?"

"I have to study it, check if it's booby-trapped."

"How in the world did you become a thief? That makes no difference at this point. Just do whatever you'd do if it wasn't. Don't look back. Trust me on this. Concentrate on the lock."

Ignoring Yella's curses and the sound of struggle, Sangr pulled out his picks. The link between their minds would tell him if she really needed his help; all he was getting from her was grim determination, not true alarm.

His mind descended into the lock. He'd seen dozens like it, usually in equally dim light. There was always treasure on the other side. The treasure behind this one was nothing less than the possibility of surviving the next few minutes. He probed the door with the two picks he normally used on locks of that design. He was expecting to break something, or to be burned to a crisp by a magical thunderbolt.

To his surprise, the second combination he tried resulted in movement within the mechanism. Could it really be that simple? He used a third pick to hold the position and pressed again with the first two. The lock popped open with an audible click.

The door, clogged with grime and mounted on rusted hinges, took a certain amount of persuasion but, by applying his back to it, he was able to create an opening wide enough to squeeze through.

A sense of urgency came from Yella. He turned back and saw her covered in blood from head to foot. A rat the size of a large dog faced her, staying just out of range of her short sword. The bodies of four of its companions littered the landing, dark with gore.

Without verbal warning, Sangr grasped her arm and pulled her through the opening. Then, with Yella's help, he pushed the heavy wooden door back into place. They piled some broken pieces of wooden banisters against it to keep it shut and Sangr wedged bits of wood under it.

"Do you think it will hold?"

"One of them? Maybe."

"You mean there are more?"

Yella laughed. "The mountains of junk were crawling with them, all coming this way. I thought I saw some bigger ones too, but was hard to tell in the dark. They'll come after us even if they have to gnaw through that door."

They were on an illuminated landing. It was impossible to tell where the light came from. It seemed to emanate from everywhere at once. Neither the two thieves nor anything else cast a shadow. But it was easy enough to see square staircases leading up and down.

"Which way?"

Sangr looked down the well of the stairs and then upward. Both holes were blanked off after a couple of levels. "I get the sense we're in a cellar."

"Yeah. Me, too. That's probably because of the rats."

As if on cue, the door behind them began to shudder as if a large army had applied a battering ram. The blow shook the whole building and the door scraped along the floor an inch.

"Let's go."

They ran up the stairs, trying to ignore the crashes, growing ever louder, from behind.

Sangr raced to the next level, and then the next and a third. By the time they'd ascended five floors he was panting, by the tenth the only thing that kept him moving was the thought of a rat twice his size pouncing on him from behind. He could clearly visualize one of the monsters tearing out his throat as he lay on the ground while another gnawed away his shirt and ripped out his guts. They could feast like kings on his remains.

His wanderings had taken him as far south as the port of Fairybottom. Even the jungles there held no rodents similar to the ones he'd seen sprawled at Yella' feet. The only explanation was magic, and that meant that Ki was making life difficult for them—probably for her own amusement.

Sangr ground his teeth. He hated when magicians insisted on playing games. But unless you could catch them off guard—preferably while they slept—there was little one could do other than grin and bear it.

Finally, after an eternal climb which left his legs burning like they'd been set aflame, they came to a long flag stoned corridor. Wood paneling and portraits indicated that they'd reached a part of the house that had been inhabited at some point. The sheer normality of the surroundings made the skin on the back of Sangr's neck crawl.

Once more, they had little choice but to go on. No matter what misgivings he had, the corridor was infinitely preferable to the giant rodents behind. They advanced slowly.

Nothing happened. They'd traversed half the hall without incident and Sangr began to eye the door in front of them. As ornate as the one in the cellar had been simple, this one looked like it would cause a large amount of trouble.

As sudden as it was unexpected, the thought from Yella, behind him made him turn around and pull his rapier from its scabbard in one motion. He was just barely in time to see her disappear into one of the picture frames, dragged along by some kind of spectral arms that stretched to near invisible thinness before snapping back into position, taking his companion with them.

Sangr ran to the frame and tried to jump in after her, but all he encountered was rough canvas.

He raised his sword to cut away the picture—there had to be a secret passageway beyond—but bands of steel suddenly wrapped themselves around his waist and immobilized him.

Sangr felt himself being pulled… straight into the portrait behind him. He struggled with all his strength, but there was no question of getting loose. For the second time in an hour, darkness fell.

The world around him seemed to have turned into some kind of liquid. Sangr felt as if he was underwater, but he could breathe normally. He moved his arms around in a panic, but only succeeded in turning himself upside-down. Or had he righted himself? It was impossible to tell.

Sangr let himself drift, trying to calm his raging heart and get his bearings. There had to be some landmark, some way to understand how to get back to the normal world—assuming that was even an option.

No bubbles emerged as he breathed, which meant he wasn't in water. Light—the same strange sourceless light as on the stairs—illuminated the space around him, but it was completely empty. He appeared to be floating in an infinity only occasionally interrupted by floating dots that looked like dark stars in a bright sky.

Desperation threatened to overcome him again. He pushed it down firmly. Logically, this was part of the sorceress' game, which meant that there would be a way to get out of it. Otherwise, what pleasure could she possibly derive from watching the struggle?

He floated in the aether, racking his brains for a solution. A thought nipped at the corner of his awareness, but he couldn't quite get a grip on it.

Again.

He tried to listen in on the thoughts, but they slipped away. He cursed his gift and cursed his lack of knowledge about it. He wished he'd listened to Yella when she explained the quirks of the ability she'd saddled him with.

Hunger.

That inhuman thought came through loud and clear, and he turned his head to see where it came from. Just in time he realized that one of the floating dots was growing, and that, more than a dot it was a creature of utter blackness. On second glance he realized that it wasn't just made of utter blackness: it was made of utter blackness and *teeth*.

Instinctively, he raised his hand. His rapier, still in his grip after being dragged into the picture with him, embedded itself deep inside the approaching sphere. Dark liquid poured out of the sphere.

More movement flashed in the corner of his eye. He thrashed to get out of the way as dozens of the dots converged upon their stricken comrade. In moments, as Sangr watched from a few arm lengths away—not feeling safe by any stretch of the imagination—the newcomers tore his original assailant to pieces. There was nothing left but a cloud of blood that drifted away on unfelt currents.

He swallowed and raised his sword, aware that he would die there, but hoping to at least make a fight of it.

Strangely, however, the black spheres showed no interest in him. Instead, they suddenly darted in the direction he thought of as up. He craned his neck to see what was happening, but the swirling mass of dots made it impossible to make anything out.

Alarm reached him. Yella's alarm.

He willed himself towards the mêlée and, to his surprise, found that he moved through the strange liquid air very effectively, just by thinking of his destination. Even so, he could never arrive in time. Considering the speed with which the things had destroyed the first one, he would be lucky if there was enough left of Yella to allow him to guess where she'd been by the time he arrived.

But he had to try. He thought of the thickest of the fray and found himself drifting in that direction. He could see movement… and not all of it consisted of black dots.

He willed himself to move faster. A leather boot suspended above his head was still connected to Yella's leg and, he was relieved to see, to the rest of her. He moved up and took his place beside her, rapier at the ready. She looked over at him, did a double-take, and then smiled with genuine warmth. He returned it.

As he'd feared, the dots had just finished tearing someone apart. By the look of it, there was much more blood in a human than in one of the attackers.

Directly ahead of them, two more people were fighting the black orbs. The battle was unusual in the extreme, as every time one of the men scored a hit on their attackers, the rest of the spheres would descend on the wounded member of their tribe and rip it to pieces. Only then did their attention turn back to the men.

Favored, Yella thought at him.

Ah, so they were the followers of Qalnoth, desperate to retrieve the diamond that, despite everything that had happened to them, was still safely ensconced within Sangr's pouch. But hadn't there been three of them?

His eyes stopped on the still-dissipating bright red splotch in the center of the fracas, and smirked. Two against two was better odds.

How do we get out of here? he projected at Yella.

I caught a thought a while ago. We need to make them spit us out.

What? What does that even mean? And who could have thought that?

But Yella was already moving. She approached one of the inky enemies and, deftly dodging its teeth, wrapped her arms around it.

Are you coming?

Sangr reacted without thinking. He reached out and took hold of the belt around Yella's waist just as the black ball began to buck and swerve. They held on doggedly as its attempt to throw them off became more and more desperate and violent.

Whatever you do, don't stab it.

Alarmed at the ever-faster motion, afraid that Yella's grip would slip and land them both in the thing's teeth, Sangr had been about to do precisely that. Thanks to Yella's warning, he realized that the only effect attacking the dot would have been to bring all of its peers to bear and probably get them both killed in the process. Maybe this mind-reading thing would be good for something after all. Well, it would after they got rid of Qalnoth's Favored, a group conspicuous for the fact every member of it could also read minds, which made the advantage moot.

Sangr saw the muscles on Yella's forearm tense as she applied pressure. He wondered if she was trying to strangle the thing. If so, he couldn't imagine what she wanted to achieve.

It bucked again, even harder than before. The thing clearly wasn't kidding around anymore. But Yella held as the struggle became titanic.

And then the thing stopped. It wiggled once more, speculatively and then the world around them stretched and Sangr found himself flying across the corridor onto the hard cold stones. Yella landed on top of him, straddling him in a most unmaidenlike way.

She sat up to look around and then gave him a sharp look.

"Can't you ever think of anything else?"

He grinned. "Not when you sit on me like that."

A sound at the end of the corridor made them look up.

"Run."

The sound of claws skittering for purchase on the wooden floor followed them down the passageway. The rats were so close that Sangr could feel the breath of the nearest one on his back. It was the size of a small pony.

In his panic, he ignored the portraits and crashed hard into something in the way. For a second, Sangr's blood froze: he was sure that grasping arms would pull him back into the incomprehensible world of the black dots—and this time, Yella wouldn't be there to pull him back out following telepathic instructions only she could hear.

The image of a slowly dissipating cloud of blood—his own—filled his thoughts and Sangr fought like a demon before he realized that what he was tangled in wasn't a disembodied set of arms or a spherical monster, but a man just as frightened as he was.

Sangr disengaged and, without looking to see who he'd run into, headed into the door at the right of the corridor. He'd seen Yella slip into the door on the left, but couldn't reach her. The pony-rat snarled and scratched at that one.

To his immense relief, the door opened easily, and he bowled through, followed immediately by the man he'd run over.

As they struggled to close the door against the weight of the oncoming rodents, he realized that his companion was one of the Favored, the servants of Qalnoth who'd followed them to Ki's mansion. The man seemed to comprehend the situation at the same time. Swords, never sheathed after the episode with the dark spheres, came up into defensive positions.

"Give me the Eye," the man said.

"Come and take it."

The man took a step forward, foolishly thinking he would be able to do just that and Sangr casually flicked out his sword. It was a move he knew would catch any opponent completely by surprise because it wasn't meant to kill or maim, only to draw a little blood on the man's sword arm and distract him in the ensuing fight.

The man parried and grinned at him. "You forget. I can read your thoughts. All the skill you might have is useless. You're going to die."

As sword clashed against sword, Sangr used every trick in the book to attempt to disable his opponent, but always found steel at hand to block his thrusts. It seemed the man's prediction would come true—Sangr's skill at reading his opponent's intentions was not yet at the point where he could react without thinking, which meant he had to rely on his training to catch the counterattacks. Sangr's skill would eventually fail, the man's telepathy would not.

Just as his opponent drew blood, a nick on the chest, the door crashed and splintered. It was barely holding.

"We need to stop. The rats are coming through. We can continue once we get out of here."

Whether it was his tone or his thoughts that conveyed sincerity, the man believed him and stepped back. "What do you suggest?"

"We should go that way." Sangr pointed left.

"Why?"

"Because the rats are that way." The Favored seemed to find this a reasonable suggestion and sprinted ahead across an enormous room. When they reached the end, he stopped. "There's a landing up there, but the stairs are gone. What now?"

"I'll give you a boost to the landing. You can pull me up after you."

The man gave him a strange look. "Why would you trust me to do that?"

"I've got the diamond. And unless you want to dig it out of a rat, you'll pull me up after you."

"All right. We sheathe our swords on three."

Watching each other like hawks, they did so. Sangr breathed easier once the man's blade was out of sight.

"Stand on my hands, I'll give you a leg up."

With this assist, the Favored managed to get his fingers onto the rough ledge and pull himself up. Then he took a firm grasp of a post with one hand and dangled the other towards Sangr.

Sangr jumped for it but missed by a handspan.

"I can't reach!"

The man leaned further out. "You'd better make it this time. Sangr looked back and nearly fainted. A brown wave bore down on him from the other end of the room. He took three steps and jumped.

He almost didn't make it. His fingers didn't quite close over the man's wrist. With a sickening lurch he began to fall back.

An iron grip took hold of him just as the lead rat scratched his boot. Sangr found himself being pulled up.

He lay panting on the boards, safely out of reach of rodent teeth for the moment. "You must really want this diamond," he panted.

"It is the center of our faith, the key to our religion. Any of us would gladly die to retrieve it."

"It's the tool that, by making you mind-readers, allows you to terrorize and subjugate the plains."

The Favored shrugged. "There are many who don't understand our creed. Enemies at every turn. We do what we must."

Suddenly, he whipped his sword out and, with a metallic clang that echoed around the chamber, he parried the thrust that Yella had aimed at his back. "As your friend here discovered, I'm well-practiced in the gift. You can't sneak up on me."

Yella stepped back, out of his reach.

"I'm sorry to hear it," she replied.

He gave her a hard look. "Where's Erival?"

"Your friend? I think he's rodent food."

"How did you get up here then, traitor?"

"Didn't they brief you? When your order bought me, the first thing you did was to train me as an acrobat for the high priest's entertainment. That served me well as we tried to climb out of the way of the rats. Perhaps you should have trained Erival as well."

The argument soon descended into a three-cornered sword fight, but even with numerical advantage, Sangr and Yella could do no more than hold their own. Finally, Sangr became exasperated. "This isn't getting us anywhere. Let's deal with the rest of this labyrinth and we can kill each other when we get out."

Again, the man peered closely at him as if trying to read his true intentions. A surprised look crossed his face and he grunted. "Fair enough."

They crossed the ledge to the only available door and found themselves outside… in a maze of colossal hedges. "We stick together," the man said.

Sangr sighed. Why was it that every magician on the planet had a maze in his cellar or somewhere on the grounds? Was it the fumes of magic powders that caused the need to annoy the hell out of visitors and marauders? Wouldn't it have been much easier on everyone involved if unwanted visitors were simply burned to a crisp by magical fireballs?

"We need to turn left at every junction. That will get us out eventually."

"That will take forever," Yella said.

"Do you have a better idea?"

"Yeah, let's hack through these plants." She attacked the nearest hedge with her sword and flew backward into the one behind her. It took her a couple of moments to get back to her feet and brush herself off. She shook her head. "All right, let's turn left."

The maze was typical of the breed. The moon barely illuminated the dark corners, out of which wolves, bears, and boars occasionally emerged, where the creatures found they'd been betrayed by their own thoughts The three fighters made quick work of the animals.

More than two hours passed before they reached another door which opened onto a banquet chamber holding a long trestle table laden with food and drink. Pitchers flanked a roasted boar which smells divine and could have fed an army.

"What if it's poisoned?"

"Then I'll die happy. And I plan on drinking all the wine. Unless you're sharing with me?" he addressed this last to the Favored.

"If you're thinking of blunting my ability, you can forget it. I can read your thoughts and predict your moves just as well dunk as sober."

"That's fine. I'm planning on blunting my own skills, not yours." Sangr poured himself a cup of wine and drained it. "It's excellent. You should try it." He sliced a portion of the boar away and chewed. "This is good, too. But the wine is simply incredible." He drained another glass.

Yella seemed about to remind him that they shared the room with an armed enemy and needed their wits about him, so he gave her a warning look. She tilted her head at him but stayed silent. She even sipped her own wine.

The Favored, seeing that Sangr was intent on getting drunk, smiled and partook in some himself. Nowhere near as much as the thief, but he was clearly a man who enjoyed a good vintage.

Finally, Sangr staggered away from the table and pulled his rapier out of its scabbard. "All right. It's time to resolve this once and for all."

The man chuckled. "Hardly sporting, but I won't complain. You deserve everything that's coming to you for taking that diamond." He pulled out his own sword.

Sangr approached. Even drunk, he knew that he was a better swordsman than any of Qalnoth's Favored. He'd trained for hours every day before he'd touched the diamond and been infected with its magic, while the god's minions relied on their ability to know what their opponent would do before they did it. His body would know what it was doing. Muscle memory and a perfect sense of balance was what made him great, not trickery.

Sangr parried an attempt to disembowel him and then quickly slashed at his opponent's chest, opening a gash along his ribs.

"What? You didn't think of that!"

"Can't think..." Sangr smiled at him. "Too drunk."

Sangr pressed his attack, his body working independently of his nearly absent mind. Bloody streaks crisscrossed the Favored and he soon fell to the ground.

"Won't kill you. You saved my life," Sangr said. He took the man's blade and walked back to the table. Swordplay was thirsty work.

A door hidden in the paneling opened beside the table and Ki walked into the room. She gave the prone Favored a disgusted look, raised a hand and burned the man to a crisp with a fireball. Then she turned to Sangr and Yella.

"I was wondering how you'd get rid of him. That was quite resourceful."

"That's the only way to be safe in the towns they control. I heard the trick from a farmer," Yella said. "I didn't think he'd be able to fight that way blind drunk, though." She radiated approving thoughts.

"Good wine," Sangr said.

"Thank you. It's from my own personal reserve. You earned it both for the entertainment and for bringing me that stone. I've wanted it for the longest time, but the Favored, on their own turf, are quite formidable. You have my gratitude."

"Want your money… Can't eat gratitude."

Ki laughed, genuine mirth. "Most people would be lucky to find themselves alive in my keeping," she said. "It's unusual for anyone to be so bold."

"Forgive him," Yella said quickly, staring at the ashes of what had once been a strong and resourceful enemy, "he's drunk. He doesn't know what he's saying. Just let us go and we'll take whatever fee you deem fit."

The sorceress waved a hand. "I'm not offended in the least. I find honesty refreshing." Then she turned serious. "And I gave you my word that you would receive a fee. My word is my bond."

Yella bowed her head. "I'm glad to hear it."

"A thousand in gold. I can't have it bandied about that I pay less than Kragler, can I? I wouldn't want people to offer him all the good stuff." She tossed a purse on the table. It landed with a heavy thud.

Sangr gave her the leather-wrapped stone.

Ki held it gingerly. The sorceress knew of the power the pink diamond bestowed on anyone who touched it. She would think long and hard about what she had, both about the power it would give her and the price that came associated with that power. She turned towards the door and called back to them over her shoulder. "Enjoy the food. It isn't poisoned. Then leave through that door over there. If you get lost or try to take anything that doesn't belong to you, all bets are off."

Sangr headed for the table, but Yella cut him off. "We're leaving now," she informed him in a tone that brooked no argument.

Pausing only long enough to grab their money, she herded him through the indicted exit, along a path, and out the main gate. By the time they had made a few hundred paces along the highway, Sangr's head was beginning to clear because of the exertion.

"Hey, what's the big rush?"

"How long do you think it will take before she touches the diamond?"

He shrugged. "I don't know. Not long. All that power."

"Exactly. And when she did, she would have been able to read exactly what you were imagining. I assume most sorceresses don't play that kind of game with thieves."

"Oh. But she's so pretty." Sangr regretted the words as soon as they came out of his mouth. Yella would make him eat them later.

But for now, she contented herself with: "Maybe I should let you go back. After all, you remember what happened to her last lover, don't you?"

Sangr swallowed and followed her. He didn't even care where they were going, so long as it led them away from Ki.

Bane

"There's only one way to remove the curse," the dying man whispered. He paused, taking shallow breaths. The fireball had burned away most of the skin on the right half of his body, leaving a blistered, blackened patch. Three ribs could be seen, shining whitely in the charred wreckage of his chest. "Get the bane."

"The bane? But that's been lost for five years. There has to be another way." Sangr resisted the urge to shake him.

The man tried to shake his head, but his strength failed him. A single sigh escaped, a near-silent epilogue to an episode filled with noise, violence, and terror. Sangr let the body drop to the ground in disgust.

"Fuck," Yella said.

Tengut was a beautiful place. The spires rising around the square were ethereal things of airy wonder, taller than any buildings Sangr had seen before. The overall impression was that of a colossal sculpture made of cloud.

The festering rot was well hidden, just below the surface.

He could feel the fear rising in waves from the people in the plaza. Their thoughts were focused on one thing, and one thing only: to sell whatever they had in order to raise the City Tribute – the tax that would allow them to remain inside the walls one more night, and not have to face the horrors beyond. Here, an old man's thoughts were filled with hope and fear – hope that the trinket he'd found on the street would be enough to gather the coin he needed, fear of the things beyond the gates. There, a young woman's contained considerably less fear, but more disgust with what she had to do, every day, to come up with coin for herself and for her baby.

Sangr blocked off the random thoughts that assailed him from every side, allowing them to become part of the background. What he was searching for would not be found in the stray thoughts of some poor, scared soul walking through the square. He needed to get further in, get near the corridors of power.

To this end, the man beside him would be useful, if not pleasantly so. Karet the wine merchant was fat, sweaty, and loomed over the short, wiry thief. Most tellingly, though, he was willing to betray his city in exchange for the ability to read other people's minds. His thoughts were a chaotic mix of greed and fear of betrayal.

"Relax," Sangr told him. "We never renege on our promises."

Karet jumped. He knew about Sangr's ability, but that didn't seem to stop him from believing that his own thoughts were sacred. "I know this," he replied hastily. "Your reputation precedes you. Where is Yella?" His agitation was evident in both his clumsy attempt at changing the subject, and the enormous faux pas he committed in the process.

"Yella is camped out in the hills. She wasn't willing to pay the entrance fee." Women from outside the city weren't given the option of paying for their sanctuary in gold, no matter how long they'd been inside the city. It was the city's way of keeping foreign families from settling there.

"Outside? But that's suicide! The Shanna own the night."

"Yella can take care of herself. She thought she had better odds against a few specters than if she had to take on the entire garrison for the privilege of entering the city without being passed around like a wineskin."

The truth was that Yella was wearing an amulet that made her invisible to any magical search. It had cost them a lot of gold, but with the Favored searching for them, it had been a necessary expense and one that was now paying dividends. Sangr wore its twin hidden inside his jerkin.

Still, he worried about her. Over the past few months, their occasional dalliances had turned into something stronger, something he'd never had with any other woman… and he hated the thought of her beyond the walls.

Unfortunately, she'd been adamant that he had to go in without her. You didn't argue with Yella when she told you something like that.

Karet grunted. "If you say so." He didn't sound at all convinced.

They kept walking towards the inner city, a complex of terraced palaces rising between the spires, growing out of the hillside beyond the square. The elite of Tengut lived there. Sangr would have sworn that nothing could be more beautiful than the buildings around the plaza, but the palaces certainly made the attempt. Though less delicate than the common buildings below, the inner city made up for it by having bands of every color of the rainbow woven into the very material of the walls. The city shimmered in the afternoon sunlight.

"Are you sure you can get me in?" Sangr asked.

Karet nodded, but Sangr could feel his doubt. The merchant was getting nervous as they approached, having second thoughts. But underlying the fear was the determination to go through with it, if only for the fabulous reward. *It was so nice to have reliable companions,* Sangr thought.

They had no time for further conversation. The tunnel leading under the thick wall which separated the ordinary citizens from their masters loomed in front of them, and they had to deal with the two armored and feathered spearmen standing guard at the mouth.

Sangr opened up his mind and was immediately reassured. This trooper was a ceremonial soldier: he was more curious than suspicious, serene in the knowledge that his back was covered by elite guards inside the wall.

"State your name and your business," the plumed guard boomed.

Sangr suppressed a smile and tried to look bored but earnest as Karet explained.

"I am Karet, vintner to the ruling houses of the land. And this man is Lord Santos of the Geno, owner of a million slaves whose only task is to nurture the finest grapes in the north."

The Song of Sangr

The guard looked Sangr over. A hard look, steady, tempered by years of weighing miscreants attempting to invade the sanctuary of their betters. But his mind told another story: the man had already decided to let them through. Evidently, Karet went in and out every day, and if his guest was unwelcomed, that was a decision to be taken above the guard's pay grade. He moved aside.

The tunnel ended at an iron gate. Murder holes lined the entire length of the roof and at least one section of the floor boomed hollowly as they passed over it – sign of a pit trap.

Sangr took careful note as he passed; even if all went well, he would be leaving in a hurry with the garrison hot on his heels. What he saw made him decide that the tunnel would only be used as an exit strategy of last resort. Boiling oil tended to disagree with him, and sharpened spikes were even worse.

The gate swung open as soon as the man on duty recognized Karet. Smiles were exchanged, a few gold coins changed hands and even if he hadn't been a mind-reader, Sangr would have been able to tell that the final obstacle had been surmounted. In no time at all, they were walking through corridors of spun glass.

"Hanet is a good man. A family man." Karet grinned evilly. "Of course, he has two lovers on the side, and is always in the mood to help some poor woman in the outer city pay her fee, so my gold is always welcome. We were lucky to find him on duty – the guards change randomly."

Sangr wasn't listening to the other man's babbling. He was preoccupied with the surroundings. Long corridors led to inner courtyards surrounded by high walls, with only tiny patches of sky visible overhead. The complex would be very difficult to escape from.

The people they passed could have been from a different planet than those in the city outside. They strode confidently, with no worries about city tax. Their stray thoughts showed that most of them were involved in the clerical work of the palace, either rushing to an appointment or plotting how to gain favor with their superiors. Most that took notice of the mismatched pair ignored them – the rest simply dismissed them as supplicants of no particular note.

Which was exactly the way Sangr wanted it.

Before long, the pair reached Karet's home, a collection of small but luxurious chambers off one of the minor corridors. Sangr dumped his pack unceremoniously on to an empty chair and faced his host.

"Now what?"

"Nothing until dinner, in an hour or so. I, myself, am going to take a bath. Smuggling people into the inner city is a nervous business. The baths are communal, I'm afraid. Only the Great Ones have private bathing chambers."

"I'll come with you. The dust from weeks on the road won't sit too well with your guests."

Karet didn't know what Sangr was looking for in the inner city. They hadn't told him about the bane, captured years before by the Supreme Great One of Tengut – even Sangr wasn't quite certain about its nature. All they'd told him was that he would be rewarded handsomely for getting them into the city and into the presence of the most important people in town. Sangr could get the information he needed directly from their minds.

A communal bath might not be a meeting place of the upper echelons, but even servants might have information relevant to his mission. And besides, Yella would have a fit when he told her that he'd been living in luxury while she'd had to scrub in a cold mountain stream.

The baths had yielded no information, but dinner promised much better. True to his word, the wine merchant had assembled a congenial group of mid-level Great Ones. Men who wished to impress their betters by always having the best vintages on hand, and who had the coin to pay for it. Even without Sangr's reward, this dinner would have been profitable for Karet.

But it only took ten minutes for his enthusiasm to turn into frustration. None of the Great Ones at the table were thinking of the bane. It should have been, to some extent, on their minds. After all, the bane was the only thing that kept Tengut from the attack of the Mage Lords to the northeast. Only the wizard's fear of the single thing that was known to destroy their power absolutely kept this city safe.

Outside the walls, everyone knew about it. Was it possible that the Great Ones had kept something that important secret from their own people?

That might be good news. Maybe the bane was a small item, easily concealed, which might explain why no one seemed to have heard of it. And it went well with what Sangr had learned of the world of magic – the most powerful objects were generally small, inconspicuous things that had had spells woven carefully into their fabric by master sorcerers.

It made no difference how it had been achieved. What mattered to him was that a small piece would be much less cumbersome when trying to flee than a medium sized one. If the bane was some heavy item, a largish statue, for instance, he would be in deep trouble indeed.

But as the night wore on, it seemed that the size of the bane would be the least of his troubles. No one had so much as thought about the thing by the time dessert rolled around. Sangr knew what he had to do. Mentioning the bane, even casually, was a risky course of action, but there was no other choice. He didn't have days to spend on this mission. While he was wining and dining in luxury, his friends were falling, one by one, to the battlemages of Oixx.

"What a great city you have here," Sangr said. "Such stability."

"Yes," one of the Great Ones replied. "Our supreme Great One has much to brag about."

"And getting his hands on the bane must have helped."

Even as he said it, Sangr tensed, ready to defend himself if necessary. Ready to run, if the situation turned truly serious. Fortunately, none of the guards had asked him to give up his rapier, so it would be child's play to hold this particular group of soft nobility. But the world was full of surprises.

"Oh, the *bane*," the man to his right said with a smile. "While we're all thankful for her presence, we don't think our protection is the primary use the Supreme is putting her to." Other faces around the table smirked at this, at least one looking more like a leer. Only Karet's face registered slight suspicion. A quick probe of his ally's mind revealed that this was one inner circle secret he wasn't privy to.

At the word 'her', an icy ball formed in the pit of his stomach, a sensation made worse as he sifted the information from the minds of the men at the table, whose thoughts were suddenly filled with very graphic imagery. Most of what he got was a product of overly vivid imaginations, but it was enough for Sangr to know that the mission had just become much more complicated.

He didn't like it one bit and had a feeling that Yella was going to like it even less. Especially if he was successful.

The chambers of the inner city changed completely at night, as the light washing in from above was replaced by darkness punctuated by the occasional torch or patch of moonlight through the semi-transparent walls. The effect was eerie, and it was difficult to see the walls clearly. The passage was as silent as a tomb, but Sangr was unconcerned. As soon as he'd mentioned the bane, everyone's thoughts had immediately focused on the same thing: a white door covered in lace and frills. Even better, it was nearby, just a couple of corridors to the west – he'd seen it as he passed.

His only concern was how the harem would be guarded. It seemed unlikely that the supreme Great One would leave something like this to chance, and Sangr was expecting at least one, probably two guards. They would be eunuchs. The kind of supreme leader who would keep his women in a separate wing of the palace would also be the kind who'd place eunuch guards.

His plan was extremely rough, because there were simply too many variables that had to be taken into account. How many guards would there be? He was betting on one on the outside of the door and one on the inside, but there could be any number of them.

What was the layout of the harem? Would the bane be willing to come with him? If not, was she small enough for him to carry? Would there be any other way out of the chambers?

Close now. It was easy to be silent on the carpeted hallway, but it was also easy to get overconfident. And a eunuch's spear could be just as deadly as the sharpest sword, and some of them were both big and nasty.

Only a shadow moving in the darkness alerted him, at the very last moment, to the fact that there was someone lurking in the passageway. It came as a nasty shock that he hadn't detected anything from the man's mind – he could normally sense the thoughts of anyone in his vicinity, even those deeply asleep. But nothing came from this guard. The corridor could have been empty.

Was the man dead? Sangr stood very still in the deepest shadow and studied him. He thought he could hear soft breathing. So intent was he on keeping perfectly silent that when the guard moved, walking down the corridor in the opposite direction Sangr was momentarily too startled to move.

But he hadn't survived this long by freezing in the face of unexpected situations. Reacting quickly, he sprinted silently across the carpet, struck the guard as hard as he could on the back of the neck, and caught him before he hit the ground. Sangr was satisfied with the outcome; the operation had produced little noise, and the guard was still alive.

Looking at the man, Sangr thought it would be safe to assume that there would be another guard inside; this one was not a eunuch.

Despite what had happened earlier, he just couldn't believe in the existence of a guard. He could sense nothing whatsoever through the door. No guard concentrated on his job, no Great One's women dreaming of what they'd like to do with their lives if they weren't trapped in the Harem. Nothing. The room might as well have been empty for all the information he was able to gather from it.

Just like the guard at his feet might have been dead, except for the fact that he was breathing.

Sangr felt his heart race. Could he have lost his power? He'd become completely dependent on it ever since the day, just under a year ago, when he'd touched what he'd thought was a valuable diamond, only to find that it was cursed, and gave him the power to read other people's thoughts – a power he couldn't turn off, no matter how much he wanted to. But now, he could get nothing. He couldn't help thinking that it was a very inconvenient time to have his power fail him. Getting out of this warren of passages without knowing what the myriad guards who knew the place better than he did were thinking was going to be … interesting.

Nevertheless, he had no choice. The bane was the only way to counter the incredible magic set against his adoptive people, and Sangr was their only hope of getting their hands on the bane. The bane which, as far as he knew, was on the other side of this doorway.

The door presented a problem. He didn't know whether it was locked or not, didn't know if the guard behind it would open to a knock. It didn't look all that solid, so he could break it open, but that would alert the whole palace that there was something going on here. And it was unlikely that the harem would have a back entrance. Too much temptation.

A quick search of the man on the floor revealed no keys. Should he knock? Or just run into the door with his shoulder? He decided that it was better to perhaps alert a single guard than to wake the entire palace. And he had to act quickly; anyone could stumble onto him at any moment. He rapped softly, three times.

"Yes?" The whisper, male, came through the door.

"Food," Sangr replied, hoping his foreign accent would be hidden by the short word or muffled by the wood.

"What?" the voice said, but Sangr could hear the latch undoing on the other side. The guard evidently wasn't suspicious yet. A small crack appeared in the doorway, and faint light shone through.

Sangr acted immediately. He jammed his shoulder against the door as hard as he could, trying to make as little noise as possible. The door encountered resistance, as if it had met with a solid object and then he heard a thud. The movement stopped suddenly, held in place by something that yielded slightly, but not enough to open the door fully. Sangr pulled his rapier and slipped through the opening, which was not narrow enough to stop him.

The guard was blocking the entrance. The door must have hit him in the head and knocked him out. Soft, bloated flesh marked him as a eunuch as clearly as if he'd been holding a sign. Sangr knew he had the right chamber at least. He kicked the guard in the head, hard, just to be on the safe side.

He sniffed. The chamber smelled of unemptied chamber pots, of perfume, and lots of people, and two things were immediately apparent: it was unlikely that the room would have any windows he could climb out of, and his gift was not working – he couldn't sense a single presence. It was just his luck, he grumbled to himself. Whenever he was in a crowded marketplace surrounded by farmers, peasants, and beggars, he couldn't keep their incredibly boring thoughts out of his mind for a second, but when he needed his gift to work, to help him identify a single woman in a large harem, it was gone as if he'd never had it. The only positive aspect was that it hadn't failed him earlier; he would have looked extremely silly if he'd gone to all the trouble of sneaking in just to have to sneak out again empty-handed.

What would follow would be a little callous, and could possibly get messy very quickly, but he could still achieve his objective if he was careful. Sangr stood silently in the room for a few seconds, letting his eyes get accustomed to the deeper darkness and trying to ascertain whether anyone had noted his presence. Time was of the essence – the two guards wouldn't be out for long, and he preferred not to have to kill them if they woke.

Dark shapes began to coalesce in his vision, large rectangular forms that loomed in front of him. Beds, he thought, with tall posts and curtains pulled – fit for use by the Great One's many wives. He shrugged and walked towards the nearest one, rapier ready, and pulled the curtain aside.

Sangr could make out a flowing mass of hair, so he made a quick calculation and clamped down with his free hand. It took some fumbling, but he managed to cover her mouth before the eyes popped open, wide with terror, and clearly visible even in the gloom.

"If you try to move, you will die," he whispered, pressing the point of his rapier into her side for emphasis. "Do you understand me?"

She did nothing for a few moments, and Sangr felt an icy ball form in the pit of his stomach. All the cities near Tengut spoke the Common Tongue, but what if this girl was a trophy piece from some far-off land? He would have to silence her and then find one who did speak his language. And he didn't have time for that kind of thing at all.

Finally, eyes even wider, she nodded. Sangr sighed with relief.

"Good. Then if you do what I tell you, you'll be all right. Nod if you are going to help me."

She nodded, quicker this time.

"Good. I'm going to take my hand off your mouth. If you scream, I will drive my sword into your stomach. It will kill you, but not right away. You will take days to die, and you will suffer horribly. Am I clear?"

Another nod and she trembled. Sangr could feel moisture on his hands. Tears. He pulled his hand away. "I don't want to hurt you, and if you do what I say, you won't be harmed. I have just one question: do you know where the Sorcerer's Bane sleeps?"

"The Bane? Yes, she's…"

"Shh! Not so loud. Get out of bed quietly and show me."

The woman complied, walking softly over the carpeted floor to indicate a bed near the left wall. He kept a careful grip on her arm, the point of his rapier pressed softly into her side – softly, but present, lest she forget the consequences of any ill-advised attempt at flight.

"Is this the one?"

The girl nodded, and Sangr smiled at her. He wasn't sure whether she could see him in the dim light, but wanted to try to reassure her. Then he let go of her arm and punched her hard in the jaw.

He caught her as she fell, and thought to himself that, for a smallish thief who prided himself on his wits and his planning, he was certainly using quite a bit of brute force. At least he could take comfort in the fact that the rapier remained unbloodied. Sadly, though, such mercy put him at greater risk – any of the people he'd knocked out could come around at any time. He had to move quickly.

It was the work of a moment to clamp a hand over the mouth of the woman lying in the bed and manhandle her, struggling and kicking, out of the room. Fortunately, she was built along similar lines to his own – small and very thin, although quite evidently well-endowed. He shuddered to think how he'd have managed her if the woman had been Yella's size.

He needed to regroup and make a break for it, and the only place that offered even the slightest temporary safety was his own room. He dragged her down the hall and through the door, ignoring the fact that she was biting his hand hard enough to draw blood. "Will you stop that?" he hissed as soon as he'd closed his door. "I'm trying to rescue you from this place!"

She tried to speak, but his hand was over her mouth. "I'm going to let go, but if you scream, I'll have no choice but to kill you. Do you understand me?"

It was a lie, of course. This girl was absolutely critical to the survival of his adopted people. He might beat her senseless and tie and gag her, but there was no way he could afford to murder her.

But she didn't know that. She nodded, eyes huge.

"Good." He pulled his hand away, keeping it close enough that he could clamp down again quickly if necessary.

She calmed down long enough to give him a haughty look. "I was saying 'what makes you think I want to be rescued?'"

Sangr smirked. "I understand you were the spoils of war, handed from soldier to soldier until the Supreme Great One decided to keep you. Even now, I hear he often lends you to those courtiers who please him."

She shrugged. "It certainly beats the way I lived before. Smelly rebel camps, unwashed soldiers, always scared that some sorcerer's troops would find us. And, before you ask, the men in charge of guarding me handed me around back then as well. They couldn't care less that I was just a little girl. Now I have safety, warmth, all the food I can eat, and men who bring me gifts." She gave him a piercing look. "And whatever you're trying to do, stop it. It won't work."

Sangr flinched. "What do you mean?"

"The magic. I don't know what you're trying to do, but it won't work on me, or even anywhere near me. So, the love spell, or whatever, isn't going to do you any good."

"I'm not doing anything," he protested.

"Don't give me that. I can feel it. I've known how to identify when people are trying to use magic on me since the day I was born. I can feel it in my sleep. Your magic is trying to break into my head."

And suddenly, it was clear. That was why he couldn't sense her thoughts. He'd thought she was a magician in her own right, but that wasn't it at all. All one had to do was put her in the presence of a magician and the magic went away. That was why she was valuable to the rebellion against the sorcerers, and also why she'd been little more than a prisoner in the hands of every power that had ever controlled her. They didn't need her cooperation, just her presence.

Sangr could also tell that she was going to be trouble. Even if he managed to convince her - in the next few minutes, before the alarm sounded – that she was better off with the rebels than as a pampered prisoner in Tengut, his life would be forfeit as soon as Yella sensed the things he was thinking about her. The Great One had known what he was doing when he picked her for his harem.

"So, you're the bane." That, at least, was a relief.

"No. I am Maluz, just one of the Supreme's women."

"Whatever. We need to leave now." He headed for the door.

She stayed where she was. Only moving as he dragged her. "Why?" she asked.

"Because you are the only person who can overthrow the sorcerers and free your land."

"Do you really expect me to fall for that? What did my land do for me? I've suffered much more at the hands of the so-called freedom fighters and Max's Hounds than I ever did at the hands of the sorcerers. So, what if they don't allow the common people to make decisions? Would Max be any better?"

"Max is dead, his Hounds hunted down, and their heads placed on spikes above the gates of Rewd. The men who came after them are just farmers and innkeepers, people like your father."

"And don't even think about using my father as a goad. Where was he when they came for me? He believed them when they spoke of freedom and sold me into slavery. I have spent every night over the past seven years cursing his name."

"He's dead, too. Failed to move quickly enough when a necromancer ordered wine."

Her face fell, the jaw that had jutted out in defiance lost its set. He didn't let her get a word in edgewise. "And besides, I'm not giving you a choice. You can either come willingly and take your place among the people who win their freedom – an honored place among equals, this time – or I will take you with me by force, and you can go back to being a slave. Either way, you will come."

"And if I scream?" She was far enough away that he wouldn't be able to stop her.

Sangr shrugged. "I can kill you easily enough, but I might not bother. Maybe it would be better if I left you here. That way the next time a sweaty man who sees you as nothing but a piece of flesh has his cock in your mouth and is telling you how he likes your tongue to move, you'll know that it was your choice. You'll know that you're there because that was what you wanted. You'll remember that you had an option. I wonder how long you'll last, knowing that."

She glared at him in silence.

He smirked. "I thought so. Now, we're in a bit of a hurry. If the guards haven't realized you're gone yet, they will soon."

A shout in the distance seemed to reinforce his point and he pulled her to the door once again. "Do you have any way to turn your bane-ness off?"

Now she was the one who smirked. "No. What's the matter, little man not so tough without his magic?"

"It would have been helpful." Now they'd have to do this the hard way.

The rapier, which he'd avoided using so far, was a bloody mess as he pulled it out of the guard's neck. He still would have preferred to keep things non-lethal, but the guards had given him no choice. Their first encounter had yielded a clatter of arrows against the translucent walls. At least the dead man at his feet one had been facing the other way.

Sangr wondered where the opening the man was guarding led. The strange cloudy-walled hallways had disoriented him to the point where he had no idea where he was. Any opening was a welcome sight.

They stepped out cautiously, but there were no guards in sight. It seemed pursuit was confined to the interior of the palace for now, although how long that would last was anyone's guess. The night was chilly up in the mountains, but clear skies exposed a wealth of stars.

They were on a ledge about a hundred feet wide and twenty deep, surrounded by a waist-high wall. The only exit was the way they'd just come through, and that corridor would soon begin to spout armed angry men.

He ran to the wall and looked over. The side of the palace beneath him was built of the same decorative, smooth material as the rest of the building, and joined the wall at a steep angle. Not flat enough to try to walk down, certainly. Sliding might be in the cards, but it would only take a small protuberance to send him into a roll – which they wouldn't survive. He and Maluz exchanged glances and ran back towards the door. Maybe they'd be able to find another corridor before the pursuit arrived.

The first guard arrived at the door the same time as they did, but Sangr was ready for him. He sliced open the man's relatively unprotected belly with a quick stab and drag of the rapier, then turned to face the next. He was no longer fighting to escape – his blood was up, and he wanted to take as many of them with him as possible before they took him down.

Suddenly, unexpectedly Maluz pulled his hair, causing him to stumble away from the surprised guard.

"Just my luck," she said, as she pushed him over the wall. "I get rescued by the idiot of the litter."

They slid down towards the city below.

Sangr hit the ground hard. At some point his uncontrolled slide had turned into an uncontrolled tumble, and he'd done himself quite a bit of damage against the side of the palace, and a bit more than that against the hard-packed earth at the end of their trip. He'd been peripherally aware of Maluz sliding along in perfect form beside him, although he probably imagined the superior look on her face.

As he came to his senses, a familiar, whiny voice was complaining at him.

"I knew you were trouble the moment I laid eyes on you. It's a good thing I packed my stuff when I did, or I would have had to leave everything behind."

"Karet?"

"Who do you think? If I'd known the deal included saving your sorry ass, I would have asked for more."

"But…" Sangr began, but stopped.

They seemed to be in a wagon, in the soft glow of early dawn, heading for a peak he recognized, the one where Yella was waiting for them.

"I packed everything as soon as you left dinner. I knew you were up to something, and I would be blamed for it, so I'd have to leave anyway. It didn't take much imagination to deduce who might be sliding down the wall of death in the middle of the night."

Sangr was speechless. "Thank you," he said.

The other man grunted. "Just protecting my investment. You owe me my payment, after all. And a lesson to you: even if you can read minds, you should know that a merchant must always keep his thoughts hidden, even from himself, lest his face betray him."

"So, you were trying to read my mind? That's a neat trick." Maluz' head popped up from beside a barrel of wine. "There was a sorcerer who used to do that. But he liked little girls, and when he saw me, he followed me into the woods, trusting his talent to warn him if there was anyone about."

She smiled evilly and Sangr found himself hoping that her power was as effective against Yella as it was against him. Because if Yella got an inkling of what he was thinking about this girl, she would kill him.

Very, very slowly.

Summerland

"Are you sure you're all right? You look like you need some rest," Yella said, concern mixed with frustration on her features.

Even weeks after they left Tengut, Sangr knew that she was still coming to terms with being unable to listen in on other people's thoughts. He had to admit that it was something of a relief to know that whatever was inside your head remained in your head.

But it had its drawbacks, too. If he'd known that the group of brigands pretending to be merchants were planning to attack them, they might have taken the initiative, Karet might still be alive, and Sangr himself wouldn't be nursing a long gash along his ribs which ached every time he moved. The only reason the brigands had been defeated is that they'd made the mistake of ignoring Yella when they charged. Yella had responded to this insult by calmly hamstringing three of them from behind and letting the men deal with the rest.

"I'm fine. I can go on until nightfall."

Yella frowned at him. She peered into his eyes intently, as if that would be enough to overcome the blanket that kept her from reading his mind, but said nothing more. Sangr was well aware that what was an inconvenience for him must be driving Yella mad. She'd been cursed with the ability to read minds since her adoption by the Favored as a child. She must feel like she was blind.

But there was no other choice. They had to get the bane to Amesta; it was the only way they would ever overthrow the Shadow Witch, rumored to be the new queen of the Mage Lords.

"Poor Sangr. Are you hurt? You were so brave back there!"

Of course, Sangr reflected, it would be better if the bane could just shut up sometimes. The ideal situation would have been that the bane hadn't turned out to be one of the Supreme of Tengut's concubines. It was too late to wish for that, so Sangr just wanted her to shut up before Yella murdered them both.

He replied brusquely. "I'm fine. Less talk and more walking." He just hoped Yella would buy it. He wondered how far away Maluz would have to go for the effect of her power to wear off.

The path they'd been following seemed to be taking them into the depths of a sweltering jungle, something that Sangr was at a loss to explain. Why was it that his own village, on the western side of the continent, was surrounded by monumental glaciers while, just as far to the north, but on the opposite coast, the climate seemed to be permanently hot and humid? He could have sworn that it was warmer than down on the plains despite moving north for endless days.

"Magic," Yella said. "The unholy god-gift of the Mage Lords. The legend says they're from the deep jungles of Cat-Seneriel, that they were scattered when the demons they called up grew too strong for them to control and they ended up here. But they've recreated the jungles where there should be ice."

Sangr nodded – he'd heard the stories – but then he did a double take.

Yella smiled at him. "I don't need the Favor to know what you're thinking Sangr. Someone else, maybe, but I've been with you too long. Plus, you've been looking around like you don't know what's happening for the past two days."

His grin was sheepish. "I guess you're right. But it's just weird. I grew up at about this same latitude, and we had to wear all our sealskin even in summer. Here, I want to strip down all the way."

"I wouldn't recommend it. These bugs would probably get into places in which you really don't want them."

Sangr shuddered. The flying things were bigger than anything else he'd ever seen, and they seemed to grow bigger as their small group climbed higher into the hills.

Suddenly, the path crested a rise, and they could see the clear blue sky stretching out ahead of them, and a green carpet beneath them, broken only by a broad expanse of muddy river in the center of the jungle valley below.

"How are we going to find anything in there?" Maluz, the bane, asked.

It was a good question. "We'll follow the path for now. It looks wide and well-travelled. That means people have to live on it or near it. We'll ask them."

"What if they aren't friendly?"

"They probably won't be," Yella answered, "but I don't think they'll come after us either. In my experience, villagers won't risk attacking travelers unless they're sure they can take their money without harm to themselves. My guess is that they'll try to sell us what they know. And all we really need to know is where the displaced tribes are."

The first order of business was to get down off the mountain into the valley floor. They suspected that any villagers – friendly or otherwise – would probably live near the river itself.

The path meandered all over the place, with wide loops to avoid sudden hillocks and sinkholes. Hours after they crested the rise, the trio was covered in sweat and the bites of countless biting insects.

"How come we didn't notice this jungle the last time we were here?" Sangr asked, swatting at some flitting thing the size of his fist.

Yella shrugged. "I guess you can't see it from the coastal road."

"But someone should have mentioned it."

"They did. The fish-preacher over at Seahaven must have talked about 'Summerland' a hundred times. He would spit every time he said it."

"I must have missed it."

"That might be because you were completely drunk on seaweed ale all the while."

"Please don't be judgmental. Seaweed ale reminds me of home." Sangr feigned indignation. "Besides, I wasn't drunk all the time. There are a couple of nights in which I quite clearly remember a beautiful moon over the sea and a certain girl from Krenn whose ideas would have shocked the most jaded streetwalkers on the plains."

"You little…"

Sensing movement in the trees, Yella had her rapier halfway out of its sheath when the net fell over Sangr's shoulders. Two quick cuts made short work of the strands, and both of them turned to face the attack, looking for cover. Without some protection, there wasn't much hope – an enemy which wanted them dead would only have to pepper them with arrows from within the thick undergrowth.

But no arrows came. Instead, the rustling of vegetation preceded a sudden storm of small, grey-skinned creatures; roughly man-shaped, but covered in tendrils of some sort. The top of the tallest one's head, had he stood upright, would have reached Sangr's breastbone. They charged straight towards the group, wielding nets like the one Yella had destroyed.

Neither Sangr nor Yella would have been the obvious choice for a pitched battle against numerous opponents. Both were of slender build and both wielded rapiers instead of broadswords. Their philosophy was stealth and trickery. Maluz, though taller than Sangr and more voluptuous than Yella was armed with nothing but a walking stick, which she had no idea how to use as an effective weapon. She stood behind Yella; her eyes wide.

The creatures from the forest, however, seemed unable to grasp the concept of strategy, attacking one at a time with little regard for their lives. Sangr stepped forward, slashing down towards the first one's neck while Yella impaled the second on the tip of her sword. As she pulled the blade free, another tried to throw its net over her, but Sangr reached out and caught the webbing in midair with one hand, opening the creature's bowels with the sword in the other.

The fight went on like this for less than a minute and soon all seven creatures lay prone on the path. Even the last one standing hadn't tried to flee, running at them despite the fact that *it* was now heavily outnumbered.

Sangr used his toe to turn one of the creatures onto its back and knelt to have a closer look. "Ugly little buggers, aren't they? And they smell awful."

"This one's alive," Maluz informed them.

"What? How?"

"It was distracted watching you and Yella, so I hit it over the head." The former palace concubine shrugged, a movement that was so delightful that Sangr once again thanked whatever gods looked over him that Yella couldn't read his thoughts right then. "They didn't really seem dangerous, so I thought I'd help."

Of course, he thought. For a woman who'd spent her entire life being traded and captured as a pawn in the eternal struggle between the mage lords and the cities on the plains, something as commonplace as a group of suicidal midgets attacking from a jungle would hardly cause raised eyebrows.

The Song of Sangr

They huddled around the fallen creature, waiting to see what it would do when it woke. The thing smelled even worse from up close and seemed to have extremely thin scales covering most of its body. It had a slightly elongated face which gave the impression of a snout. Sangr thought they looked much less human at rest than they did in motion.

One leg twitched and the grey scales seemed to regain some of their color. Their captive emitted a soft whistle and tried to sit up. Sangr's boot on its chest prevented it from doing so.

"Hello," Sangr said.

The creature struggled with all its strength, twisting this way and that and pelting Sangr with dirt and clumps of grass it pulled from the path. Sangr just grinned at it, showing a large number of teeth. It soon realized that it wouldn't be able to break free and kept still.

"Ready to talk yet?"

The only reply forthcoming consisted of another series of incoherent noises. No intelligence illuminated the enormous yellow eyes.

"Just let it go, Sangr," Yella said, disgust evident in her features.

He did as she asked, removing the boot and moving back. But instead of scampering off into the woods, the creature lunged, trying to bite into his thigh. Sangr, blade already in hand, dispatched it quickly with a single cut to the neck. He turned back to Yella. "Happy."

She shuddered. "Come on, let's get as far away from here as we can."

A few hours later, light was beginning to fail – much later than Sangr thought it should have that far north – and they decided to make camp. Once a cheerful fire was burning with dry wood salvaged from beneath the sheltering canopies of the huge trees, they ate the last of the rations they'd brought along. Soon, they'd have to hunt and cook something from the forest – an experience none of them was looking forward to.

Maluz volunteered to take the first watch, and the other two agreed. Anything waiting to strike wouldn't attack them immediately, but would wait until the passing of the hours had lulled them into a false sense of security.

The sounds of the jungle pressed in on every side, but the night passed in complete tranquility.

When dawn finally arrived, Sangr found Maluz blue and shivering, lying in the middle of a patch of dead vegetation on rock-hard, frozen soil. She barely had enough strength to move.

As he pulled her off the icy turf, he called out to Yella, who rose immediately, bleary eyed but with her sword ready. "What?" she said irritably when she realized that they were not under immediate attack.

"It's Maluz. I think someone must have tried to attack her while she slept."

Concern replaced the irritation. Yella had no particular love for the bane, but she knew the other woman was necessary to attack the Mage Lords. "Why, what did they do to her?"

"I don't know. By the look of it, someone must have tried to freeze her in her sleep with a spell." He turned to the shivering girl, now safely settled on the grass of the path under the warming rays of the rising sun. Some color had returned to her cheeks. "Did you see who did this to you?"

Maluz shook her head weakly, seemingly ashamed by her failure to spot her assailant.

Sangr knew there was something he was missing. First, they'd been attacked by monsters – but in a decidedly non-lethal way. The attack had been designed to capture them, but the creatures seemed amazingly ineffective at defending themselves when the attack went bad. And now this. It was obvious that the little net-wielding savages were unlikely to have that kind of magic available to them, but he still couldn't shake the feeling that they were somehow connected. He said as much to Yella.

Maluz laughed at them both, weakly.

"It wasn't a magical attack," she said.

"Why not?"

Maluz just cocked her head.

"Oh, right," Yella said. But then she peered hard at the girl. "But maybe your particular talent doesn't work here. After all, even the weather seems off."

Maluz smiled again – less weakly this time. "So, if my power's gone, tell me, what am I thinking?"

Sangr chuckled and Yella gave him a look that promised dire retribution. Still, it was a point for Maluz in the struggle between the two. "All right. You still seem to be able to nullify all the magic around you, so how do you explain that? *Something* got through the shielding?"

The bane seemed to have no answer to that.

"That's it!" Sangr said. "Maluz' power still works. She's nullifying the effects of magic around her – so that means that the ice was formed because of the lack of magic. This jungle, this Summerland is here because magic keeps it here. Without the magic, we wouldn't be walking through a jungle straight from the depths of Cat-Seneriel. We'd be freezing our butts off in a snowstorm on a glacier. So, when our little princess here lay down to sleep, the cold just under the surface managed to break through."

Both of the women looked surprised at this deduction, but mostly, Sangr suspected, because it had come from him. Even though Yella looked to him to solve most of the puzzles in their lives, she always acted like he was some bright child when it turned out he was right.

"But wouldn't that happen all the time. Wouldn't she be creating snowstorms wherever she walked?"

Sangr shrugged. "It's too hot for snow."

Yella looked at him as though he was a complete idiot, but Maluz came to his aid. "He might be right. Perhaps the magic is causing it to be warm, but the warm air isn't exposed to my magic long enough to cool. That's why the ground only froze after I'd stayed in one place for a long while."

Seeing Sangr's expression, Yella snorted. "Do you think you'll be able to walk today?"

Maluz nodded. "I'll be all right. I've stopped shaking already, see?" She held out her hand. Then she locked eyes with Yella. "I'm not the soft little flower you seem to mistake me for. I've been chained and beaten and raped before I was a pampered concubine. My own father traded me for vague promises of glory and freedom for our people. I've endured things a lot worse than a little cold."

"Then let's go," Yella said and set out.

The path continued through the leafy tunnel. It felt as though each step was through the spray of a waterfall. But instead of being refreshing, the droplets stuck to their skin and soaked their clothes. The air was alive with gnats, and Sangr tried to convince himself after every breath, that he'd only imagined a swarm of tiny insects flying down his throat, that what he was feeling was the effect of the humidity in the air.

Hours later, they finally came to the first signs of a village. An obvious, well-beaten secondary trail led away from the main path. Sounds of human activity came from the forest all around them.

Sangr motioned them to be quiet and set off down the branch. Only a few dozen yards in, the path went around a small hill and opened into a clearing. Several open-sided wooden huts with dark straw roofs occupied the opening.

Sangr relaxed when he saw that the people around the huts were human as opposed to the creatures they'd encountered earlier, and sheathed his sword when the villagers noticed them. Three small girls, skin white as paper and red-haired ran towards them, but stopped short when a sharp voice called them to heel. A woman who Sangr thought could only be the girls' mother because of the obvious resemblance stepped into view from behind one of the huts. She wore a peaceful expression and sported a wicked-looking crossbow. "Good afternoon," she said, seeming a bit surprised by the fact that two of their number were women. "Are you just passing through or are you looking for trouble."

"Neither, really. We need a bit of help," Sangr replied, hoping his winning smile would not be taken for a show of teeth, which was likely to get him speared.

"We can't spare much, here. We're barely surviving as it is."

The crossbow never wavered. It seemed to Sangr like quite an advanced piece of armory for a village in a jungle. Of course, he was standing squarely on the wrong side of it, which might have tainted his objectivity just a little.

He suspected that the village's men were hiding just behind the tree line. There was no point in bandying words. "We're looking for someone," he said.

"And who might that be?"

"A man named Hemery." Sangr fervently hoped that Hemery's band of merry murderers who called themselves freedom fighters hadn't done any 'liberating' in this village. "He leads a small band of wanderers that live in these woods, and on the coast. Claims that his family once ruled these lands."

"And why would you be wanting Hemery, then?" All trace of the relaxed wait-and-see attitude had disappeared from the woman's features. Her eyes had tightened, and the color had gone from her face.

Sangr balanced his weight on the balls of his feet, hoping that the woman would give some twitch, some sign before she pulled the trigger. A split second might make the difference between a direct hit and perhaps a quarrel in the arm. There was no way she would miss at that range, no matter what he did.

Of course, if he answered correctly, maybe she wouldn't shoot him at all. "Hemery saved our lives a year ago. He took us into his heart, adopted us into his family. Now we're trying to return the favor. We brought something he needs."

The crossbow was still steady, and Sangr let his breath out slowly. The trees to both sides of the village suddenly came alive with men dressed in green. One tall blond man with a long scar on his cheek walked to where Sangr stood. "How do we know you're telling the truth?" he asked.

"My name is Sangr. He should have left word for you to wait for me. The girl behind me with the sword is Yella."

The man grunted noncommittally. "And the girl? Lunch for the jungle beasts?"

"The girl isn't just a girl. She was born accursed. You might know of her as the sorcerer's bane."

Sangr watched in satisfaction as the man's eyes widened. The legend of the bane, told even in the cities of the plains, was the central myth of the northeast. The reason for that was simple enough: only the bane would free them from the Mage Lords. "Can it be true?" the man whispered, eyes misting over.

"It is. And we're here to help you put her to good use." He looked around. "Now where is Hemery? We need to get this girl into his hands."

Rapture disappeared from the man's face. "The old men have him."

"The old men?"

"It seems we need to talk. Come into my hut."

The glade below them seemed to have been created out of pure dreams, or perhaps the vision of heaven of some desert religion. There were grassy clearings bisected by crystal-clear streams, wooded terraces and colored flowers. It had a tame quality that the rest of the jungle simply didn't possess. It seemed domesticated, somehow.

Dusky men with white hair that matched their robes could be seen ambling alone or in small groups.

"Those are the old men?"

"Yes."

"They live in that place?"

"They live in a network of crystal caves under this very mountain."

"And the Shadow Witch?"

The blond man, whose name was Ernst, laughed. "Oh no. She lives in the far north, well beyond Summerland. Her castle is nestled among mountains so sheer that even the ice can't get hold."

"Oh. Great." *Fortunately*, Sangr thought, *that was not his problem.*

Once they sprung Hemery out of the clutches of these old guys – who really didn't look as though they would be much good in a fight, and any magic they might have been hoping to rely on wouldn't work the way they were expecting – he would be heading somewhere without jungles. He just hoped Yella would come with him. "So how do we get down there?"

"We don't. Anything that tries to cross the barrier will be burned to the bone."

"A magic barrier?"

The Song of Sangr

The man looked into Sangr's eyes. "I know we have the bane, but are you willing to risk your life on the power of one girl against the collected might of the council of elders of the Mage Lords?"

Sangr thought of how the magic of his telepathy, something he'd attempted without success to have removed by every wizard on the plains, had simply vanished when he came into her presence. He was almost afraid it would never return. "I think I am," he replied.

The other man shrugged. "The path you followed to our village crosses the glade. It's a trap meant to lead outsiders to their deaths."

They climbed back down from their vantage point, Yella complaining all the way that they could have done without the long climb if all they had to do was follow the path, but both of them knew it was just for show. Yella was a warrior at heart, and she would have memorized the lay of the land and the position of the landmarks, as well as quick ways in and out of each place they could see. But she was playing dumb for some reason, and Sangr knew her well enough to keep quiet about it.

The barrier Ernst had told them about was visible in the sunlight if one knew where to look. A slight shimmering in the air ahead of them, like heat mirages on a hot plain, indicated its location.

Maluz had been forewarned, but Yella pulled her aside again. "Are you ready to do this? There's no need for you to cross. Just get close enough to the barrier to make it disappear. Then wait till we cross. All right?"

The former concubine gave Yella a hard stare. "Do I really have any choice? This is why you brought me here, and the only way I will avoid going back into the chains is if I help you, so let's not waste any more time." She strode towards the barrier.

Sangr and Yella were a few steps behind while Ernst's group lagged. It was obvious that they didn't want anything to do with the barrier, but soon, probably shamed by the fact that the three strangers were not shrinking from their duties, they moved.

They advanced cautiously, holding their breaths and expecting to come under attack at any moment, but reaching the barrier proved anticlimactic. As Maluz gingerly reached out with a finger, the shimmering vanished. Sangr and Yella were unable to keep the younger woman from stepping forward into the place where the barrier had been.

"Well, are you coming, or aren't you?" the bane asked.

As the group filed through and walked past the last of the trees into the first glade, Yella turned to

Ernst. "I assume there are more defenses in place than just this. What can you tell us about them?"

"Er… We never really imagined we'd ever make it this far. As a matter of fact, no one who's ever tried to come this way has made it back."

"Well, they definitely know we're here now, so the faster we move, the less time they'll have to throw everything in their arsenal at us," she replied.

"Too late," Sangr remarked.

The beautifully maintained grass ahead of them seemed to be crumbling and splitting to reveal the earth beneath. The brown mulch, in turn, seemed to be writhing as if it was made of worms.

"What is it?" Yella asked.

"I have no idea, but it can't be good."

Ernst, standing beside them, had blanched noticeably. "Oh, no," he said.

"What is it?"

"That area, that place…. It was the place where our fathers would leave the dead to freeze in their cairns. It was covered with piles of stone before the Mage Lords arrived. I was only a child – but we used to challenge one another to walk through the stones to the far end and then come back. I don't recall anyone actually making it."

"So, lots of dead people."

"Hundreds."

"This is going to be fun." Sangr pulled the rapier from its scabbard, wishing not for the first time, that he was big enough to effectively use a war axe, a much better weapon against reanimated corpses. He also reflected that it was probably time for a career change. For now, however, he sighed in resignation.

One of Ernst's men, on the other hand, had a much more logical reaction. As soon as the first grey, grasping hand broke the surface, a man turned and ran.

He didn't get very far. From the screams and the smell of burning hair that reached them, Sangr surmised that the barrier had closed up once Maluz couldn't affect it anymore.

There was no time to check on the poor fellow, since the glade in front of them had sprouted a number of surprisingly well-preserved corpses that came at them. Sangr assumed that, like most of their kind, they would be relentless, but slow. There had been one ensorcelled corpse, in the mountains east of Tengut, that had followed them for several leagues before they realized it was still with them. It only managed to catch up as they rose for breakfast… He'd had to hack it apart to stop it.

"Try to take off their arms," Sangr shouted.

Ernst looked at him like he was completely insane, but Yella just nodded and turned back to the attackers. They were mere paces away. Sangr screamed an incoherent battle-cry and launched himself at the nearest; a bearded man who looked like he'd died the day before. Other than the bluish cast to his features, there was little decay evident on the body.

Sangr's first stroke explained the cause for the preservation of the body, the ungainly lurch and the way the dead men creaked as they approached. His rapier should have been more than heavy enough to cut most of the way through the thickest part of the dead man's forearm; the blow, after passing through a small chunk of skin, stopped short, caught in flesh that should have been soft and yielding but was instead rock hard. Frozen.

He had to give the blade a mighty tug to get it free.

"It looks like Summerland doesn't go as deep as it looks," Yella said grimly. They were being pressed into the vegetation around the clearing, hacking at fingers, wrists and anything else that seemed thin enough to break.

They had plenty of targets but had to be careful not to fall victim to the urge and stab the creatures. That was a good way to lodge a blade in a set of frozen ribs, and get pulled into the mass of advancing dead. So Sangr and Yella did what they had to do, dancing this way and that to avoid the clutching hands, removing fingers as they went. They tried desperately to stay between the ghastly advance and the lightly armed Maluz, whose stick seemed little threat to them.

The undead were slow, but they didn't seem to feel any pain; eventually the inevitable happened. Ernst, hacking at a dead forearm to free one of his men who'd been too slow to retreat, was grabbed from behind by another corpse. Both men were pulled screaming into the press of bodies.

A voice came from behind. "Let me through, you idiots!" Maluz screamed.

Sangr felt a hand grip his hair from behind and pull him none too gently aside. The girl rushed through the gap and, looking back at him with no concern whatsoever said, "You people don't do much thinking, do you? I just hope I can get to your friends before they get torn apart." She walked straight into the wall of clutching hands, which immediately gave way before her.

As it had to, Sangr realized belatedly. The animated corpses were obviously magical in nature. And the whole point of dragging the girl all the way from Tengut was exactly to provide protection against this sort of thing. However, instinct had caused them to attack a physical enemy the way they always had – with steel and skill.

The episode served to remind Sangr that this wasn't his fight, or even his kind of war. His own major talent was deception and slipperiness. There was also the fact that he could read other people's minds – except when the bane was around. It seemed to be ever more obvious that they had to get back to the plains.

The girl made short work of the nearest living dead, and was extricating the two bruised, but breathing members of the party from their clutches when Sangr and Yella caught up to her. She took the time to give them a withering look before leading on once again, scything a path through the unholy horde.

They were no sooner clear of the dead than an ear-piercing keening broke out ahead of them. Three gigantic creatures, lizards the size of a man, but furred like bears, bounded towards them out of the forest.

"They never learn, do they?" Sangr asked.

He wondered what would happen when they encountered Maluz. Would they shrink back to their normal size? Or would they take the form of regular humans?

The group watched as the bane stood her ground, ready to pounce on whatever remained after the magic dissolved. Or so Sangr assumed.

"What are you doing? Help her! Those are Byrits, they aren't…"

The rest of what Ernst tried to say was lost as the lead creature bowled Maluz out of the way as though she were made of paper and slammed into the tall blond man. His followers immediately attacked it with their knives, but sharp teeth made short work of Ernst's throat. He fell screaming, blood spurting everywhere, and the lizard worried the carcass the way a cat will with a mouse.

Sangr had little time to mourn the man. The second lizard attempted to give him the same treatment but caught only air as Sangr twisted to the side and brought up his blade. A small section of the lizard's tail fell to the ground at his feet, twitching.

Out of the corner of his eye, Sangr noticed that the third lizard was attacking Yella. He wanted to go help her, but his own opponent had turned. It was not affected by the loss of its tail, except perhaps that it was angrier than before. It circled around him, trying to come at him from an angle that wouldn't be covered by the sword. Sangr circled in the same direction.

Suddenly, mid-turn, the lizard lunged. As Sangr instinctively defended his more vulnerable torso, the reptile attacked his left foot. A single swipe of a claw shredded boot leather and left a deep bleeding gash in his ankle. He could feel the blood pooling under his sole.

It pulled back out of his reach and simply looked at him, seemingly trying to gauge its next attack. Sangr stared at it for a moment. This was pretty advanced thinking for a lizard, but it also represented an opportunity.

Sangr pretended to stumble to the left, only to realize that no pretense was necessary as his weakened foot gave way. The lizard was already springing for his neck as he began to fall. Despite expecting it, Sangr barely managed to get his blade up in time. It was sheer luck that he managed to get into position, allowing gravity to drive the blade into the monster's palate.

The furred lizard collapsed on top of him, its enormous weight pinning him to the ground. He pushed at it frantically. Yella appeared beside him, bleeding from a scratch in her forehead. "Are you all right?" She seemed a lot more concerned than he would have thought.

He tried to smile, but the effort of pushing the lizard turned it into a grimace. "I think so. It just nicked me."

She hugged him, cutting off his air in the process. "I thought I'd lost you."

"I'm not that easy to kill," Sangr replied. He tried for a gruff tone, but he noticed the catch in his voice. He hoped she didn't. "Help me move this thing." He pushed again and, with the aid of the three surviving members of Ernst's party, they got his legs free and got him back on his feet. "I'm going to need someone to lean on."

They limped to where Maluz lay. She was just beginning to regain consciousness, whimpering with pain as she held one finger up. It was bent at an alarming angle.

Yella rushed to her side, took a look at the finger and pulled. Maluz yelped, but then smiled with surprise as the pain faded. "Thank you," she said.

Yella had already turned back to Sangr. "So, do we go back and lick our wounds, or do we go on? We're in no shape for another fight."

"True, but if we leave, nothing short of an army is going to get us this far again. I think we caught them napping."

"Onward then?"

"Yes."

Yella smiled, the first time in days. "You see, that's why I like you. You're completely insane."

"You're one to talk." He smiled back at her. Had he really been thinking of getting into another line of work?

Without the benefit of their magic, the old men attempted to fight, but a limping Sangr stepped forward and sliced one's belly open in an instant. He ran through a second. That was all the rest needed Before they saw reason.

One of the old men threatened Hemery with a knife, but Sangr simply shrugged and advanced.

"If you kill him, you die an instant later. If you drop your weapon now, I promise you we'll spare your life."

The knife hit the floor.

Hemery was released into their care less than an hour after the lizards were dispatched, and he immediately selected two more ringleaders. He made them kneel and beheaded them with an axe that one of the dead men had dropped.

"We have to destroy this place," Hemery said, his grim expression inviting no discussion.

Sangr rolled his eyes. "And I suppose you want us to burn it down or something?"

"That won't be necessary. You see, this whole place is built on magic. Where there were majestic glaciers and clean air, now we have a fetid jungle."

"A jungle that is actually capable of supporting life," one of the old men interjected. The council members that had survived Sangr's demonstration, and the subsequent round of extreme violence by the newly freed Hemery, were sitting in a loose circle, arms shackled behind their backs with their own chains. "When we came here, there was nothing but lichen."

Hemery kicked the man in the mouth, sending a trail of blood sailing over the others. "And people who ruled themselves, without having to fear the wrath of the Shadow Witch and her Mage Lord puppets."

The man on the ground wasn't done. "That's only because you insist on attacking them. If you would just live in peace, you'd enjoy a much easier life than your people knew before."

"A life of slaves. I'd rather die in mage fire."

"We can arrange that."

"You won't be arranging anything," Hemery said.

He kicked the prone man once, twice more; again, and again until all hint of movement disappeared. He looked across the rest of his old, pale enemies. "Does anyone else have any interesting comments to make?"

None did.

Sangr took Hemery's shoulder. "Come on, man. This isn't like you. We can do what we have to do without killing helpless old men."

"Those old men are anything but helpless. Perhaps you should have been here when they demanded two young women from each village to warm their beds. Or maybe when they set all the men from the single village that resisted alight. Or when they tortured me to learn where my people were. They hate resistance so much that they consider us their enemies, even though all we want to do is to hide in the jungle and live as we choose. You should have been there when they sent the wraiths after me, should have felt how their touch burned when they captured me. Then you'd understand."

"You're probably right. But still, it does us no good to lower ourselves to their level."

"All right," Hemery sighed. "The first thing we need to do is to get rid of this Summerland."

"Why? I have to agree that it's a lot better than the ice."

"This is a cursed place. Time stands still here, which is why the winter can't advance – and why these abominations," he pointed at the old men, "are still alive after a thousand years. The simple act of removing the spell will kill them. Not immediately, but they will die of old age soon enough."

"So, you'll kill the jungle and everything in it just to get revenge on the old men?"

"No matter how easily they fell, you have to remember that those men are the core of the Mage Lords. They've kept us enslaved for more than twenty years. Without them, the Shadow Witch is weakened."

"All right. How do we do it?"

"We need to halt the magic of the heart."

"The heart?"

"An enchanted ruby. I'm sure we can convince one of the councilors to show us where it is."

The Mage Lords didn't want to give up their treasure. Hemery began to torture one of them. He resisted, staying silent until Hemery lost patience and beheaded him.

"That won't work," Sangr said. "If they think they'll die quickly, they'll resist until you kill them."

Hemery didn't make the same mistake with the second man. He used his sword to slice open an eyeball, and then cut off the man's little finger without even asking a question.

The other little finger went next and, when he began to slice away the man's breeches, the Mage Lord broke and began to scream directions.

Five minutes later, Hemery, Yella, Sangr and Maluz were standing in front of the pedestal which held the stone.

Hemery's eyes gleamed. He spoke to Maluz for the first time. "Go on. Touch it."

Maluz gave him a piercing look, seeming to look all the way into his soul. "No," she replied.

The word echoed around the chamber, the rocky walls sending it back to them infinite times.

"What?" Hemery's eyes widened. "You will do what I tell you. And if you won't do it willingly, you'll do it in chains." He took a step towards her.

Sangr's rapier stopped him. "I don't think so," Sangr said. "I gave her my word that she wouldn't be a slave this time around, and I intend to keep my word."

"You owe me your life," Hemery spat.

"I'm trying to give you a kingdom. I think you'll agree it's worth more than my life."

Hemery glared at them.

"So, what do you want in exchange?" Yella asked.

Maluz jumped guiltily. It was obvious that she'd been caught out. Yella laughed. "I've been reading people's minds since I was a little girl," Yella said. "I've learned how people think, even if your power blanks out the Favor."

"I… if I'm going to free this place, I want to be queen." Maluz held up a hand. "And I guess that means I'll have to marry this lout."

Hemery, caught about to protest, stood there with his mouth agape.

"Well," Sangr said with a smirk, as he pulled the blade away, "how about it?"

"I guess I could do worse."

"So, you'll marry her?"

"Yes."

"Swear to it," Maluz said.

Hemery did.

"Good. Now let's turn off the magic jungle." Maluz reached out and closed her fingers around a ruby half the size of Sangr's fist. She studied it for a moment, contemplative. "I think I'll keep this, too." Even deep inside the cave, the sudden loss of life energy in the jungle outside could be felt. A humming that they hadn't been aware of ceased.

Although he knew it was only his imagination, Sangr thought he could feel the cold winds of his childhood sweeping into the valley.

As the newly betrothed couple had their first real conversation, Yella pulled Sangr aside and whispered, "I think the sooner we get out of here, the better."

"Why?"

"Hemery was bitter enough, and all they did was take his kingdom. Can you imagine how much hate that girl is holding in? She was taken from the cradle, swapped between powerful men who only wanted her magic and a bit of occasional sex. Now that she'll have power, I don't want to imagine what she'll do."

Sangr remembered the cold look on Maluz's face as she'd condemned the billions of creatures outside the cave to a frozen death with a single gesture, and the chill he'd imagined settled deeper.

"Maybe you're right," he said. "Maybe you're right."

Gina

The girl – young, voluptuous, nubile and dressed only in streaks of ceremonial paint – screamed and struggled. She tried to scratch at the jailer's eyes, but the enormous man simply swatted her attempts aside as he pulled her inexorably towards the red glow of the pit. A single heave was enough to send her tumbling over the edge.

Her final shriek of pure desperate terror ended abruptly.

It's about time, Gina thought as the guard turned back to the remaining captives. She'd waited with ill-concealed impatience as nearly a dozen girls – she thought that to call them maidens would have been a bit optimistic – were sacrificed to the fire-demons of Hell's Gate. It hadn't been a pleasant wait. The heat in the bowels of the mountain under the city was oppressive and the red light from the pit and flickering torches, not to mention the continuous begging for mercy and screams of the women, were giving her a headache. She couldn't *believe* some of the things that the girls offered to spare their lives. The guards just leered at them and tossed them into the pit.

Fortunately, *finally*, her turn had come.

The huge man, streaked with soot and paint that had come off the struggling victims, undid her shackles and grabbed her arms very tightly. "No need for that," Gina said. "I'll come quietly."

The guard looked into her eyes, shrugged and let go. There was nowhere for her to run, as soldiers blocked the only exit. Trying to escape would only delay the inevitable.

Gina had no intention of making a break for it. She hadn't come all the way here just to chicken out at the last minute. The heat, already oppressive at a good distance from the fires, beat into her brow. At least the paint on the rest of her body seemed to be shielding her more sensitive parts from getting broiled. Five paces from the end of the ledge, it began to be painful even through the paint.

Seeing that she truly was walking to the edge of her own volition, the guard decided that he didn't have to get singed yet again. He stopped dead and encouraged her to walk on with a very intimate shove and a deep chuckle. She walked.

Out on the ledge with her back to everyone else in the room, Gina smiled. The absence of the guard would give her additional time – time that would make little difference in the outcome but would mean that she didn't have to rush.

Toes over the edge, Gina pretended to hesitate as she looked down into the swirling redness below. Molten rock mixed with tongues of flame, but the darting movements beneath the surface left no doubt that something in there was alive. The demons knew that more souls were coming their way and they were hungry to consume them, tear the bodies to shreds, take the astral power for their own. The peace between the citizens of Hell's Gate and the things that lived beneath the mountain had been kept this way for centuries.

The guard, fed up with the delay, shouted at her to get it over with.

Gina looked down again and smiled. She said a few words under her breath. Out loud she said: "Haggan," and took that final step forward.

She did not fall.

The guard's footsteps rang out behind her as the man realized that something had gone wrong and rushed towards her to correct it. Not only was he much too late, but he was also running in the wrong direction. Any intelligent person living in a city as infested with magicians as Hell's Gate would have taken one look at the floating woman and run the other way.

Sadly, dungeon-keepers were not selected for their intelligence. The man kept coming as Gina turned back the way she'd come. A contemptuous flick of her arm brought a tongue of fire from the depths. A gesture sent it towards the rushing defender, who could do nothing but look down at his chest in horror as a searing lance thicker than his arm penetrated his sternum and emerged from his back.

Steam rose from the wound, all that was left of the man's heart, and he collapsed without so much as a whimper.

Gina smiled again, but this time with true pleasure. She'd waited more years than she could count for this moment. She was going to enjoy it.

She stepped slowly towards the rest of the people in the cavern. The naked girls chained to the rock watched her wide-eyed, but the palace guards at the foot of the stairs that led to the surface were less cowed. They had charms against sorcery and magical weapons. A single witch was not going to do them much harm. There were six of them, and they advanced with purpose, drawing their swords.

Gina laughed. "I'm glad to see the men of Hell's Gate are not cowards. I'd hate to rule a city of sniveling, worthless pigs."

The captain of the guard said nothing. His hard eyes bored through her as he led his men forward.

Another gesture from Gina brought the demons out of their pit. They emerged from the lava like ants from a threatened hill. Small demons that glowed pink; winged demons that circled in the shadows in the cavern roof; but mostly demons of glowing rock, whose skin turned black in the cooling air.

The men fought valiantly, and their charms did protect them against the heat of the demon hordes, but there weren't enough guards. The demons didn't need magic to overrun a paltry six defenders. They simply overwhelmed them through sheer force of numbers and crushed them with their magnificent strength. Soon, only the captain stood, one arm hanging limp, but still struggling.

"Haggan," Gina said, "Stop toying with the men. I want the captain alive." Two huge demons, living, walking boulders, materialized behind the man, and had him on the ground in seconds. Gina looked down on him, and then at her own body, covered in ceremonial paint. "Bring him with us." The man glared at her.

Not looking to see whether her orders were being carried out, Gina strode toward the exit. One of the women chained to the rock tried to touch her arm. Tears welled in her eyes. "Thank you, my lady. Thank you for saving us. I will be your servant forever. Anything you want, you only have to ask it of me." The other women also looked at her, a mixture of terror and hope in their expressions.

"I thank you for the offer," Gina replied. "But I already have servants. They are strong, they are faithful." She paused. "And they have been unfairly deprived of part of their prize. I will not deprive them of the rest." She made another gesture with her arm, wove a string of elemental magic and spoke, barely more than a whisper: "You may feed."

As she began to mount the long, dark stairs that led to the palace far above, the screams of sacrificial lambs meeting their allotted fate followed her.

She smiled, content in the knowledge that things were finally being put into their correct places.

The fireball came from an unexpected quarter, blowing a dozen of Gina's demons into screaming fragments. But there were simply too many of them, and the mage responsible for the attack had made the same mistake as every other enemy they'd encountered so far: they attacked the fierce-looking demons and ignored the tiny, naked slave girl in their midst.

The logic behind that escaped her. Did they think the demons were bringing her along as a snack?

Whatever the reason, it served her purpose. A dozen demons more or less were nothing to her and, as their comrades bore the wizard to the floor and tore pieces off until he stopped struggling, Gina was able to watch in complete safety.

She was tired. They'd climbed from the subbasement where the sacrifices were made to the tenth level of the palace. By now, resistance, other than sacrificial snipers such as the one they'd just neutralized, had solidified around gates, doorways, and especially staircases. There would be another few chambers to take before she could reach the throne room at the apex of the castle. The Tyrants of Hell's Gate did not believe in building on a small scale.

Or maybe they were well aware of what lived in their cellars and wanted to be as far away from it as possible. It was also possible that they'd designed it this way to make military assault impossible. Gina had lost hundreds of demons already, and they were not easy to kill; the combination of booby-traps, ambush points and magic assault was lethal. A human army would never have made it past the first few flights of stairs, but the demons were driven by magic. Her magic.

The corridors, growing more and more ornate as they advanced, had morphed into column-lined and lavishly decorated marble avenues. Just a year or two before, she would have grabbed any one of the treasures on display and been content to live off the proceeds for the rest of her life. But two adventurers, a man and a woman named Sangr and Yella, that she'd met along the way had taught her the true value of the wealth around her.

They'd seemed to be able to read her mind and had quickly discovered her deepest secret. She still burned in shame when she recalled the conversation.

"So, you can control elemental spirits," Yella said. It hadn't been a question.

"Why do you say that? No one can control the spirits. They are wild and unpredictable."

Sangr casually backhanded her, drawing blood from her lip. "Don't lie to Yella," he said. "She gets cranky when you do, and then I have to put up with her. Now tell us about this magic. Where did you get it – and what have you been doing with it?"

Gina made up a story about having observed a wizard beside a river, calling to river sprites and ordering them around. Sangr and Yella shared a smile, and then Sangr punched Gina in the stomach. "It's pretty ungrateful of you to lie to us, don't you think? We could have just left you to hang in that little village back there. No one would have missed you overmuch, I think."

Gina tried to give him a defiant look, but her heart wasn't in it, partly because of the pain – he hadn't held back when he hit her – but mainly because this was a new experience for her. No one had ever been able to see through her like that before. She'd often been praised for her honest, open demeanor, even when she was still sticky from teaching the stable boy a thing or two behind the barn.

Back then, no one ever suspected anything. Perhaps these two were just guessing. They expected her to lie to them, knowing her type. She tried an experiment. "I studied with the priests of Wasyl, down on the plains. They taught me how to sing to the spirits." She tensed, expecting the blow. It had been the truth, but they had no way of knowing it.

The blow never came. Sangr grunted and walked off to tend to his horse, and Yella smiled. "There, doesn't it feel better when you tell the truth? Now, tell me, what did the priests do when they found out you weren't... let's just say eligible... to be a priestess?"

Gina had felt her cheeks flush. How could this woman have known? She was so surprised that she actually answered the question. "They never found out. I ran away before they tested me in my final year."

"Impressive. It's not easy to get away from those elementals."

"I was their best student. None of my teachers could control the most powerful spirits. I could, from the very first day my mother abandoned me at the temple. I was four, and I had more skill than any of those old men. And, despite what they said, it never went away, even when I… even when the stable boy…" Her voice fell away.

Yella chuckled. "Men in positions of power like to spread false rumors about the importance of virtue. It makes them feel like they can control us. I would ignore it in the future." The older woman gave Gina an appraising look. "What are you going to do now?"

Gina paused. She'd expected to ride along with the notorious duo, learning as she did, becoming a part of their team. She thought that was why they'd saved her. But it seemed silly somehow to put it into words. Yella saved her the embarrassment with a sad smile. "We ride alone, Gina. We have too many secrets from everyone else and too few from each other to allow strangers into our midst. And I especially prefer that the strangers not come in the form of pretty young thieves."

Gina thanked her silently for not finishing the phrase with the words 'of questionable morals' and just said, "Then you might as well have left me to hang. There isn't much I can do on the plains. I can't go back to Wasyl, can I? And I'm not welcome in any village between here and there anyway."

"You have magic. You can survive."

"Magic? All the elementals can do is tell me when people are coming. Even the strongest of the air elementals can barely pick a lock. It's handy, yes, but not much use to me when I get caught."

"True. But do you know why the priests have their monastery on the plains?"

"Because it allows them to look into the distance from their towers and contemplate the enormity of the world?"

"Because they can't control their wards in the mountains."

"Why, because there are more places to hide?" Gina well remembered the feeling, as she slipped into the night, that when daybreak came, she would be visible from any of the towers.

"No, because there are spirits, powerful spirits that live in the mountains. And even more so underneath. Spirits that truly can make you powerful, but only if you can control them."

"What happens if I can't control them?"

"Then you'll be dead, and it won't be a problem any longer."

They sat in silence for a few moments until Gina got the courage to ask the first and less uncomfortable of her two questions. "Why did you tell me this?"

Yella actually laughed at that. "Mainly, it's because I don't think we'll be riding through this part of the world again and won't be in any danger from whatever you do. But it's also because I think that, if you don't get yourself killed, you can irritate the hell out of the local Tyrants, which would make Sangr happy. He's pretty upset with them right now. The reason we saved you is that I wish someone had saved me at your age. I wasn't on a path to goodness, and neither are you, but at least you'll have a life of some kind for a few more days. Maybe you'll do someone else a kindness one day."

That had been Gina's other question. And she sat silently as night fell.

The following morning, Sangr and Yella had set off towards the Casin pass, leaving her with strict instructions to walk in any other direction. She had complied.

By now her demons had broken down the ornate doors, and an older and harder Gina could only spare a second to wonder what had become of Sangr and Yella before the tide of angry, animalistic bodies propelled her through the opening. The demons smelled victory, and they were becoming harder and harder to control.

They emerged into the formal antechamber. The Tyrant's bureaucrats would belittle lower nobles and even some common-born petitioners for the amusement of the unwashed, allowed to spectate from the balcony around the room. Though there was no connection between the balcony and the chamber, and crossbowmen to deal with anyone trying to climb down, it allowed the poor of Hell's Gate to feel that they were part of something important. Gina herself had watched from the galleries, before learning the city's dark secret.

Those balconies, hundreds of paces long and completely in control of the high ground, were now packed with soldiers in the Tyrant's livery.

Inhuman screams filled the air as thousands of magically fortified arrows landed among her troops. Gina hastily ordered the beast next to her to turn its heat down to bearable levels and cover her with its body. She was amused to note as she dropped, that the captain of the guard, beaten and trussed but still breathing, had been dumped beside her.

She thought she heard her demons attempting to rally, thought she heard them climbing the ornate walls, imagined there were human screams among the beastly ones, but there was no way to know. The demon above her shuddered with arrow and spear impacts, and its temperature soon went from comfortably controlled to the cold of death. Still, the sound of battle raged.

When the noise subsided, Gina peered out from beneath her improvised shield. The balconies were empty of defenders, but also, it seemed, of demons. Blood and ichor spattered every visible surface, and bodies of every sort littered the ground around her. She tried to sense her demons and quickly located some on the upper level – they must have given chase when the men on the balcony retreated – and some behind her. The ones behind trickled in as she sent out her will, but did so reluctantly, as if the recent slaughter had calmed their bloodlust.

Haggan, notably absent from the front ranks, stepped through the ornate doorway and gave the massacre a critical look. "You don't seem to have much respect for your troops, my lady," he observed in a surprisingly human-sounding voice.

"I didn't know you could speak," Gina said.

"Of course. All the underworld lords can speak. I would have thought that anyone with the power to command us and had taken the time to study our race in enough detail to know my name would have been aware of that."

This gave Gina pause. She wondered what other little tidbits her teacher had forgotten to tell her. He seemed very enthusiastic about what Gina had offered in trade, but less so about his teaching duties. She would have to have a nice long talk with old Carle when this was over.

But now wasn't the time. "Why didn't you speak to me before?"

"You didn't command me to." Was there a mocking gleam in the demon's huge black eye? She couldn't tell, but she also couldn't recall commanding him to speak at any moment. Perhaps it was just reflected torchlight.

The doors at the end of this room represented their destination: the audience chamber, the Tyrant's throne room. It would be the most heavily defended of the chambers. Any really nasty surprises would be on the other side.

Gina thought they would need to improvise some kind of battering ram to get through the barrier but, just as she was about give orders to create one, the doors opened by themselves, gliding silently apart. A glowing cloud spilled into the antechamber from the other side of the doorway.

Haggan walked towards the opening, ignoring the vapor. Gina was about to order him to stop, to turn back, but two things halted her. The first was that there really was no reason for the demon to turn back. It wasn't her life that the elemental spirit was putting at risk, after all. The second reason, though she hardly even dared admit it to herself was probably the stronger of the two: simply stated, she was afraid that the demon lord would ignore her command. And then what would she do?

She looked around at the numerous human bodies in the antechamber. None of the bodies were in one piece, showing the price one paid for not being able to command demon magic. She considered making herself scarce, simply gliding through the hordes and out of the palace into a deep dark hole somewhere.

The press of demons behind made the decision for her. Accidentally or not, one of the demons jostled her forward, and then the mass of hot flesh pushed her all the way through.

The throne room of Tyrant Menthragincar was magnificent. A colossal crystal dome rose up above them, allowing sunlight to soften the dark reds and blacks of the décor. The clouds along the floor were streaked with magical blues, yellows and greens, and the throne itself was mounted on a dais twice as tall as the demon lord himself. A small man with a white beard and blue robes sat there, his head resting on one hand. Without knowing how she knew, Gina sensed the presence of countless troops hidden among the shadows, in the mist.

"So, Haggan, the day has come." The Tyrant's voice belied his size and age. It echoed in the enormous chamber and seemed to make the floor vibrate. Gina's legs trembled at the sound, and she fought to keep them under control.

Haggan was unaffected. "You will find the outcome very different this time around," the demon replied.

"And why would that be? Have the elementals of the Earth sunk so far that they would foreswear their most ancient and sacred obligations?"

"Obligations? Only the fact that your ancestors tricked us when we were innocent of the world has kept us bound all these years." The demon lord seemed to be holding himself back from attacking by sheer force of will. Gina would have sworn she could see the waves of pure hatred radiating from the elemental.

"Be that as it may, you agreed. And it was you, Haggan, not some forgotten ancestor, who bound himself to the terms in the Rite of Anari. I don't even know how you've managed to come this far. Killing a single member of my household other than the offerings should have dissipated your essence."

"I came because I was commanded to by a human bearing the magic."

This pronouncement was met with silence as the Tyrant looked into the crowd at the foot of his throne. His eyes lingered on the captain of the guard, who had regained consciousness and was now standing unsteadily under his own power. "Do you mean to say that the loyal Engris has had the talent of magic, hidden all these years from our screening?" The tyrant's eyes glowed green for an instant, and the guardsman stumbled slightly. "No," the Tyrant said, there is no magic in that one." His eyes alighted on Gina, and he smirked. "Then who? The slave girl? I thought you'd brought her along as a snack. Let's see…" Gina felt a wave of cold rush through her. The Tyrant sighed contentedly. "Ah, yes. A moderate talent. Not the kind of thing one normally encounters among the peasantry, but strong enough, even so. It's a pity this one couldn't have used her discretion. Or worn something a little more according to her rank. Witches can't go around the world covered only in paint, little one."

Gina tried to glare at him defiantly. This was the man who held the entire range of the Hell's Gate Mountains under his thumb and thought nothing of sacrificing its people to the creatures that dwelled in the fire pits below. She found it impossible to hold the Tyrant's gaze.

"So, you've found someone to command you to come here. Have you told her that you only follow her commands because it suits you? And that when it no longer suits you, you will consume the essence of her very spirit, dooming her to eternal torment?" The eyes found her again. "Has he told you that, little girl? You would have been better off dying poor and alone in whatever hovel you were born in."

"Don't listen to him," Haggan said. "He's just trying to save his own skin. He knows his end is near."

"Ah, but that's not quite true, now is it? The command to attack me or any noble must be given separately. You can't just walk in here and slaughter us. She hasn't given it yet, has she?"

Haggan said nothing, and the Tyrant chuckled before continuing. "But I have no such constraints. I can reduce all of you to cinders floating on the wind with no need to get a command from a trembling pleasure-slave who's walked into something she could never comprehend. And the girl won't do it, because I promise her that she'll be made a noble and train beside our children if she just stays where she is, silently, while my magicians finish you off." He raised a hand, and a group of grim-faced men stepped out of the mist, their outstretched hands beginning to glow orange.

Gina knew she had to act immediately, but still hesitated. Could the Tyrant be telling the truth? Would Haggan turn on her when the deed was done? Would the Tyrant honor his promise?

She looked out over the magicians, bearded and hard-eyed, and something inside her snapped. She exerted her will over the demon. "Kill them," she whispered. "Kill them all."

The demons leapt into action immediately. The front line attacked just as the magicians grew ready, and were incinerated, but some of the second wave got through. Human screams mixed with the animal grunts of the demonic horde. Gina found herself surrounded by a press of demon bodies, which pushed her against a wall and pressed the hapless guardsman into her. They were pushed with no heed to their surroundings and almost fell out an arched window, unshuttered in the cool air.

Gina felt an instant of panic, convinced that the demons were going to take advantage of the confusion to kill her, that she would be eaten where she stood, but then she realized that the outer layers of surrounding demons were being hammered by fireball after fireball, and other kinds of magical energy. Waves of cold, waves of strange light, broke on her shield of bodies. She realized that these attacks, far from being calculated to thin the elemental ranks, were aimed at eliminating her. The press of bodies was all that kept her alive.

She turned to the guardsman. "Would the Tyrant have kept his promise? Would he have treated me as one of his own? Did I misjudge him?"

The captain seemed dazed, barely able to comprehend what she was saying. She screamed into his face. "Do the Tyrant's daughters get magical training? Would he have given it to me?"

It seemed as if the man wouldn't respond, but he finally realized that Gina was speaking to him. "The Tyrant's daughters were each sold to noble houses as pleasure slaves, cementing alliances, on the week after they had their first moon-blood. Each was ceremonially deflowered in the public square by their new owner and his brothers when he took possession. But I truly doubt the Tyrant would have given you such pleasant treatment after all the trouble you've caused."

Gina had known that would be his answer. The Tyrant was not known for his mercy, nor for his honesty, but that wasn't what had given him away. It was simply the fact that of the hundred mages that had stepped forward to fight the horde, not one was without a beard. Not a single witch among the hundred warlocks. "Kill them faster!" she screamed over the din of battle.

Haggan must have heard her, or the magic linking them must have transmitted the urgency, for suddenly, every demon remaining launched itself towards the dais at once. The carnage was incredible, and the losses to the horde were atrocious, as demons were vaporized in masses.

But the numbers were just too great, and the mages in defense fell, one by one, under their sheer weight. Finally, Haggan himself, smoke pouring from multiple wounds on his enormous torso, reached the top of the platform. The Tyrant held his arms above his head, an instinctive gesture to protect himself, but Haggan brushed them away. The crack of snapping bones echoed across the chamber.

The Tyrant had time for one final whimper before Haggan's fangs buried themselves in his throat.

As soon as the Tyrant's body had been consumed, Haggan stood and turned to Gina. "That last command of yours was unnecessary and foolhardy. We could have won the fight with fewer losses. Your impatience has left us with less than thirty elementals to do my bidding. I cannot hope to hold Hell's Gate with that."

"To do *my* bidding," Gina corrected. She could feel the magic binding them. Strong, vibrant, like a rope of glowing warmth. She would command the demon lord forever.

"I meant what I said," Haggan replied.

The cord cut. Gina gasped. It felt like a physical bolt to the gut, and she understood that Haggan could have overcome her magic had it been a hundred, a thousand times stronger. In that, at least, the Tyrant had spoken truly.

Now she would die, but not like this. She turned to the guardsman and whispered. "Please. The window. See if you can push me out."

The captain seemed to be caught by surprise again but recovered quickly. He wrapped her in his arms and rolled out of the opening. Air rushed past them.

"You didn't have to come," Gina said.

"I think a clean death is preferable to that, don't you?"

Gina knew she was going to die. There was no way to avoid it. The flagstones were coming up at them at a huge rate, and they were nearly a hundred and fifty paces away. There was no surviving this fall.

Air elementals, numerous among the mountain winds, pulled at her hair. She smiled and touched them as they shot past, strangely calm at the moment of dying. She had tried. She had failed. Life would go on for others.

But suddenly, a sense of urgency filled her, and she screamed a silent request, backed by the full force of her talent to the air elementals around her, a desperate plea to magical creatures who, individually, would never be powerful enough to shrug off her wishes.

At first, nothing happened but, when it looked like their time was up, the air around them thickened, and their fall slowed. A little at first, and then more, as the air itself seemed to pull them back. The ground met them not with crushing finality, but with only enough force to knock the wind out of them.

The guardsman's eyes were filled with awe. "You saved us."

She thought quickly, her heart racing. "You made the right choice in coming with me. Never underestimate me. If you are willing to follow me, I will give you magical protection."

"I will not cross you. I've seen your power."

"Good." Gina felt relief pour through her. The guardsman could have killed her, raped her, beaten her, and there was nothing she could have done to stop him. An air elemental wouldn't stop an angry man. "Then let's get out of this city. People are going to begin asking questions soon. And I need to have a long talk with one of my old teachers."

The man hesitated, unmoving, and Gina's fear rose again. "What is it?" she said.

"I wouldn't question your wisdom, but…" he seemed afraid to speak further.

"Out with it, man. We need to move." A small crowd of passers-by was already forming around the witnesses who'd seen them fall from the sky.

"Don't you think you should get some clothes before leaving Hell's Gate? Those mountains are cold as the devil's heart."

Gina smiled. Maybe this one would be useful after all.

A Frozen Heart

The expression on Hemery's face as Maluz plunged the blade into his chest almost made her regret the decision. He wasn't a bad man, hadn't been a terrible husband. In fact, he had treated her with a degree of respect and kindness that she'd never believed possible.

Unfortunately, he had to die. If he didn't, he would come after her, and that would be inconvenient.

"I'm sorry," she whispered to the dead man. "It has to be this way."

Maluz quickly threw the final items into her pack and shouldered it. The wind outside would be murderous, but the snowstorm would hide the signs of her passage from any of her subjects who tried to follow her when they found her gone the following day. After living here two years the cold held few terrors.

As she emerged from the well-heated central chambers of the palace, the air turned frigid. Her breath hung before her like the spirits of all the jungle creatures that had frozen to death on the day she banished the spell that held the ice at bay.

Outside, the stars weren't visible because of the storm, but she knew the paths between the trees well enough to navigate for the next few hours. Once she reached the coast, she could follow the shoreline. She knew exactly which way she wanted to go. South.

Maluz smiled. She was a creature of the plains, of warm sun and open-windowed palaces, but she'd still managed to choose the right storm to make her escape: flurries of snow would cover her tracks and make her lamp invisible from any distance, but it shouldn't last long enough to kill her.

She took one last look at the castle carved into the mountain and sighed. It had been good to be the queen after so many years as a pawn and a bargaining chip among the potentates of the plains.

But her surprise when she realized that a queen was just another type of slave had slowly hardened, like the ice of her realm, into a rock of determination and, finally, a decision. She would live her life on her own terms, and she'd do it somewhere warmer.

Unfortunately for Hemery, he'd woken up to find her packing her bag.

A blast of hot, humid air emerged from the tavern. Even three days after leaving the ice, Maluz still stopped to savor the glorious warmth. For a while in the north, she'd been certain that the chill would never leave her bones; even beside the fire in the deepest chambers of her palace, her body had believed that heat was a temporary, fugitive thing, to be tasted and then lost, like the fine liquor made from the tropical fruit that had once stood where her kingdom held sway.

Two dozen men turned to look at her and the noise level dipped noticeably. Maluz didn't flinch or look away and things gradually returned to normal. She knew she might have to fend off unwanted advances, but that was what her knives were for.

The man behind the bar appeared out of place among the trackers and hunters that made their living in this frontier town where the warm plains met the frozen woods. He seemed to be about sixty years old with only a few strands of grey hair remaining on his head. Kindly eyes studied her.

"Are you sure you want to be here?"

"Yes," she replied. "And before you ask, I'm also sure I want a decent glass of the strongest thing you have."

"That will be the Ruby Fire, then." He pulled out a plain earthenware jug and poured the contents into a pewter mug. Despite the drink's portentous name, it was a clear, colorless concoction that smelled strongly of alcohol.

She took a sip and smiled at the way it burned. There was none of the disguised sugary taste of the refined drinks she'd had to endure both as a queen and as a pleasure slave in the plains. "Thank you."

"I suppose you can take care of yourself," the barman said.

Maluz could tell that he was still concerned for her safety, or perhaps for his own should she cause an incident. No, she decided, the man had a kindly look to him. He would be worried about her. "If you want a room, I have plenty, and you can go up right now. I'll have my wife take the food up."

"That's very nice of you, but I need some information. I suspect some of your clients will be able to help me on my way."

"You're *sure* you can take care of yourself, right?"

"Just go. There's a man over there trying to get a drink. I can't take up all your time, now can I?"

Almost as soon as the innkeeper moved along, the stool beside sprouted a dark-haired man with a well-trimmed beard. Clearly some kind of village pretty boy. A low-level swell for a low-level town.

"Unless you can tell me the latest news about where Sangr and Yella are, you're wasting your time."

"I don't know who you're talking about," the man said with a smile that showed off a mouthful of white, clean teeth. "But I'm sure there are much more interesting things we can discuss."

"I doubt it."

"Don't. Many women have told me what a delight my company is to them."

"I'm not interested." She pressed the curved blade of a particularly sharp and wicked jungle dagger against his side. "But if you'd like to tell me one of your delightful stories that should give me time to decide which bits of you to cut off."

"You should have said so before, madam. I see you're truly not interested." He turned and walked stiffly away.

The next guy was more promising. Scruffy and unkempt, clearly a man who'd spent some time on the road. "I couldn't help overhearing your question about Sangr. I can tell you something about his whereabouts."

"What's your price?"

He shrugged. "My news isn't too fresh. I can probably share in exchange for a drink."

She smiled. "That sounds fair." She motioned for the innkeeper to match the man's drink to hers. "What do you have for me?"

"He and the woman were down in Ka Surana a couple of months ago. One of the Emir's counselors wound up dead at the same time. Not saying the two things are connected, but I hear they're not in Ka Surana anymore."

She grimaced. Ka Surana was stuck down in the southwest corner of the continent, a good distance from anywhere she was. It would take months to catch up to them.

And that damnable Yella was still with him. That was going to be a problem.

"Thanks, enjoy your drink."

The man looked like he was about to say something more, but she gave him a look and he smiled and nodded. "Thank you."

Maluz dropped some coins on the bar and turned towards the door, only to find her path blocked by a scrawny guy with drooping eyelids and a scraggly ten-day beard. She'd expected to have to deal with at least one other unwanted advance before reaching the door… but had been hoping for something a little more impressive.

"Would you like to pay for a room so we can use it now?" the guy asked.

"What? Are you insane?" Maluz replied. "I'd rather sleep with a gump lizard. It would probably smell better, too."

She expected anger, possibly violent anger. But instead, the man seemed genuinely puzzled. "I don't think you heard me right. I suggested that we should go upstairs. You want to pay for a room for the night."

Suddenly, Maluz understood. She looked him up and down until she saw a small carved stone in the shape of a heart that hung from his neck on a chain. "Magic pendants don't work on me. You're wasting your time."

He backed away a step. "I don't know what you're talking about."

She fingered the heart. "This little thing here. I wonder how many poor women you took just by telling them what you wanted." Maluz held it for a moment in her fist, hoping that the charm was as cheap as the rest of him. If it was, it would never work again after spending a couple of seconds in her hand, under the influence of her particular power. Then she raised her voice. "I've heard about you. Dozens of women have warned me that… well, that you have been issued unimpressive equipment."

That got her a laugh from the room, a dark look from the little guy and, most likely, a concerned sigh from the bartender. She didn't turn around to find out.

South and west. Everyone she spoke to, every rumor, from the most unfounded and vague to those that sounded authoritative agreed on that one detail: she had to go south and west if she wanted to find Sangr. Her horse—bought in the first town she'd encountered that boasted a decent stable—had grown to know the way instinctively. It would find the sun in the sky every morning, put it behind and to the left of them, and begin to walk with no prodding.

As the excitement wore off, Maluz grew weary of the road and angry at Sangr. It almost felt as if the man was doing it on purpose. It was a large continent, and most of the important stuff was right in the middle, on the plains… but he seemed to be exactly on the other side, as far from Maluz's starting point as possible. She told herself that she was being ridiculous, that the man had no clue that she was attempting to find him. But it was hard to shake the idea that he'd gone as far away as he could.

There was also the question of Yella. On her own, she was a formidable opponent, well-trained and with the ability to read minds. Well, to read everyone's mind other than Maluz's, of course. With Sangr to help shore up her defenses, she was almost unassailable. Separating them would be a neat trick and whoever she chose for the job would need to be very good.

She wondered how anyone would go about that… it would likely take some powerful sorcery.

Her own abilities were more limited. She had no ability to perform magic of her own—she could only nullify the magic of others. It was a valuable characteristic if you were a king afraid of magical assassination, so she'd been bought and sold several times.

That all ended when Sangr, attempting to steal the Wizard's Bane and grievously misinformed about what it might look like, had liberated her from a harem in Tengut. He was clearly unhappy that his objective wasn't particularly portable… and Yella was absolutely furious that the talisman they so desperately needed was shaped like a man's deepest desires.

That particular episode had ended with Maluz as Queen of Summerland… as inapt a name for as forsaken a patch of ice as any she'd ever imagined. She'd jumped at the chance, only to quickly discover it was just another form of slavery. Freedom, she'd decided, lay in living a life of adventure with the only man who'd ever treated her as anything but chattel. The adventurer she'd tagged along with for a few glorious weeks after her liberation.

Unfortunately, that man seemed determined to stay down in the southwest, a region she knew almost nothing about.

Maluz gave the horse its head. It seemed to have a better idea of what it was doing than she did.

Tyrrha was different from any place she'd ever seen before. Nestled between the mountains and the sea, the city was built on a narrow strip of salty marshland that fronted the ocean. It was a pitiful place to live, better suited to the plentiful—and enormous—insects than to anything human. And yet, the people rushing along the walkways and canals that connected the rickety wooden buildings appeared both happy and numerous.

The hills behind the town belonged to the sorcerers. Each had his own palace somewhere on the heights, commanding a majestic view of the sea as well as its own warren of tunnels dug out of the mountains. No one could agree as to what the magicians kept inside their caves, other than to say that they were creatures and spirits out of nightmares. Having known a magician or two in her time, Maluz thought barrels of cheap wine were more likely. Good wine if the magical trade was in a good phase.

"I want to talk to a sorcerer," she told the boy who offered to guide her around the city as soon as she arrived. He looked perhaps fifteen years old, and Maluz was certain that he would only guide her into the nearest alley where his friends would be waiting to take her for everything she had. That would be a terrible idea, but she'd explain that if the time came. "That interests me more than seeing the town. I can see the town from right here."

"But you'd be missing all the good bits," the boy protested.

"What's your name?" Though she wasn't all that much older than he was, she felt sorry for him. How could anyone be so inexperienced? His earnestness—even if that earnestness was being used for the express purpose of luring her somewhere to be robbed or worse—seemed sad. At the same time, it was also refreshing. Everyone she'd met on the road seemed to her older than their years, eyes decades past the age of the body they looked out at her from.

"Parru," he replied.

"Well, Parru, let me explain. If you take me to the sorcerer, I'll pay you for the service, and what you receive is yours. You won't have to share it with the men you work for." She smiled at him and had to stop herself from laughing at how his expression changed, from earnestness to greed in a single instant. "And besides, I'll be grateful to you. You'd like that, wouldn't you?"

For a second the boy looked torn. Finally, he sighed. "All right. I just hope I don't get caught. Narya hates it when anyone disobeys her commands."

"We won't be. Now, which one of those guys," she waved her hand in the direction of the hill, "is the deadliest magic wielder around?"

"That would be Urianna," the boy said with a shudder.

A woman… Maluz could deal with a woman, of course, but she had more tools for dealing with men. Men, after all, were much bigger fools where young women were concerned. "All right. Who's the second worst?"

The boy grinned. "Heard of her, have you?" He thought for a second. "It's probably Abren. That's his palace, over there." The boy pointed to a stone compound set against a mountain on which lush greenery grew. She could see huge gardens inside its walls.

"Lead the way."

The boy did, traversing the city crosswise, against the flow of traffic that seemed to be moving along the length of the town, which, though lengthy, was only a couple of city blocks wide and ended abruptly among the thick trees at the base of the foothills. She saw movement among the green leaves an instant before a group of five or six long-haired men wielding knives blocked her path. A graying woman wearing a patch over one eye stood behind them whistling commands.

"Parru, was this your doing?" Maluz asked.

"I swear it wasn't, Lady. They must have been watching me."

Once the men had finished surrounding her, the woman stepped forward. "What have we here? A girl from the plains? Your type always has a little bit of gold on you. Might be that it's yours from years back, might be that you earned it on your back just last night, but there's always coin somewhere. Just a question of looking for it. Maybe if you give it to me, I won't let my boys look for it too deeply." She turned her gaze to Parru. "And you? I knew you'd turn as soon as you thought you could get away with it. What did she promise you?"

"Only that I wouldn't have to smell your breath anymore," the boy replied with a shrug.

The men sniggered but, Maluz noted, took care to hide it from the woman. She admired the kid for his spunk, if not for his intelligence; with these odds he probably would have been smarter to kiss up to the harridan.

The older woman sneered at him. "I'll deal with you later," she said ominously. "Now, what have you got for us, girl?"

Maluz put a hand inside her jerkin and pulled out a single glowing orange ball of magic slightly smaller than her fist. Four of the men—the ones who knew what it was she was holding—flinched back. One of them broke and ran. The woman's tawny skin paled.

"So, instead of giving up a little gold, you've decided to curse us all. At least your torment will be as awful as ours."

Maluz smiled. "Perhaps. Or perhaps not. Have you asked yourself why I can stand here and hold this without suffering any ill effects?"

The woman said nothing. Another of the men ran for the woods.

"I'll tell you. The curses are contained in a glass egg." She paused, savoring the fear of these people, these tiny, insignificant people, who'd wanted to rob her and hurt her and humiliate her. She was done with that. "You might be thinking that it's there to protect me from the curses. You'd be wrong. It's there to protect the curses from me. You see if they touch me, they will die. So, I had a magician spin me some glass bubbles with curses inside. Pretty, aren't they?"

And with a final smile, Maluz let the bauble roll to the end of her finger and fall to the ground. The delicate shell hit an exposed root and burst.

The doors of every hell opened at once.

Maluz turned and put her arms around a frozen Parru. The curses didn't care who they landed on and if you got in the way, you were a dead, or worse, even if you were just a bystander.

Out of the corner of one eye, she saw an orange streak hit the man nearest her. He dropped his blade and fell to the ground. His skin bubbled as sores formed over every patch of exposed flesh she could see. She assumed he was screaming like a stuck pig, but the sound was lost among that being made by his erstwhile compatriots.

Parru's yell, on the other hand, caught her attention. Green lightning had just grounded itself onto his back. His thrashing nearly succeeded in pulling him out of her grip."

"Relax. They can't hurt you while you're with me."

He tugged and bucked all the same.

"I mean it. If you throw me off, you're going to die."

The lad whimpered, but he stayed still. Or still enough: Maluz was able to hold on through the occasional shake.

As soon as it had begun the storm of lights and screaming was over. A couple of charred mounds smoldered to one side. A soft keening came from the man with the blisters. Small pieces of limb lay where the woman had once been and two men were actually twined together, still alive, with their faces contorted in a pain so profound that they were unable to make a sound. She looked away from where their skin had fused together. They would never move from that spot without assistance and certainly never walk again.

Parru looked around, stunned.

She grinned at his expression. "Yeah. Thank your stars that I believed that you weren't responsible for the ambush. Now, let's go see this Abren guy."

The gate wasn't locked, and there were no guards in sight, a clear sign that the gardens beyond—and the magician's palace deep in the grounds—could take care of themselves. It also gave her a glimpse into the sorcerer's personality: he was the kind of man who made it easy for the ignorant and greedy to get in and then enjoyed the show as they ran into whatever awaited within. Uninvited guests to this kind of place tended to fail to make it out.

She turned to Parru. "Well, you've done your part. Here's your fee."

"Are you going in there?"

"Of course. I came all this way to see Abren. It would be silly to stop now."

"But…"

"Don't worry. You don't have to come with me. I can take care of myself."

He still seemed uncertain. "Should I wait for you here?"

"No thanks. I can find my own way back. Really, relax. There's nothing in there I'm worried about. Now go."

Maluz would have enjoyed the walk through the gardens much more if the wizard's defenses hadn't been there. Lights hit her from all sides. Blasts of strange air that wilted the vegetation around her. She couldn't really tell whether the magic was supposed to slow her down or to kill her—all magic was exactly the same in her eyes: ineffectual. She only knew it was there because of the light and the effect on things around her.

Finally, a huge creature, glowing and scaly with five rows of legs barred her final few paces to the palace. She approached fearlessly and it brought an elongated, fanged monstrosity of a head down to her level and peered at her curiously.

"Good doggie," Maluz said in a soothing voice. She placed her hand on a bony ridge above the creature's eyes, and it disintegrated into a scintillation of light.

She sighed and headed up the stairs, wondering how long the magical creature had been alive, happily haunting this and other gardens like it, occasionally eating an intruder. It wasn't the creature's fault that Abren was too cheap to spring for someone to answer the door and separate the legitimate visitors from the ones who were there to waste the sorcerer's time.

"I'm impressed," a dark man with a goatee, but otherwise clean-shaven, said, emerging from the shadows under the porch. "But whatever magic you're carrying; don't think you can use it to harm me. I keep my truly strong spells for defense." He smiled, a man speaking to an equal, at ease enough that Maluz was inclined to believe he was telling the truth about holding something back. "So how can I help you? Whatever it is, I'm telling you now that the shadow-dragon is going to be included in my price. I'm Abren."

She held his gaze, completely unintimidated. "Maluz. Do you enjoy it?"

That caught him off guard. "Enjoy what?"

"Watching people die in your little fun house out there."

"Of course, I do. Why shouldn't I? Most of them are assassins too dumb to know who they've been hired to hit, and the rest are thieves. The ones with actual business to discuss generally have the means to come through those little spells." He cocked his head. "Though I'll admit that I've never seen a spell that can disperse a shadow dragon quite that effectively. I might lower my fee if you teach me that one."

"You'll need to go back and be born again quite different to what you are now."

"You mean it will only work if I'm a woman? That can be arranged, but it's always a nuisance. The main problem is that I'd have to give up all the male-only spells I currently use."

Maluz was taken aback. Even after a life spent among potentates who enjoyed surrounding themselves with magicians of all types, she'd never imagined that was possible. She held her features steady, though. No need to let the man know he'd scored. "Not that. I was thinking you'd need to be born again not only immune to all magic but in such a way that magic doesn't work in your presence. At all."

"That's ridiculous. The only thing I've ever heard of that works that way is the Bane, and that's locked up in a treasure room up north somewhere."

"You mean it *was* locked up. And not in a treasure room. In the harem."

Realization hit him. "You… so the silly rumors were true," then he shook his head. "And here I thought whatever you'd come here to ask for was going to be a straightforward job."

"It could be, I guess."

"Not with you around." Abren pointed at a candle, but his magic failed. He grunted. "That's not going to make it easy."

"I won't be around for the job."

"Yeah," he seemed preoccupied. He pointed to the candle. "How far do I have to be for that not to happen?"

"Ten paces are usually enough. A little less for really powerful wizards."

"All right. Tell me what you want."

"Have you ever heard of a woman called Yella?"

He sighed. "Miss Maluz, please don't assume I'm an idiot just because I live far from the plains. We all know she runs with Sangr which means that any job involving her has to account for him as well. And pay for the privilege."

"Not this one. I don't want Sangr harmed in any way. In fact, I'd prefer he wasn't involved at all. I just want Yella taken out of the picture."

"By out of the picture…"

"Do whatever you want. I need Sangr alone, with no complications. Kill her if you must, do something else if you prefer. I'll pay when you can prove she's gone."

He shrugged. "I suppose I can find a way. But now we come to the unfortunate topic of price. This won't be easy. And Sangr isn't the kind of man I want out for my blood."

"That's something you'll have to deal with." She pulled a green crystal out of her pouch. It was the size of both her hands together. "And here's your price."

He looked at it. "Impressive rock. I'll need to have one of my jewelers look it over. I can't tell if it's worth anything."

"I don't know either. The monetary value isn't why I brought it. You won't be selling this one."

He peered at it. "Why not?"

"It's a magic stone. Or at least it was before I grabbed it. Have you ever heard of Summerland?"

"The jungle kingdom up in the ice? Of course. I heard it died off a couple of years… oh." He looked at the rock more intently. "And you say this is the reason it existed in the first place?"

"Yes." She handed the stone to the magician. "Why don't you step away and test it?"

Now he looked away from the rock. "And what's to stop me from attacking you once I'm out of range of your power?"

"Attack me? With what? As a child, a prince decided I would be the perfect tool to remove a number of magicians who were annoying him, so I was trained as an assassin. If you try to steal it, I'll take it back."

Abren nodded and took a few steps away. Maluz watched him poking and prodding the thing. She assumed he was studying it with some kind of magic, too, but other than the fact that it was an obvious thing for him to do, she had no way of knowing. Many people had told her that they felt a tingling in their bones when someone was using magic nearby, but not Maluz. Her immunity extended even to that.

Abren returned to her wide-eyed. She chuckled. "So, you'll do it."

"Yes," he whispered, holding the stone out towards her reverence and reluctance visible on his face.

"Excellent. Then you can keep the stone. Just remember that if you cross me, I'll come looking for you, and your magic can't touch me."

"I wouldn't dream of it. Besides, I need to try out the power of this crystal, and I have an idea that will both test it and get your woman out of the way."

"Remember: Sangr doesn't get harmed. And you should know that both of them have the power to read minds. That's what makes them so dangerous."

"Yes, yes. Leave that to me." Abren had obviously dismissed her. His attention was elsewhere, creating spells in his mind or whatever it was sorcerers did. For a second, she felt a pang of guilt for whatever would happen to Yella. The woman had never liked her—with cause, as they both knew—but she'd also never done anything to harm her.

Then she shrugged. Yella was standing in the way of the life she wanted.

As she showed herself back out through the mangled gardens, Maluz wondered what life on the road with Sangr would entail. Based on the chase he'd led her on, one thing was for sure: she'd see a lot of different places.

All she had to do now was wait for news that Yella was gone and that Sangr was wandering the dusty roads alone.

She stepped out of the gate and back onto the garden path and sighed; for the second time that day, she was surrounded by people she didn't particularly want to see.

"I'm going to have to start looking out for ambushes," she told the group in front of her.

Unlike the brigands, she knew the people in this group very well. Kaliin, her handmaid, stood a few steps ahead of Thomas, the senior squire of Summerland, a boy she'd spent hours grooming until he had the best manners and grasp of protocol of any person in her palace. She wanted him to be Chancellor someday. With her gone and Hemery dead, he could even have taken power for himself. The others were men from her personal guard, armed to the teeth. She nearly laughed at the way they looked around nervously. Even crossing the entire continent hadn't disabused them of the notion that every land outside their own little glacier was populated exclusively by barbarians intent on dismembering everyone who visited their lands. "So, you finally caught me," she said.

"You didn't take many pains to hide your progress," Thomas said, stepping forward so he was even with Kaliin.

"You want to take me back." It wasn't a question. "I'm not coming."

"The council got together. We're supposed to take you back even if you don't want to," Kaliin said. There were tears forming in the corners of her eyes. "Won't you please come quietly? You're still our queen, even if you…" she choked off.

A great sadness gripped Maluz. These were people she knew and liked. A lot, in the case of Thomas and Kaliin. Why couldn't they have given her up for gone and been done with it? "Just go back. Tell them you didn't find me. I command you."

"We… we can't do that," Thomas said. She was proud of the firmness in his tone. He'd adored her from the moment she walked into their lives; it must have been an inhuman effort for him to stand up to her. "We have given our words. It will hurt me more than you can imagine, but if necessary, I'll ask the guards to tie you to a horse and drag you back. I know you're deadly with those knives, but not even you can stand up to four trained men who know what you can do. You can't surprise us. I only hope you will forgive me someday."

"It's not you who needs forgiveness," Maluz said softly.

The glass globe she'd plucked out of her pocket as he spoke shattered at her feet, releasing its deadly contents into the midst of her friends. As they looked down to see what was happening, she walked away from them, not hurrying, not fast enough to make them want to pursue. As she got out of range, the curses flew among them and they fell, writhing with unspeakable pain, to the ground.

Maluz forced herself to listen to the screams and watch them die.

It was the price she paid for her freedom.

Gustavo Bondoni

Green Hell

Sweat ran down Sangr's face in rivulets that threatened to become floods. There was no escaping the ever-present wetness in the air, but he resisted the temptation to brush the moisture away. A single movement, any chance of being spotted, might be the difference between life and death.

The High Councilor moved slowly through the thick air, showing no discomfort despite his great bulk. It was obvious that the eunuch had been born there, and that he was comfortable. He walked secure in the knowledge that – other than the king himself – there was no one who would ever dare to challenge his power. He walked across the open courtyard, over stones eroded by centuries of rain and feet, between two pillars and onto the dock.

Sangr heard a boat approaching on the river, its oars making tiny splashes. He couldn't turn his head to see what type of boat it was, didn't dare to move. As long as he didn't lose sight of the fat man on the wooden pier, he could afford to let other details go.

A conversation, held in the mellifluous language of the deep Seneriet, ensued replete with raised voices and the unmistakable sound of bartering.

Finally, the fat man in Sangr's field of view shrugged and a second man appeared, carrying a wicker basket an arm's length across which he laid at the eunuch's feet. They argued again, but this time the courtier lost, since the second man retreated, holding his arms in front of him and making warding gestures. Moments later, Sangr heard the sound of the boat moving away. The eunuch grunted and picked up the unwieldy basket.

Good, he thought. *It will be much easier if the man is alone.*

But Sangr didn't move yet. The foliage covering him would make quite a bit of noise when he emerged. It would be more than enough to get him spotted by someone who'd been raised to understand the nuances of the jungle. He waited, alone in the undergrowth with his heartbeat for company, his rapier's familiar weight comfortable in his hand.

The eunuch approached once again, and Sangr held his breath until he was certain that the other man would spot him, then burst from his concealment.

The fat man moved much faster than expected. With a high-pitched squeal, he jumped back and, simultaneously, threw the basket towards his assailant.

It was Sangr's turn to jump aside, and that leap was the only thing that saved him. The round wicker lid came off the flying basket and the contents emerged. Three serpents of colors that could only mean poison, sailed through the space he'd just vacated. Upon landing, they struck out at whatever they could find – each other in this case.

Strangely, Sangr hadn't been able to hear the man's thoughts, just a strange muted mumble.

The eunuch, undistracted by the snakes, dove at Sangr's throat, brandishing a small dagger he must have had concealed upon his person.

The man was fast, but he wasn't that fast. With reflexes schooled on the ice and perfected on the plains, Sangr reacted. He ducked just enough to avoid the thrust and drove the point of the rapier deep into the man's stomach, twisted and pulled it back before it could get caught on something.

Unfortunately, it all took place before his mind could intervene. By the time he stopped to think, the High Counselor was striving vainly to staunch the flow of blood.

Damn, Sangr thought, *I needed him alive*. He knew it was useless to try to negotiate with a man who knew he was dying. He ended the man's misery with a final slash to the throat and straightened.

I guess I'll have to do this the hard way.

Sangr beat back the instinct to charge straight into the royal compound and looked in the direction he had to go. The only sign of civilization – much less the very center of an ancient monarchy – was the columned courtyard from which the eunuch, still twitching feebly at Sangr's feet, had emerged. Beyond that, the jungle seemed impenetrable.

The trees were taller than any he'd ever seen, and their trunks seemed to be made of solid masses of creepers. High above his head, leaves that seemed black even in direct sunlight blocked off all illumination. Far below the canopy, plants that could evidently survive on nothing but the spotty light that snuck between the leaves created a solid wall of undergrowth.

Actually, it wasn't quite a solid wall. At the far end of the courtyard, Sangr could see a well-maintained path leading into the forest, a gash in the underbrush.

It looked like the opening to a very deep cave.

He sighed, but there was little choice. The life of the only person in the world that he truly cared about hung on his ability not only to brave the jungle, but to survive and to succeed. Pausing only to wipe the sword on a wad of grass, he strode towards the path.

As soon as he entered the forest, all sound ceased and a chill wind began to blow from the depths of the jungle ahead, freezing the sweat to his forehead. Sangr, born and raised on the glaciers far to the north, could easily survive a cold that was little more than a lessening of the heat, and silence bothered him not at all. But it didn't feel natural – it was the silence that living creatures make when there are predators about – and Sangr didn't feel like much of a predator.

He walked for an hour that felt like an eternity, jumping at each sound – most of which were simply the echoes of his own clumsy passage. The path, though, seemed clear of any obstruction. It was obvious that either the king felt it was important enough to have a maintenance detail to clean it, or it was enchanted.

Please let it be human workers. He could deal with human workers – and capturing one would help him answer many of the questions that plagued him. Sorcery, on the other hand, was usually… sticky.

But he had few hopes in that regard. The man who'd taken Yella, the man who'd turned off Sangr's curse of telepathy in order to keep the adventurer from sensing his plans, wasn't the kind of man who would worry about the mundane. He wasn't the kind of man who would go to all that trouble to recruit an assassin to kill a man a thousand leagues distant unless there was sorcery involved. After all, sorcery had been involved from the very beginning.

The Song of Sangr

The assassin brooded, thinking about how he was going to get through the royal guard in order to murder a man he had no quarrel with.

Sangr brushed aside what he thought was a thick vine, semi-occluded by the darkness; it dropped onto him from above and immediately began to coil itself around his chest. Faster than he would have thought possible, leagues of serpent began to squeeze him. He could feel his ribs creaking.

With a gasping cry that was probably heard in whatever submerged palace served as home for the court, Sangr fell to the ground, fighting for his life.

His right arm was still free, but he was completely unable to get any leverage to pry the serpent off his body.

Sangr stumbled. The snake's weight was driving him to the ground, but Sangr refused to fall—his terrified mind was telling him that if he fell, he would die. He ran his hand along the snake's body, feeling between the coils, trying to get a grip he could use to pull it off, but there was nothing. Hands slipped off the slick scales of a killing machine designed to deal efficiently with food that objected to being crushed. The darkness of the jungle seemed to grow deeper as he rolled on the floor in hopeless struggle.

In desperation, he struck with a closed fist and encountered unexpected resistance, the resistance of metal. Somehow, in the struggle, his rapier had slid partially out of its scabbard, and he'd bruised his knuckles on the pommel.

Smiling despite the pain, Sangr pulled the blade out, making sure to angle the edge in such a way as to slice deeply into the snake's body as it emerged. Thick blood coursed onto his side. The snake seemed to take forever to realize that it was defeated. It held, gradually pulling tighter for several agonizing seconds, even as the assassin hacked desperately at any part of it, he could reach.

Then, perhaps because of the pain, it slithered away, leaving him panting on his knees.

He listened to his breath, glad for each lungful of air, enjoying the humidity and the smell of rotting leaves. The sound of his breathing seemed to fill the jungle.

Beneath his ragged panting, a more sinister sound emerged: the jangling, rustling sound of large animals moving through the forest in numbers. Though Sangr was a man of the ice, he'd spent enough time in forests over the last decade to know that only one animal made that much noise when it moved through the woods… an animal that didn't care about stealth, because its spears and arrows ruled supreme against even the greatest predators.

The royal guard – or whatever passed for it in this jungle – was coming to get him.

Even though every muscle in his body screamed at him to stay where he was, that death would be preferable to movement, Sangr stood. His chest ached badly, but a quick examination failed to reveal the sharp, localized pain of a broken rib. *Good, I'll just hurt all over, then.*

Running back towards the river seemed like the best option. He could try to outrun them, escape on one of the spare boats. Once across the river, they wouldn't dare follow him – not unless they wanted a war against the sorcerer who controlled the neighboring islands.

But if he did that, Yella would die. There was no doubt about it, no possibility of another attack once the king's guard was up. There was no choice.

Sangr ran, off the path and as silently as he could, towards the sound of the approaching pursuers. It was the last thing they'd expect and might give him the element of surprise. He was considering tactics – try to climb a tree and drop on them from above? Or just to attack the first man he saw and try to punch an opening in their lines that would allow him an unencumbered suicide run to the court, wherever that might be? – when an opportunity presented itself.

A stream, no more than three or four paces across, wound its way through the jungle. He almost blundered straight into it – *and wouldn't that have made me an easy target?* – before he saw it. He was about to jump over it as quietly as possible when he changed his mind.

Although every instinct urged him to hurry, Sangr slowed down. He lowered himself carefully into the muddy water, relieved to see that it moved sluggishly, and was no more than hip high. He sank until only his head remained above the surface.

Sangr listened. He listened with the intensity of a man who knows that his life depends on being able to hear every tiny sound. Fortunately, the men in the jungle behind him – either afraid to lose him or confident in their numbers – were not concerned with stealth. They were nearly on top of him.

The timing would be tricky. If he drowned, he would be just as dead as if his pursuers cut him to ribbons – and so would Yella.

A nearby footstep decided the question. Sangr took a deep, silent breath and allowed his head to go under. He opened his eyes but could see nothing through the suspended silt.

The slow-moving water, however, meant that he could hear every movement. A ripple in the distance signaled that one of his pursuers had entered the stream. It was quickly followed by three more, possibly representing steps taken to cross the water – or perhaps meaning that Sangr had been spotted, and that, even as he lay there helpless, a jungle warrior was approaching to stick him like a pig.

But there was no pain, just the faint sound of another pursuer crossing the stream.

The third splash sounded as though the pursuer was right on top of him. It took all of Sangr's self-control to keep from lashing out and attacking blindly, hoping to injure the unseen man before the other could react. But he kept still.

His tortured lungs were telling him that, unless the enemy moved quickly, it would be a moot point.

The other man seemed disinclined to oblige. There was no more movement for five heartbeats, then ten. Sangr was convinced he'd been discovered and wished he could read the other's mind, as he'd been unable to since that fateful day in Tengut.

But he'd lost that ability on the same day that he'd lost Yella, and the fire in his chest told him that there was no more time. Sangr gripped his rapier and tensed to strike. He opened his eyes again, hoping that some shadow would give some clue as to his pursuer's position.

Three splashes in quick succession followed and Sangr's leap turned into another few heartbeats of waiting. Only when he was sure he would pass out if he didn't move did he allow his head to break the surface, gratefully – but silently – drinking in the sweet, moist air. He believed his enemies had moved on but was beyond caring whether they had or not.

He took stock of his surroundings. Apart from the sounds of his pursuers moving away from him, the forest was silent.

Sangr struck out again, hoping it would take the men a few more minutes to realize that he'd slipped through their net and doubled back. Of course, if he was wrong and they weren't hunting him, they would never even know he'd gone. Certain they actually were after him, though, Sangr moved as quickly as silence allowed in the direction from which the pursuers had come. He knew that without being able to follow a path, the likelihood of getting lost forever in the jungle was very real. Although, in this case, forever was likely to last only until his next encounter with a choking snake – or something worse.

Sangr's anxiety was short lived. A dim white glow seemed to emanate from the depths of the forest ahead. His heart sank. *Sorcery!*

There was no question of turning back. Moving more slowly, Sangr made his way from one tree to another, diving behind a bush at one point, using a natural rise in the land at another, all in the hopes of casting no shadow, and remaining undetected.

As he approached the light, cover became scarce. The dense undergrowth gave way to patches of some kind of serrated emerald grass and the trees thinned out. At times, Sangr could even see sunlight in large patches as opposed to pinpoints. The yellow of the sun, however, couldn't compete with the white light from whatever lay in his path. The original dim glow had become a nearly blinding glare.

A large clearing ahead held a stone edifice: a truncated pyramid with circular towers at each corner. The walls were made of dark grey stone, and it looked as if it might be possible to climb them without undue effort. Not the most defensible of structures, but then again, the fact that it was lost in a trackless jungle would be more than enough to discourage invading armies. Besides, Sangr didn't like the look of the moss and vines that grew over the stone in patches. It had the look of something that, combined with the moisture in the air, could turn even an easy climb into a nightmare of slips and slides.

But climb he would. There was no other choice. The only opening in the walls consisted of a large doorway, sealed with a portcullis of rusty metal bars, from which the light emanated. Sangr thought anyone with that light at his back would be invisible to an adventurer trying to get inside. And anyone inside was unlikely to welcome said adventurer with anything short of lethal force. The frontal approach was clearly out of the question.

But this wasn't the first time Sangr had arrived at a palace uninvited. He moved through the woods, making his way around the edifice, until he stood along one of the lateral walls. Next, he studied the top of the wall and the two towers at the corners, trying to spot lookouts. He preferred not to attempt the climb at night, but any kind of guard presence would make a daytime assault suicidal.

There were no visible sentries. *Strange,* he thought, *what kind of royal guard abandons its king to fend for himself?* But that thought only led to all sorts of speculation about the fact that, just maybe, the king was perfectly able to fend for himself. He stopped the second-guessing by launching himself across the open grass that separated the forest from the wall, half-expecting to be pierced by a dozen arrows or blowgun darts – he felt fortunate that he had yet to learn what weapons the natives used – as he ran.

No death rained on him from the walls, and he made it to the base unscathed. It became immediately apparent that the climb would be even easier than he had thought. Little or no maintenance had been done here; the stone was worn and cracked, and the mortar had long since eroded in the tropical rain. To any determined assassin, the wall was a series of handholds linked together by some stone between them.

Why did that make Sangr feel no better?

Just before the summit, he pulled out the rapier. It wouldn't be much use against arrows or spears, but it would be better than nothing. He didn't expect his luck to hold to the point that there would be no guards on the top of the wall.

But, incredibly, it did.

The roof was a flat expanse, hundreds of paces to a side. A smaller structure lurked in the center: two stories tall, a floor plan that occupied about half the available surface, with two columns bookending an opening on the side facing Sangr. He didn't need to see the intricately painted and carved reliefs to know that this was the abode of the king. Royalty always lived at the top.

He sprinted towards the opening, still amazed that no one had challenged his presence, and nearly ran into the spear that appeared as he approached the doorway. He managed to jump aside at the last second – earning a long gash along the ribs for his efforts – and lunged towards the butt of the spear, where its wielder should be. He pulled it away with a wrench, much too easily, and found himself face-to-face with a young girl, no more than fourteen or fifteen summers old. Her eyes were wide with fear, and her body petrified, but Sangr clasped his hand over her mouth just before she screamed. The sound of her muffled terror made it out around his fingers.

"Do you understand me?" he whispered in the trading tongue of the plains, the closest thing to a universal language he knew of. She seemed to calm down at the sound of his voice, but it was a false impression: almost immediately, she began to struggle anew. "Nod if you can understand me," he hissed.

She ignored him, writing like the serpent he'd encountered earlier.

"If you don't stop, I'll have to kill you. Do you understand? I'll kill you."

But it was obvious that either the language was beyond her, or that she was too scared to respond. Sangr sighed, closed the fist that wasn't covering her mouth and drove into the exposed side of her jaw. She went limp and he allowed her to fall to the floor, hoping that he hadn't hurt her too badly.

What kind of king would use frightened girls as palace guards?

The Song of Sangr

Sangr walked into the building, and it was like being back in the jungle. The air seemed even more humid than it had been outside, the floor was covered with plants – growing out of the rock itself, as opposed to being in pots – and there was no roof. The sun beat in through the top unhindered.

He expected another interminable slog, that the large room would somehow magically transform itself into an actual forest through which he would have to spend hours wading before he reached the court, but he was in for a surprise. He reached the end of a row of thick bushes and turned, to find himself looking at a boy no older than the girl guarding the door. He was seated on a raised golden throne, on a pedestal in the center of a circular clearing among the trees.

The young man's bare chest was covered in necklaces, and a headdress – a solid gold headdress by the looks of it – topped the image off. Sangr was shocked by the absence of guards. Had they all run after him like a pack of hyenas?

The boy on the throne, however, didn't seem surprised to see Sangr. "Are you here to kill me?" he asked, in a lilting, singsong voice, but in the language of the plains. There was no fear in that voice.

Sangr, unable to reply, just stared. He'd imagined some kind of powerful warlord. A hulking pillar of a man who would let fly with all his accumulated magic as soon as the assassin showed his face. And though Sangr had plenty of protection against magic, he had still come prepared for a titanic struggle.

A pale, weak, underage ruler was the last thing he'd imagined possible.

"Well, here I am. It would be a kindness," said the boy on the throne.

Sangr believed him, believed it to the core of his being. The boy on the throne was a threat to no one, just a victim, a pawn in the game of power. "I have no quarrel with you," Sangr said.

The king nodded sadly. "It's always the same. We're nothing but pawns in the game of power." His eyes were so deep that Sangr could have sworn that the boy's soul was visible beneath.

But then he stopped to think about the king's words. He was amazed at how they echoed his own thoughts, nearly to the very word. He and the king must be some kind of kindred spirit. He took a step toward the throne, ignoring the armed men, probably the same who'd run after him in the woods, who suddenly arrived and stood at the edges of the clearing around the throne.

"Come to me, my assassin friend. You don't want to kill me."

Sangr walked, showing no emotion, all the way to the steps. "Of course, I don't want to kill you. I have no quarrel with you," he said.

"Then you may ascend," the king replied, his eyes black as night, deep as the deepest ocean.

Sangr obeyed. There was no question that the king expected it, and it would be of no use to resist. In a moment, he was standing beside the golden seat of power in the jungle abyss.

"Kneel before me," the king said softly. Then, glancing at the rapier in Sangr's hand, he continued: "You won't need that. There is nothing but love in my jungle."

"Ah," Sangr replied. "But I do need it." He drove the point of the rapier deep into the young king's chest, making certain to keep the blade horizontal so that it would slide between the ribs. "And more especially Yella needs it."

The king's eyes, no longer deep loving pools, widened in pain.

Sangr watched the young boy's face. Lines appeared, shallow wrinkles that soon became deep crevasses. The skin went from a light, almost ghost-white tone to a dark brown, and turned first to the texture of leather, and then to that of old parchment before dropping from the muscle entirely. "How?"

the ancient creature managed to whisper, a sound like a distant wind.

"I was a telepath, too," Sangr replied. "I can tell when my thoughts are being warped without my consent." And he understood why the sorcerer had chosen him, and why he'd taken his most valuable ability. If the king had sensed Sangr's own telepathy…

The monster on the throne crumbled to dust.

But, Sangr continued silently, *I would have killed you anyway, even if you'd been a babe in arms. Yella is more important to me than any statement of morals. My only regret is that I will die before seeing her again.*

He turned to face the palace guard, men who'd hunted him, and who would now avenge their ruler. Mercy would not be given. He would not ask it.

But the men were gone. In their place stood a motley assortment of carrion eaters, wild dogs and apes. The creatures slunk off into the vegetation save for one large serpent who eyed Sangr speculatively. Pound for pound it could have been the twin of the one that attacked him in the jungle, and Sangr showed it his blade.

It slithered away, moving quickly, and not looking back.

The Love of Another's Life

"Hello Abren. You sent me on a suicide mission," Sangr growled.

"And yet, here you are," the sorcerer replied. He spoke carefully, trying to keep the blade of Sangr's rapier from drawing any more blood than it already had. There was little else he could do with a sword against his neck. "I trusted you would be up to the task."

"You trusted I'd get myself killed."

"Not in the least. I wanted you to assassinate the king for me. That's why I went to the trouble of hiring you in the first place."

"Hiring me? You kidnapped Yella."

"You wouldn't have taken the job otherwise."

"Of course not; it was madness."

"But now that you've completed it, you can collect your fee and live a life of comfort."

"What if I decide I want your liver for my fee?"

The sorcerer showed that ice truly did run through his veins. "Then you'll never see your little lady again."

"Damn." Sangr pulled the sword away. "A thousand. In gold. And Yella."

"That is what we had agreed," the sorcerer said. "I am as good as my word."

"All right. Lead the way."

Abren led him through torchlit hallways and staircases, always heading downward. To Sangr's surprise, their path led through a sally port in the outer wall of the keep and into the moonlit garden. The wizard kept up a running commentary all the while.

"I must compliment you on the ease with which you penetrated my defenses. I'd heard that you are quite good at this sort of thing, which is why I hired you in the first place, of course. But I'd also planned my defenses against the possibility of a skilled thief scaling the walls… so I'd venture to say you had a little outside help? And to get through my defenses, am I correct in guessing that it cost a small fortune?" The man paused and took a few steps. "And that the money is a direct result of the mission I sent you on?"

Abren waited for Sangr's reply but, as none was forthcoming, he chuckled. "I'm beginning to think I should be miffed at you for acting all annoyed with me. It appears you made out pretty well from the deal."

"Don't push your luck."

Sangr followed the wizard's laughter down a gravel path that led towards the mountain. A cave yawned open before them but, unlike most caves in his experience, this one wasn't a darker patch in the already dark wall. The cave glowed blue, like a beacon of wizardly light, and Sangr suddenly felt too tired to go on.

Everything. Every single thing he'd done over the past three or four years of his life, since he'd made the awful mistake of leaving his tiny village in the frozen north, reeked of magic. The parade of magical monsters, ensorcelled jewels and even inherently magical people had left him exhausted. All he wanted was to take Yella, walk to some isolated village far from the centers of power and magic and simply grow old. They had enough treasure put away for several lifetimes. There was no reason to go on as they had.

He wasn't relishing putting that argument to Yella, but he'd cross that bridge if he ever came to it.

"I assume she's inside?"

"Yes. There's something I need to tell you, though."

Sangr's rapier flew out of its scabbard like it had a life of its own. The sorcerer threw up his hands.

"Don't make me burn you to a crisp, Sangr. I gave you my word, and I intend to keep it."

"Tell me."

"Yella is inside, and she's perfectly all right."

"Then why do you need to talk to me?"

"Because… well, I can show you."

They walked into the cavern. The place seemed to be made entirely of crystals and, if Sangr's mind hadn't been on Yella's safety, he would have been assessing the potential value of the shards that covered the floor.

As they penetrated deeper into the cave, the images became more polished, and the huge crystals, freestanding, vertical and taller than he was, would have fetched a pretty price anywhere on the plains—even if they'd been nothing more than quartz.

But they weren't quartz. The interior of each crystal looked like quicksilver, eddies swirled within to create patterns that almost seemed to coalesce into faces and figures. It felt like looking for shapes in the clouds.

Then he no longer had to look. The figures in the countless crystals coalesced unmistakably into faces and bodies. No. Not into faces and bodies. Into *face* and *body*, singular. Every crystal contained the delicate features and knowing smile of his beloved Yella. None of them looked happy to be inside a crystal. Several were banging on the surface, but none of them acknowledged his presence.

"How do I get her out?"

"That isn't the right question, Sangr. Look closer."

He did. At first all he saw was Yella, trapped in a crystal, angry at the indignity, repeated a thousand times, or maybe more. Certainly, as far as the eye could see.

But as he concentrated on the individual crystals, Sangr realized that they weren't all the same. To start with, they didn't all look alike. Most of the Yella's he could see wore the familiar tan breeches and green shirt she always sported, but some were dressed in different colors. One sported low-cut shoes of a truly peculiar design. Another wore her hair nearly to her waist. A third, unimaginably, was wearing a red dress.

He stepped back and realized that every single one of the iterations was different, even if sometimes almost imperceptibly so.

"What… what is this?"

"These are Yella. Each and every one of them. But not all of them are from this world. They are as many worlds as there are stars in the sky and I've called all the Yella's from each of those worlds here for you."

"But I don't want the ones from a different world. Just give me the one who lives here."

Abren looked sheepish. "I'm afraid it's not that simple. Yella was trying to escape. She'd killed three of my guards and was climbing the wall. I hit her with the first spell I could think of that wouldn't kill her. Unfortunately, it was a random banishing spell."

"Let me guess… you don't know where you sent her."

"It shouldn't have been a problem. I knew I could bring her back. And I did. She's in here somewhere. I'm sure you can find her."

"Find…" the words trailed off as Sangr looked over the countless crystals. "How…"

"Preferably quickly, I'd say. The crystals are unstable, and if you dither too long, they might start shattering." So, saying, the sorcerer backed towards the entrance. "Once you find her, all you have to do is touch the crystal holding her and say her name. Easy. So… I'll see you when you're done. Here's your money."

Backing quickly, he tossed a heavy purse at Sangr's feet.

Sangr watched the sorcerer go, knowing that when a man of that kind retreated in such an undignified manner, it meant that something was about to explode or otherwise go badly pear-shaped.

For a moment, he was torn between finding Yella as fast as possible in order to get out of the cavern and running after the sorcerer to attempt to cut him into small pieces. The man, like all of his kind, seemed to have a pathological need to keep every letter of his promises. Unlike others, though, this one seemed to have an equal desire to see Sangr dead. At the very least, his actions made it perfectly clear that he was unconcerned with the thief's continued welfare.

The urge passed and Sangr looked into the chamber. The task ahead was daunting: there were hundreds of women in the crystals, and each could realistically claim to be his Yella.

He nearly froze, but the sense of urgency from the wizard's words saved him. He knew he had to be moving, and he also knew that he would know his Yella when he saw her.

So Sangr ran between the crystals. Most of the women he discarded immediately. This one was dressed wrong, this other wore her hair in a way that the original would have died before accepting. Others had a different posture, or a strange expression. He ran past dozens.

Every once in a while, he stopped for a closer look. Each time he did so, he was disappointed, but there were some women that he just had to check. He couldn't simply run past and risk losing Yella to whatever cataclysm was approaching.

Suddenly, he stopped dead in his tracks. Two crystals held nearly identical women. Both dressed in the right breeches and in the correct shirt. Both wearing Yella's shoes. Both with expressions of frustration with being locked inside a crystal that would have been perfectly at home on his love's face.

He peered closely at one.

Then he looked at the other. Something was telling him that the woman on his right was the correct choice, but he couldn't put a finger on what it was.

And he saw it: a white line across her forearm, a gift from a servant of the god Qalnoth, received in a serious swordfight that ended with only Sangr and Yella standing. The woman on the right had the scar. The other didn't.

He reached out and touched the crystal, certain he had the right one. Then, frightened by the fact that nearly a third of the room had gone unsearched, and that there were crystals he still had to verify, he stopped dead.

A crack like thunder echoed through the chamber and a crystal thirty paces away exploded into shards. Rocky shrapnel pattered against every surface and announced that his time was up. He touched the crystal and shouted: "Yella."

The rock surrounding her disappeared and Yella blinked in surprise before her eyes settled on him. Tears welled. "Sangr?" she asked. She reached out with a hand and stroked his cheek, as if to satisfy herself that he was truly there.

"Come on," Sangr urged. "I'll explain later."

She looked confused. "Explain?"

They had no time to talk. The crystals were all vibrating coarsely, and having seen what one failure could do, he didn't want to imagine what all of them suddenly bursting at the same time would entail. He took Yella's arm and yanked her towards the exit.

They'd barely taken two steps when a rock halfway between them and the safety of the gardens exploded. It was too far away for the shards to reach them, but the shock set off another crystal nearby, causing it to burst as well. That one set of the one beside it.

Despite her recent imprisonment, Yella reacted with the usual alacrity. She stopped dead in her tracks. "The explosions are coming this way."

Sangr had reached the same conclusion. "We'll need to go back, deeper into the cave."

"Is there an exit that way?"

"I have no clue. But I also have no other ideas."

"You never were one to have a contingency plan, were you?"

"It wasn't my fault this time, I swear."

"Whatever," Yella said. She wasted no more time arguing and headed further into the cave.

Sangr followed, moving as fast as possible without getting too close to the crystals. The last thing he wanted was to set off another series of explosions at this end of the cavern. He saw Yella looking at the crystals as she passed, her face growing ever more concerned. Knowing her, concern would soon turn to anger, which would be directed at him, even if they were in the middle of trying to fight off a monster as she vented.

He smiled. He was glad to have her back. The months without her had been torture.

The cave was larger than he'd been able to see from the first chamber. It grew narrower as they went deeper, and there were fewer crystals. He glanced at one and saw Yella dressed in some outlandish silver garment which clung to her body and left even less to the imagination than her breeches did.

For a fleeting second, he wondered if he could liberate more than one version of her. But then self-preservation kicked in—Yella would kill him if he tried it—and he decided against it.

A sound to their left caught Sangr's attention. He looked to see one of the crystals apparently intent on shaking itself to pieces as it vibrated against what appeared to be a wall of ice. He threw Yella to the floor and covered her with his body. Shrapnel flew through the air around them. A piece of crystal embedded itself painfully in his upper arm.

"Ow," he groaned.

"Are you all right?"

"You tell me." He showed Yella the wound and she rolled her eyes. "Just a little puncture. I've seen you take much worse and keep fighting." She said it with fond sadness. Then, with a quick motion, pulled the offending shard of rock painfully from his arm.

"We should go that way," she said, pointing. The exploding crystal had taken a good piece of the wall with it. The opening led to another cave, equally bright, but seemingly devoid of detonating rock. Sangr could hear the explosions behind them, getting inexorably louder. The sound overruled any anxiety he might have had about what else, apart from lethal crystals, might live inside a sorcerer's cave complex. He followed Yella through.

"Don't go in too deep. Just far enough that the shrapnel can't reach us. We need to go back that way to get out."

They entered the new cavern which, apart from lack of crystals, appeared identical to the first. Cool blue light came from the walls—someday he'd have to ask a sorcerer about the source less light they all seemed to use; he suspected it must be the first spell they learned in evil wizarding school—and the same rock and white sand littered the floor.

Sangr saw movement out of the corner of his eye. Some kind of crystal insect the size of a human baby scurried among the crags in the rock.

"As soon as those things stop exploding, we're getting out of here," Sangr said. In reality, though, he was relieved. He'd expected the monsters to be bigger. He could probably hold this one off for a few minutes, if necessary.

The explosions in the adjacent cavern got closer and closer before finally drawing alongside the opening. They took cover, Sangr looking behind to keep the creature at bay. A crash shook them and when he turned back, his heart sank.

"Of course," he spat.

Yella gave him an amused look. "Did you actually think it would be that easy?"

The opening between the two caverns had collapsed. Large rocks had detached from the wall and roof, and the resulting pile of rubble had completely blocked off the exit. Sangr ran up to it, hoping to shift some of the debris, but a single look at a boulder the size of a shepherd's cottage convinced him that it was a lost cause.

He turned back to see Yella, short sword drawn, sparring with the insect-thing. He took his place beside her and immediately fell into the glorious, side-by-side rhythm that they knew so well. It was almost as if no time had passed. They alternated: block, parry, strike, block, parry, strike.

Sangr smiled happily as he studied the monster facing them. As they struck it, chips flew out of the hardened carapace, but that hardly slowed it. The question seemed to be why, exactly; a stone spider would attack two humans. Surely it couldn't eat them, so perhaps it was just an expression of territorial defense.

He hated to think of the amount of grinding and polishing his rapier would need to get the nicks out. As he thought it, he realized that, now that Yella was with him again, he had no particular fear of being killed. They'd get out of this, together, the way they always did. He could afford to think about inanities in the middle of a fight.

The little monster retreated out of reach and scuttled deeper into the cave.

"I hate to say it, but we need to go after it. I don't see any other exits."

They advanced cautiously through several chambers, always trying, by dead reckoning, to move in the direction of the entrance Sangr had used. There was no guarantee that the two caves would share an exit, but at least they wouldn't be going deeper into the mountain. That was, of course, if Sangr hadn't gotten hopelessly turned around in all the excitement.

The only warning they had was a slight humming, but it was enough. As if sharing a mind, Sangr and Yella dropped to the floor simultaneously, as something flashed over their heads. Had they remained standing, both would have been decapitated.

Sangr rolled to his feet. What he'd thought was a large boulder suddenly sprouted legs and unfolded into a scaled-up version of the spider crystal they'd done battle with. It advanced cumbersomely, glaring at them malevolently through red eyes.

"Looks like our little friend came to find her mommy," Yella remarked.

"Yeah. I'm thinking we can't take that thing."

"I'm with you. Especially because there are four more over there."

"Damn. I thought those were just big rocks."

"The only way out is behind them."

Sangr grinned at her and, with a whoop, ran straight between the creatures. They reacted slowly, and the adventurers made it out of the chamber unscathed. There were no creatures in the next room, and the two laughed excitedly.

The spiders pursued them, but the result was never in doubt. The two thieves were simply too quick and, within minutes they reached a reinforced iron gate. Beside the portcullis, a door big enough for a man, but not for a monstrous spider gave them access to Abren's gardens.

They exited and embraced each other.

"Let's get out of here," Yella said.

"No. I need to do something." He fiddled with the wheel that controlled the gate until, with a groan, it began to budge. He kept lifting until he thought there was enough room for the spiders to squeeze through. "There. I hope they wreck his gardens."

They sprinted off, vaulted the wall and kept going until they felt safe from pursuit.

"Do you believe he actually paid my fee?" Sangr said. "We're rich. Even richer than we were."

"Sangr…"

"We can leave this life and try to live like real people. Rich people even."

"Sangr!"

"What."

"We're not going anywhere. Not together, at least."

"What do you mean?"

"Those women in the crystals. Who were they?"

"They were you. I mean…" he quickly explained what the sorcerer had told him.

She looked at him sadly. "You chose wrong. I'm not the Yella you were looking for."

"What? No. You're joking." He laughed nervously, but the sound died when he saw her face. "That can't be. The clothes. The way you fought beside me. The scar on your arm—"

"They gave me that scar the day I watched you die," Yella said. "In my world, in my life, you've been dead for two years."

He froze. "You mean…"

"I cried for weeks."

His world spun. "We can make it work."

"No, Sangr. You pulled me out of my life, a good life. I met another man. We were happy. You destroyed that."

"Still…"

"I loved you. But now I love someone else. And we can't be together."

"Why not? He's not here. If you loved me once, you could do so again."

She gave him a sad look. "Don't you see? If you're here and I look the same way as the Yella from this world looked, then this world must be nearly the same as mine. He'll be here, somewhere. All I have to do is to find him."

"Not if I find him first."

"You won't find him first. You don't know who he is." She gave him a hard look. "And if you try to follow me, I'll gut you like a fish."

Sangr just nodded. He had nothing to say.

As she walked away, checking to make sure that he wasn't following her every few paces, he vowed to find his own Yella.

And the way to do that was to speak to the sorcerer; Abren would be more than a little miffed to get ambushed in his own house twice on the same night.

Then he swore. Had he known he would be crossing the lawn again, he wouldn't have released the spiders.

Sangr sighed and pulled his rapier. At least those things were slow.

Elemental Questions

The guardsman took one look at their clothes and waved them through. Gina smiled to herself, amused to note that the good people of Revenn were just as quick to bow to the trappings of wealth as those of Hell's Gate. Even their famous proclamations of equality didn't seem to be proof against the maxim that some were more equal than others.

The gate led into an arched passage whose roof was dotted with murder holes. At one point, the floor on which they tread echoed hollowly, signs of pitfalls beneath.

"This should be an interesting place," Tavill said.

"I don't think things can get much more interesting than Hell's Gate," she replied.

"One can only hope." He glanced at her sidewise. "But knowing you, I sense that they might."

She ignored him and pulled at her coat. Though warm enough for the mountains, and of high quality, it was too tight around the neck. She found herself wishing they'd robbed a different couple. But then again, perhaps it was for the best. The nobility of Hell's Gate deserved to be left naked and unconscious on the street more than any other group she could think of offhand.

Besides, Tavill actually looked handsome in the man's outfit, especially now that his wounds were healing.

The passage opened into a small square from which three streets led further into the city. Gina shrugged and chose the one in the middle, on the premise that it shouldn't take them too far from where they needed to be.

"I wish I knew where the Priest of Wasyl is. It's not the kind of thing you can ask just anyone. I'd prefer it if he doesn't know I'm coming."

"I still think this is a bad idea. Hell's gate is just five days' ride away, even on those ridiculous mountain roads. I don't want to be here when whoever wins the fight between the demons and the Tyrant decides to come looking for you."

"They should be too busy holding the city to worry about that. And besides, if Haggoth's horde wins, he should be thankful to me for ordering him to leave his pit and allowing him to kill the nobles."

"I think he might object to the fact that you're telling everyone his name."

Gina shrugged. "He'll need to kill a lot more people than just me to stop that now. We'll be fine."

"Whatever. What are you going to do when you find the priest?"

"I told you already. I just want to ask him a few questions."

Tavill didn't look convinced, and she felt a small surge of guilt for what was about to happen. It passed quickly, however: they'd only met a few days before, and he'd been doing his best to sacrifice her to the demons below Hell's Gate at the time, so no matter what happened next, he probably deserved to suffer through it by her side.

"Should we find an Inn?"

"Do you have any money? The woman seems to have had all her wealth locked down in clothes."

"The man had nothing but the brooch we traded for the horses. I suppose his credit is good everywhere. I wonder who he is."

"I don't care. I hope the demons got him." Impulsively, Gina reached out and grabbed a small man passing by. Her victim spluttered in protest, but upon closer inspection of her clothing and of Tavill's hulking form and menacing glance, he became docile.

Gina smiled at him. "I'm sorry to detain you. Could you indicate where the Priest of Wasyl is located?"

"He's in the narrow streets. Walk straight up this road and ask when you get to the alleys."

"I think I'd prefer it if you would show us the way."

"I need to be somewhere else," the man protested, and began to pull away, Tavill or no Tavill. But, as a wisp of wind wrapped itself around his neck, his eyes grew wide. "I'm sorry, I didn't know… I'll take you."

Gina smiled. "Thank you." She knew that air elementals here were very weak – they couldn't have choked him… but there was no need to tell the man that. And she definitely didn't want him sending the priest a message before she got there.

With the man's help, they found the Wasyllan Sanctuary easily enough. It was just a small brown door in an unimpressive building fronting an alley that Gina could have stretched her arms across. It most certainly wasn't what she'd been expecting.

"What did you think you'd find?" Tavill asked as their unwilling helper scurried away. "Wasyl is not a big thing in the mountains. Our people have learned to fear the elementals, and anyone communing with them is viewed with suspicion at best. Revenn only tolerates them because Revenn tolerates everyone. I remember what Tyrant Menthragincar did to the last priest who tried to come into Hell's Gate. The demons complained because the pieces they got to feed on were too small."

Gina shrugged. "Let's go inside."

The door was locked, but insistent banging summoned a small, wizened servant who told them to go away. Gina ignored his words, gave him her best smile – which she knew would work on any man with a pulse, and told him. "We're here to deliver a donation."

"Deliver it to me," the man said with a leer.

"Come, come, you know better than that."

The servant sighed and opened the door another fraction in order to look them over. "All right. Come inside."

The place was no more impressive on the inside than it was from without. A small, dark front room opened into what seemed like a room not much larger, but which held a table suitable for six people. It was illuminated by a soft blue glow.

Gina sighed. "I hope you're not expecting us to be impressed by the light. From the look of it you might have one, perhaps two water elementals giving you some help." She looked around. "Definitely two, but very weak."

The old, bearded man seated at the end of the table nodded to her. "I see that this conversation is going to be a bit different from what I normally have in this place." He turned to the servant. "Gastón, please go down to the tavern and get us some wine. Perhaps the Tribellan red we enjoy so much."

Once the stunted man had left, the priest turned his attention back to them. "So, who do I have the honor of addressing? I imagine that you didn't come to give us a donation, though, as you can see, it wouldn't be amiss."

Gina suddenly wondered why she'd come. She'd always been well treated by the priests, back when she was an acolyte with talent, and before she'd abandoned their teachings to go her own way. And yet, she felt that, somehow, they were the enemy, that what they had refused to teach her – refused to teach any girl – was tantamount to stealing her birthright.

"I would like to know where to go for elementals in this city. Real ones, not like these two. Preferably fire. Water and Air are too weak, and never really gotten along with Earth spirits."

"These two are loyal, faithful servants. I'd thank you not to insult them."

"Suit yourself, but I need to know where I can find stronger elementals." Gina saw a flint and steel on a ledge beside her, with a candle in the center of the table. She took the igniter and sat on the seat facing the old man.

"Do you know how to see them?"

"I can see them," she told him. "Possibly much better than you can. I was taught the ways of Wasyl on the plain. I learned some of the secrets, but I also learned to spot the lies. I also learned that most priests are more afraid of the elementals themselves than most of the people out there." She struck a spark and created a small flame on the wick of a candle, something that was impossible to do for most people. "My theory about that is that the priests are afraid of the elementals because they can't really control them as well as they want to. And they know there are others out there who can."

The flame burned brightly, drowning the blue light in soft orange. A tiny face danced within the flame, leering at Gina, and occasionally glancing over at the priest… at whom it stuck out its flame-tongue.

The old man stared at it and swallowed. The fear visible in his eyes confirmed Gina's suspicions: this man had probably been exiled here because he could barely control the weakest of elementals, so he would assiduously avoid fire spirits. It was probably wise to send the real duffers out to these places – an ineffectual weakling was likely to create a sense of benign indifference as opposed to open opposition, and that was something the Order of Wasyl could use to its advantage if the need arose.

Of course, it might also be that they wanted to maintain control over their priests; men with power were dangerous in the mountains, since there were truly strong forces at work just below the ground.

She smirked to herself. Perhaps they shouldn't have worried so much about the men… Women with power, she knew, were even more dangerous, as the Tyrant of Hell's Gate had discovered to his cost.

She looked the old man in the eye. "I'd like to know where the more powerful elementals are. As you can see, I prefer to play with fire, so anything with a nice vent or caldera would work well. But if not, I wouldn't say no to a raging river."

"Why should I help you?"

"Because we both are trained in the mysteries of Wasyl. In a way, we are brother and sister, united by our sensitivity to the spirit world." *Of course, in that analogy*, she didn't say, *you'd be the much younger little brother.*

"But why would you need strong elementals? Our way is clear. We seek to commune, to use the elements to make lives better, but without resorting to force. Our philosophy is to guide, to commune with the spirits around us, and use their energy to create harmony between man and nature." He gave her a long look. "I can't see how the strength of the spirits we speak to could have any importance."

"It's important to me. I feel more harmonious when speaking to stronger entities."

"I think you have slipped from the path. Perhaps it would be better if you left," the priest told her, a calm air of finality in his tones.

Gina thought about that for a few seconds, and then responded in what she felt were perfectly reasonable tones. "I think that, if you don't tell me what you know, purely in the spirit of brotherly collaboration, of course, I will have the spirit in that candle burn away your beard."

"You dare walk into a sanctuary of Wasyl and…"

"I dare basically whatever I think I can get away with. Right now, I believe you aren't powerful enough to defend yourself from a small candle-fire spirit, or even begin to challenge my mastery over it. I could take your water elementals equally easily. But I won't. All I need is some information, and we'll be on our way."

The old man gave her a dark look, but then broke his gaze. "You will find a cleft behind the marketplace. It is a place of pilgrimage and worship, but it also opens into the bowel of the mountain. There are fire elementals there."

"And how do we get in?"

"It is open to all. Just be sure to take an offering."

"Thank you. I knew we would understand each other." She stood. "May the peace of Wasyl guide your steps." It was the only part of the litany that she could remember, from back when she was being trained as an acolyte. She'd always found the stable boys much more interesting than her lessons.

"Just go away," the old man sighed.

As they walked towards the market, Tavill gave her a critical look. "That wasn't nice. We probably could have convinced him without resorting to threats."

"Perhaps. But they aren't nice people. Do you believe that they expected us to be virgins all our lives? They told us that the spirits would only speak to the pure of heart and body."

"Sounds logical, I guess."

"I can assure you that they were wrong," she told him, with a wicked smile. "But worse than that, they seemed to think it only applied to the girls. So, if you ask me, they deserve whatever they get."

"Still, I don't think that priest in there has much to do with policy-making, do you? He just seemed like an old man who would have loved to be appreciated instead of insulted and threatened."

Gina turned on him in disbelief. "Have you lost your mind, or just your memory? If I recall correctly, when I met you, your main occupation was to push naked women into a pit of fire so they could be torn to pieces by demons."

"That wasn't my main…" but he let the protest die. "All right, I guess it's a fair point. What are you planning now?"

"Well, as you know, my attempt to install myself as the leader of Hell's Gate didn't go exactly to plan." She waited while he finished snorting. "And now I find myself without a city to rule. So, I was thinking what a tragedy it is that the good citizenry of Revenn doesn't have a Tyrant to guide them. I believe we can remedy the situation."

"You can't actually…"

"They were young girls, too. Most of them were barely girls that you had to push into the pit while they screamed for their mothers. Did you do it yourself or did you have your guards do it for you?" Seeing that he had no answer, she laughed. "Besides, doesn't Tyrant's consort seem a much better position for you than maiden pusher?"

"Consort?" he asked, but had the wisdom not to say anything more.

"Oh, look. That must be the marketplace."

Getting an appropriate offering was not easy. The guard at the entrance to the cave sent them back to the marketplace for some root of the blin tree, which turned out to be a series of small circular chunks of wood. The locals, wise to the pilgrimage functions of the cave, had priced it as high as they thought possible.

Gina was sure that their clothes had added a healthy bump to the price – enough that they'd had to leave Tavill's coat with the peddler in order to obtain what they needed.

Seeing them sufficiently laden with offerings, the guard let them enter the cavern.

"I hope this was worth it," Gina muttered as they trudged down a dank, long cave that seemed to be more of a path than a natural cave. The walls were made of polished rock formations that looked like they'd been worn smooth by running water. Torches in iron rings broke the penumbra, but they were much too far apart for easy navigation.

"This is a lava tube," Tavill said. "We used to explore these as children in Hell's Gate."

"Fascinating," Gina said. "What a lovely childhood you must have had. No wonder you became a professional maiden sacrificer." The cave had done little to improve her mood. She hoped the fire pits were truly something special, because if not, they'd have sacrificed a cloak for no good reason.

And then, after a sharp bend in the tube, she stopped dead. The walls of slimy rock had suddenly disappeared, and the dark cavern was suddenly infused with a warm orange glow.

When her eyes adjusted, she saw that the light was coming from the cavern walls, no longer smooth and rounded but sharp and hard. She could see deep inside them, as if looking into a cloudy diamond. And there, in their profundities, lived a flickering orange and yellow and red glow, as if the walls had swallowed a fire and somehow kept it captive in their belly.

"How…?" Gina was at a loss for words. She'd seen enough of the world, both on the plains and in the mountains, that she knew beauty, but she'd also seen enough to know that beauty was the preserve of the rich, the almighty Tyrants and petty kings. It wasn't something that would be open to the masses in this way.

She resolved, once she became Tyrant, to close the cavern for her own exclusive use.

They walked through the living fire of the walls slowly. Gina tried to take in every facet of the beauty around her, every twinkle and flame. She barely noticed as the clamminess of the cave gave way to a warm, dry wind.

The flaming diamond corridor ended as abruptly as it had begun. It opened into a cavern which radiated an angrier red than the subdued hues of the passage. A short shelf of rock opened onto a caldera in which the blood of the deep earth bubbled. It was crusted over at some points, but in others, there were burning stumps of wood from blin trees.

Despite the heat radiating from the pit, a knot of red-robed pilgrims knelt at the edge of the abyss, blisters forming as they slowly baked.

Gina walked to the edge only long enough to throw a branch into the caldera, and then stepped back from the oven-like air. She watched the wood burn and understood why it was used for offerings. It floated on the molten rock, but stood vertically, and only the area in contact with the lava burst into flame, a beautiful blue fire.

Fire elementals crawled all over the burning branches, ranging in size from the inconsequential – no larger than the one she'd summoned to light the candle in the priest's home – to monumental monsters who barely touched the burning wood with a tendril. Most of those were hidden in the molten rock, but she could feel them below the surface, calling to her.

That, of course, was the problem with fire spirits. They were always hungry for things to consume, and human flesh had long been a favorite.

But that was only if you were less powerful than they were, and Gina was not. She'd grappled with a lord of the hells themselves – she'd lost, of course, but she had survived – and nothing in this shallow pool held any terror for her. She summoned the largest, deepest of the lurking flame-spirits.

It resisted. Commanding it was like trying to pull a well-laden bucket out of a deep well. It was a slow, laborious process.

In the end, inevitably, she felt it budge, sensed the way it moved towards the surface. She saw the sudden flash as it broke through and watched all the blin branches suddenly burst into flame all along their lengths, lighting the hall with near-white radiance. One of the pilgrims, unable to stand the sudden increase of heat, toppled, falling headfirst into the caldera. He didn't even have time to scream before the monster of fire consumed his body.

"That is just the first of the sacrifices you shall have," she told the elemental. "Obey and you shall be rewarded fairly." She neglected to say what would happen if she was disobeyed. Elementals knew the kind of etheric pain that a good Wasyllan could impart. Gina knew she was among the best.

Tavill, on the other hand, seemed to have his reservations. He saw the colossus beginning to emerge from the fiery pit and stepped back almost to the opening of the crystal corridor. But, to his credit, that was as far as he went.

The pilgrims, on the other hand, were having a more difficult time of it. A couple staggered to their feet and turned to run, while the rest seemed to believe that the elemental was a god come to answer their prayers. This second group exploded into a cacophony of chanting and yelling, in a rapture of ecstasy which Gina found incredibly annoying.

"If you want, you can answer their prayers," she told the spirit. She turned to face Tavill. "I think we have the power we need to take this town, don't you?"

She ignored the horrible transformation of prayer into screams as the pilgrims paid for their unwise choice of deity.

The problems began as soon as they emerged from the crystal corridor. This was particularly frustrating because she'd seen how beautiful that place was when the source of light was actually within the corridor as opposed to just being refracted from the caldera. She could have spent days in there, telling her elemental to dance for her so she could just watch the infinite reflections.

But the guardians of Revenn had other ideas.

As soon as the elemental emerged from the crystal corridor, two solid-seeming spirits materialized and jumped at it.

The huge fire creature sidestepped them easily and plunged tendrils of flame into them, causing the new figures to hiss and spit, but Gina knew what they represented.

"Earth elementals," she shouted. "Come on, we need to get out of this cave as fast as possible. We can't fight them underground."

She raced down the corridor, cursing the organic, uneven surface of the stone, and spirits materialized around them, trying to block the path of the flame, to smother it, to contain it.

Tavill began to fall behind. Unlike Gina, he wasn't immune to the touch of the elemental's flame, and he'd already been grazed more than once. He'd have some very pretty welts to show for it later.

"Why don't you control the elementals?" he shouted. "Send them back to their master!"

"I told you already. I'm not good with earth elementals."

This was putting it mildly. Not only had she never been able to bend the servants of the soil to her will, but, more often than not, she found that they'd do anything in their power to oppose her desires. She remembered her lessons as if it had been yesterday: a shower of dirt and the laughter of the other acolytes.

This was exactly the same thing except on a much bigger scale.

The tiny earth spirits that had made up the bulk of the first wave of defenders were gradually being replaced by ever larger and more powerful elementals. Soon enough, it became evident that the sheer size and number of their enemies were herding the animate flame into a side cavern. It would never make it to the exit.

"Tavill, come on. They're concentrating on the spirit. We need to try to get out." She sprinted towards the exit; they were close enough that she could see daylight up ahead.

The earth elementals in the cave weren't the tiny brown balls of ethereal matter she'd learned with as a child. They were big, solid-seeming boulders of energy, and even the small ones were ponderous. They wove their way between the spirits.

Gina avoided one final obstacle and turned towards the light, when she was suddenly struck in the stomach by what felt like a ball of rock. All of her forward motion was arrested, and she only had time to say "Oof," before another impact swept her legs right out from under her. She landed hard.

By the time she'd recovered her breath sufficiently to stand up, the opportunity had passed. A wall of living spirit-rock pushed her towards another corridor, one she could have sworn wasn't there before. When she refused to move, not only did she get shoved, but smaller pellets of spirit bounced painfully off her head. She went where they directed.

Where they ended up being another larger cavern, about the same size and layout of the caldera chamber. But where that one was hot and oppressive, this one had a cool, humid wind blowing through it. Behind the shelf was a pool of strangely illuminated blue water. A waterfall fell from the roof into the lagoon, and it was mist from this cascade that gave the room its pleasant sensation.

The fire elemental cowered to one side of the platform, driven right to the edge of the water by the earth spirits which surrounded it. Tavill, likewise, looked as though he'd been battered pretty badly on the way, and Gina herself didn't feel particularly well either.

But she suspected that her true concern were the people seated along the table with their backs to the pool. There were seven of them, four women and three men, and none of them looked amused. The ancient woman in the center, sitting at a chair that was both larger and more ornate than the rest glared at her with ice-blue eyes.

"Is there any reason we shouldn't kill you right away?" she asked.

There really wasn't. In fact, that they were still alive showed a tendency towards leniency that was both unusual and unwise. But she knew she needed to find one, or they'd eventually come to the same conclusion. "I have done nothing to harm you."

"Nothing? Perhaps you don't feel that killing pilgrims owed the protection of the city under ancient and revered treaties is harmful to the council?"

Ah, so these were the city's revered rulers, the choice of a free people. They looked as sour and humorless as the tyrants of most of the other cities in the mountains. Who'd have elected people like this? If she'd been asked to vote, she would have voted for the bawdy mistress of the local brothel, or maybe a pleasant stable owner.

Clearly, the people of Revenn had a lot to learn.

She hung her head. "I am just a poor girl from the plains. I was enslaved by a Tyrant," this part, at least, was true, although she'd gotten herself enslaved on purpose. "When I managed to escape, I came to Revenn, hoping that in a place where people are all considered equal, I would be given a chance to build a life."

"You aren't dressed like a slave. You're dressed like a noble, and your actions mark you out as a sorceress."

Gina was about to respond, but stopped herself. If the people of this town couldn't tell the difference between a sorcerer and a disciple of Wasyl – no matter how far strayed from the flock – then she might have an opportunity. She wondered, then, why the earth elementals obeyed commands from these people. Probably ancient agreements followed slavishly despite their origins being long forgotten.

"It's true I'm a sorceress, but the clothes are just illusion. As for the fire, I tried to conjure a light, but something more powerful than expected emerged from the pool. I couldn't control it. We were running away when your army came and saved us."

This caused a stir, and for a moment, it looked like she would get away with it. But the steel-eyed woman presiding over the meeting brought her peers to order. "Do you take us for fools?" she asked.

Gina thought it best not to respond to that. Instead, she sent a tendril of summoning to the elemental of fire, her faithful servant. She ordered it to break through the spirits around it and burn the people at the table.

The flame didn't move.

"I think it would be best to end these proceedings quickly. Let it be noted that the accused was allowed to give her side of the story and decided not to cooperate. Let no one dispute this death sentence as unjust."

The words 'death sentence' broke through her attempt to make her servant move. It simply wouldn't – no longer a lord of the fiery depths, it had been cowed to the mentality of a defeated prisoner. It was useless.

"You dare to attempt to sentence me to death?" she cried, raising her arms.

Many of the people at the table flinched, but the woman in charge simply lifted a finger and two large earth elementals placed themselves between her and the table. When nothing happened, the old lady smiled. "Perhaps sorceress is too strong a word, but it is still a good thing we captured you. The world will become a better place without your mischief."

"Perhaps you're right. But not today." As Gina had expected, all eyes were on her.

Unnoticed behind the platform, a wave formed, driven by the spirits of water. It reared up to nearly man-height washed over the fire elemental. That lord of flame writhed in pain and fury, and found the strength to fight its nemesis, more than Gina thought it had left. It writhed and screamed – and created steam.

Lots of steam.

Under Gina's coaxing, air spirits spread the steam around the room, covering the chamber with a foggy soup so thick she couldn't see for more than an arms-length in front of her.

Slowing only long enough to grab Tavill's arm, Gina ran to the chamber entrance.

Without the earth spirits to block their way, they were out of the cave in moments, sprinting past a surprised sentry and through the marketplace.

Only after they'd left the city through the same gate, they'd entered hours before and put some distance between themselves and the city did they halt their brisk walk.

"They're not coming after us," Gina said.

"I know."

"So, we're safe."

Tavill gave her a dark look. "Perhaps. Except that this road only leads to Hell's Gate, where we really,

really won't be welcome. And our only other option is to walk through the mountains."

"So, we'll walk through the mountains. I'm a powerful sorceress, remember?"

"All I know is that you have a true talent for nearly getting me killed."

"I've always managed to bring you out alive, haven't I?"

"You made me jump off a tower last time."

"And here you are. Come on. We'll cross the mountains. How hard can it be?" Gina set off at right angles to the path, not caring if she was heading north, south, east or west.

Tavill followed. "I'd feel much better about this if I had a coat."

"Oh, shut up."

Gustavo Bondoni

In the Dark

Sangr cursed silently. Of all the treasure rooms in the Southlands, it was just his luck to burgle the one that was already being robbed by someone else. Furthermore, that someone else was likely a heavy hitter: while Sangr had had to rig a complicated system of ropes and pulleys, his adversary, it seemed, had decided to burn a hole in the floor and walk in.

That floor was hewn out of solid rock, and the mountain beneath it had no tunnels worth mentioning. He'd checked before deciding on the near suicidal climb through the tower.

He was dealing with a serious magic-user, then. Other than that, though, Sangr couldn't tell anything about his opponent in the dim light.

That won't matter. Everyone is pretty much the same when someone puts a sword against your throat in the night, he thought.

Lowering himself from the rafters, he dropped lightly to the floor and padded up behind the shadowy form. His opponent was not just a magician, but also well-informed: he'd gone straight to the case containing the Idol of Manista.

Sangr couldn't allow that. The Idol was his own target, and he'd spent a good amount of time and coin preparing the job.

Two steps closed the distance between them. The shadow coalesced into a human form and Sangr clamped his hand over the other thief's mouth while simultaneously laying the blade of his rapier against his throat. His opponent tensed, but wisely refrained from making any sudden moves.

"I may need to kill you anyway, but first I'll let you tell me who you are and why I shouldn't just cut your throat and get it over with. I'm about to take my hand off your mouth. I suppose you know what will happen if you try to shout for help or anything silly like that, right?"

The other person nodded, and he pulled his hand away.

"Sangr?" the thief asked. It was a woman's voice.

His blood froze. There had been few women in his life, and every single one of them was bad news. He pressed the blade deeper into her neck on the verge of drawing blood.

"Who are you?" he hissed.

"It's Gina." The voice was hesitant. "You remember me, don't you?"

Gina… she was bad news, but less so than most. At least she had no particular reason to be angry with him. He pulled the rapier away.

"What in all the hells are you doing here?"

"I suspect the same thing you are."

"Well, you can stop now. Get out while I'm still in the mood to let you."

"No."

"I'll kill you."

"No, you won't. I know you. You don't kill people just because. And you don't kill your friends."

"You're not a friend."

"That stings. I always considered you a friend."

Damn. He hated when they did that.

His eyes were growing accustomed to the darkness, and he could make out that what he thought was a helmet on her head was actually her red hair tied into a knot.

She looked around. "Where's Yella?"

"I don't want to talk about it." He glared at her. "And for that matter, where's the big lunk you always hang around with?"

"Perhaps we should talk of something else."

His eyes were growing more accustomed to the light. "Yes, like, for example, where you left your clothes."

She blushed visibly, even in the dim light. "I wasn't expecting company. Fire elementals tend to burn every stitch of clothing away, so I never wear any when I'm on a job." She looked down for a moment. "Is the light getting stronger?"

Sangr looked around the treasure room. Boxes that should have been buried in shadows had come into plain view. The mouth of the tunnel Gina had cut into the floor glowed. He nodded in that direction. "I hope that's just one of your elementals coming our way."

Gina cursed like a sailor raised by harpies. "No. I use water elementals to erode the tunnels. Those don't glow. We're about to have company."

"Well, see you around, then." He returned his sword to its scabbard and sprinted back towards the rope he'd left dangling from the roof.

But just as he reached it and began to swing himself up, Gina grabbed his waist from behind.

He tried to push her away. "The rope can't hold both of us."

"It had better, because I'm not letting go."

Sangr grunted. He pulled and began to climb, arms protesting. It was almost a relief when the rope gave way with an audible crack, and they fell to the floor in a heap. He pushed himself off the girl.

"Hey, watch those hands."

"It's your fault for not wearing any clothes. And also, for grabbing me." He cocked his head. "They're getting closer."

"But how do we get out?"

"Through the front door?"

"There are four guards in front of that doorway. Do you think they'll let us out?"

"They're supposed to keep people from entering. They won't expect us to be leaving. And besides, we don't have any other ideas and whoever is coming after us is getting close. I don't suppose you have any elementals with you that can kill them, do you?"

"No. The big fire elementals are at the bottom of the tunnel, in the caldera. And water spirits move too slowly."

"Then we'd better run."

Sangr charged for the door. About halfway there, he realized Gina wasn't with him. "What are you doing?"

"Taking the Idol. You don't think I came all this way for nothing, do you?"

He watched her. He told himself that he was fascinated by her dedication, and that the fact she had no clothes on had nothing to do with it. She was trying to pick an ornate lock on the box that held the idol.

"Give me that." Sangr slammed the iron mallet he'd brought for the express purpose of opening the lock into the metal, tore off the tangled remains, opened the lid and grabbed the fist-sized, jewel-encrusted figurine. "Can we go now?"

"Ladies first," Gina said. She raced towards the doorway.

Sangr followed, secure in the knowledge that, as long as he had the Idol, she would wait for him.

The double doors were made of iron or something equally heavy, and their attempt to crash through failed miserably. Instead, they had to squeeze through a small opening they managed to create into a brightly lit hallway. Four large guards stared at them, scimitars at the ready.

"What do you think you're doing?" the nearest one asked. "How did you get in there?"

"Get in? We live in there. We're part of the treasure. Well, actually, she is," he said, pointing at the gloriously unclothed redhead beside him. "I'm just there to ensure that none of you oafs lay a finger on her."

The guards exchanged confused looks. "We've never heard of that kind of treasure." The confusion stopped whenever they glanced at Gina. There was nothing confusing about her at all.

"Of course, you haven't. How long would she remain a treasure if people went about telling the guards about her? We'd have you morons lining up for a chance to 'guard' her." Sangr made quotation signs in the air in the appropriate place. "Anyhow, that's irrelevant right now. We came out to warn you that there's someone digging a tunnel in the rock. They're going to try to steal the other treasure."

The guard's face clouded over. "How do I know this isn't a trick so you can escape?"

Sangr nearly stamped with frustration. Why did the dimmest members of the garrison always get selected for guard duty? He suspected they really didn't have time for this. Whoever was coming out of that tunnel likely had much more authority than an extemporaneous story. "There's four of you! Send one inside to look and the rest can guard us."

"Hey, that's a good idea. Storu, you go."

The man to the right lumbered toward the door, opened the massive thing with almost no effort and peered inside. "Captain, they're telling the truth! There's a light coming up a tunnel. I can see a couple of guys climbing through."

"Come on, let's get them!"

The four guards disappeared into the treasure chamber and Sangr and Gina ran down the hallway in the opposite direction, followed by the sound of cursing and the clang of swords.

"Can I ask you for a favor?" Sangr said as he followed Gina at a run.

"Now? I'm kind of busy escaping."

"Yeah, but as soon as you can, could you put some clothes on? It's very distracting."

"If you're looking at something you shouldn't be, I'll burn you to a crisp with the next fire elemental I can find."

Sangr swallowed and kept running.

"How big is this place, anyway?" Gina asked, leaning against a wall and trying to get her breath back.

"It's the biggest fortress in the Southland. Carved out of a solid mountain. Didn't you do your research?"

"I came up from underneath. I wasn't expecting to return by the scenic route."

Sangr tore his eyes away from Gina's heaving chest and looked around the corner. "We seem to have reached the servant's passageways. That's a good thing."

"Why?"

"Because none of the nobles will think to search here, and the guards, if they come, will probably stop to squeeze the serving wenches."

"You know, when we get out of here, I think I'll kill you myself. Do you ever think of women as anything but playthings? I'm a powerful sorceress, and you're just a petty thief. You're just a pawn in my world."

"It would be much easier to see you that way if you were actually wearing something."

"I don't need clothes to be powerful."

"This isn't getting us anywhere."

Sangr stepped into the hall, grabbed a passing messenger, a boy of maybe thirteen years of age with a dark brown cloak, by the arm and said, "Here boy. Look at that." Sangr turned the lad's head towards Gina. The boy's eyes went wide.

"I hope it was worth it." Sangr hit the immobile lad on the tip of his chin as hard as he could, and the boy went down like a sack of potatoes. Sangr quickly removed the lad's cloak.

"Put this on."

"This is ugly. And it smells."

"I don't care. Either you put it on, or I'll leave you to fend for yourself."

She pouted and donned the cloak.

Sangr looked her over critically. "I liked it better before, but you're definitely less distracting now. Come on." He set off in the direction the boy had come from on the general principle that messengers spent most of their time outside, running to and from the mountain fortress. Maybe this one had just gotten back.

The corridor dead-ended at a cluster of doorways that, when opened, led into tiny cells where the servants slept.

"Maybe we can hide in here," Gina said.

Sangr shook his head. "No way. What happens when the people who sleep here come back?"

Her eyes flashed. "Then you can use that sword you're carrying around. I'd love to see if your swordplay lives up to your reputation."

"No. We'll be stuck here. Let me think. All right. There was a door to the formal section of the castle farther back. We'll have to take our chances."

Walking out of the utilitarian, stone-lined servants' area into the lush, carpeted and decorated corridor where the nobles' held sway was akin to suddenly opening one's eyes to find that the world actually had colors in it. Sangr straightened up and walked with a swagger.

"Put your hood up," he said in conversational tones. "The guards are looking for a thief and a naked redhead, not a noble and a cloaked holy man of some kind. They'll ignore us and we'll walk right past."

"There they are!" the voice came from behind, immediately followed by the unmistakable clanking of armored men running.

"Remind me never to bet on a horse you recommend," Gina replied. She was already running down the hall before Sangr had fully processed the situation. They took a sharp turn to the right, then another to the left, but the guards were too close to lose. Finally, they burst through a large, wooden double door. One of its leaves was open, and Sangr slammed it shut behind them.

They were in a large circular room, some kind of wooden chapel filled with a million lit candles. Sangr's practiced eye immediately realized that there were no doors leading out. He barred the big door behind them and set his shoulder to it.

"I'll try to hold this as long as I can. Look for a secret exit, there has to be some way for the priest to enter without being seen. Look near the altar."

"Always so brave…" Gina began before her voice trailed off. "Wait. I can use this. Get away from the door."

"What?" the thud of a body against the thick wood shook Sangr to the bone. "Are you crazy? They'll cut us to bits. Well, they'll cut me to bits and try to take you alive to save for later. I don't particularly want to be cut to bits."

"And no one is saving me for later. Get away from that door."

Gina's voice had taken on the tone of command and those weird echoes that Sangr always associated with sorcerers about to unleash things it was better not to witness.

The hair at the back of his neck stood on end and he dived aside.

But instead of a magical attack from behind, the only thing that happened was that devoid of someone pushing back from his end, the door crashed open, and some very surprised-looking guardsmen tumbled into the room and fell to the ground.

Sangr pulled his rapier free of its scabbard and advanced towards the fallen group. He hated to kill men who were only doing their jobs, but if he was going to do it, it was better to do it while they were on the ground as opposed to when they were attempting to remove your head with scimitars.

"What are you doing? Get out of the way, you idiot!" Gina shouted.

He jumped back just as a sheet of flame shot past his head and struck the pile of men still trying to disentangle themselves from each other.

Expressions of pain such as: "Ouch," and "Hey, stop that, it stings," came from the group. They all stood and started swatting at the air around them.

Sangr realized that what he'd thought was a huge fireball was, in actual fact, a collection of tiny flames sizzling against the men's skins. He also noticed that the chapel, formerly illuminated by hundreds of candles, was now mostly dark: the only light came from the pinpoints swarming around the guards.

The guards became more frantic as they tried to fight off their tiny tormentors. One guy's beard caught fire. A flame somehow got inside another man's helmet. The four men broke and ran.

With a wave of her arm, Gina gathered the tiny lights around her. She turned towards him. "Fire elementals. Tiny ones, but brave and loyal. Just powerful enough to keep a candle alight, but nothing else. Now let's get out of here before someone arrives with a bucket of water."

The elementals hugged her close, almost like a second skin, but Gina didn't seem to be affected. Unlike the guards, she wouldn't be nursing nasty welts and burns for weeks.

Sangr stayed as far from her as possible. It was never a good idea to interact with sorcerers, but it was even less intelligent to do so when you were carrying a priceless jeweled figurine that said sorcerer was particularly keen on getting her hands on. Also, she was surrounded by a wall of fire.

He checked beneath the altar for a hidden trapdoor or staircase, but nothing immediately popped out at him. Likewise, the back wall was made of solid rock. He pulled aside a curtain and saw the tiny door he was looking for hidden behind it. He would have to duck to get in, but at least it led out of there.

"Sangr… you might want to look at this."

He turned back towards the main doorway to see that it was no longer there. Or, rather, it was, but something was keeping the light from the hallway from coming through. Something big. Something ugly. Something moving in their direction with a long club.

"That's a troll, and seeing that it's in here, it's probably one of the guards," Sangr said. "You'd better do something about it."

The thing was half again as tall as they were and, once it made it through the door and straightened to its full height, it looked even bigger. The swarm of lights—despite their numbers—barely managed to cover it completely.

The troll reacted immediately. It swung its club around in a circle, attempting to drive its tiny tormentors away. The club decapitated a particularly ugly statue whose head, propelled at startling speed, whistled past Sangr's face and dented a wood-paneled wall. The monster thrashed and jumped and bellowed, but still the flames came. Finally, it shrugged, accepting its lot, and advanced on Gina.

It took Sangr three steps to interpose himself between the woman and the giant creature. "Run for the door behind the curtain," he shouted and faced the troll.

His opponent was of the grey, leather-skinned persuasion of troll kind. Not as deadly as rock trolls, and only barely smart enough to work as guards, but more than enough to polish off ten swordsmen like Sangr. It swung its club at his head, attempting to improve him the way it had the statue.

Sangr did the one thing that a troll would never expect: he ducked forward and rolled right towards it, came to his feet less than a hand's breadth from the monster and stabbed it in the stomach with all his might.

The blade penetrated an inch into the thick skin.

The Troll looked down at him in confusion, as if wondering where he'd come from. Then, with a casual backhand, Sangr was launched across the room to land beside Gina's feet.

"If you're done playing, I think we'd better get out of here," she said, pulling him through the door.

"Why didn't you leave? I told you to run."

"I couldn't just leave you."

"Wow, thank you."

"Why are you thanking me? You've got the Idol. I didn't come all this way to lose that."

They retreated ten paces down the tunnel. The troll couldn't come after them unless it wanted to crawl. Even a troll wasn't dumb enough to crawl into a hole after an armed man and a sorceress. That was a good way to lose an eye.

They paused to catch their breath. "Any idea where this goes?" Gina asked.

"Probably nowhere good. It goes wherever the priests come from."

"What do they worship here?"

"How should I know? With the way my luck has been going today, they're a death cult, or worship crocodiles, and every priest will be armed with some kind of hook and dressed in protective clothing."

"Well, it's either that or the troll."

Sangr looked back longingly, but the malevolent look the troll was giving them through the small door convinced him that perhaps the priests weren't so bad after all.

"I see you've lost your robe now," he commented as he followed Gina down the hall in the light of tiny flying flames.

"I told you. Fire elementals are hell on clothes."

He peered around the corner again. In the dim light, Sangr was pretty sure the men couldn't see him, but he didn't want to take any chances.

"There are at least twenty of them. And I'm afraid they don't look like a straight-laced order. They look like the kind of priest who wouldn't consider a day to properly begin unless they sacrificed at least two people before breakfast."

"What difference would that make?"

"If they'd been one of those gentle, prissy orders, I would have tossed you in front of them and run. Those orders tend not to see too many beautiful women wandering around their corridors." He paused. "But these guys look like they've seen it all."

"So, what do we do?" Gina asked.

"How should I know?"

"What do you usually do in these situations?"

"If the guys surrounding me are soldiers, I try to bribe them. That usually works. But these guys have more money invested in robes than I have in my purse. If they're unarmed, I try to threaten them with a sword. It's amazing how many people will back away from a single guy with a rapier and a good scowl."

"That might work."

"Maybe. But can't you think of anything better? Priests have a tendency to be willing to die for their beliefs. They're funny that way."

"No. Let's just try it."

Sangr sighed and showed himself, rapier held high. He grimaced at the sight of the point of his blade, an inch shorter where he'd left the tip buried inside the troll.

"Hello, your holiness," he said in what he hoped was a threatening tone. "You need to know something." He waved the rapier in their direction. "I'm a dangerous man, and I'm armed."

The head priest, a man with no hair visible anywhere on his head, raised what would have been an eyebrow. "Yes, we can see that. But there's twenty of us and only one of you."

"Actually, there's two of us," Gina said and stepped out beside Sangr.

On one hand, Sangr admired her spirit and pluck, but on the other he regretted not sending her out first. The way the priests' eyes nearly popped out of their heads made him think that maybe they weren't quite as worldly as they looked.

After a considerable pause to assess the situation while scanning Gina thoroughly for concealed weapons, evidence of special abilities and, quite possibly just for the hell of it, the bald man answered. "I'm pretty sure she's not armed. It's still twenty blades against one."

"Yes, but I'm a desperate criminal who's killed dozens of men. I don't want to harm you. If you just get out of my way, no one will be hurt."

The priest's lizard-like smile widened. "Ah, but it's much more fun when people do get hurt, don't you think?"

Every priest went for the ceremonial daggers that Sangr realized were conveniently hidden inside twenty sets of robes.

Sangr didn't wait for them to finish drawing. With a scream that was equal parts madness and desperation, he charged straight into the middle of the group, flailing wildly with the rapier. More surprised than afraid, most of the priests stepped back, leaving three unfortunate men in the center who were just a step slower than their peers. Sangr bowled into these, and all four sprawled into the passage beyond. He reacted first, disentangled himself and got to his feet, just as something red-haired and naked streaked past and around the corner.

Sangr started to follow, but one of the priests on the ground had his ankle in a death grip and was struggling to draw his dagger with his other hand.

"Sorry," Sangr said, and stabbed him through the wrist.

The priest's scream of pain followed him down the corridor as he ran after Gina's receding back. The echoes of twenty pairs of feet attempting to follow in the cramped confines of the hallway gave him an extra burst of speed.

Gina zigged and zagged as the tunnels turned, almost as if she knew where she was going. The sounds of pursuit began to get less immediate and eventually disappeared altogether. Either the priests weren't in the best of shape or they'd simply lost interest.

The hallway ended and they ran across the flagstones of an open terrace. The light of the full moon illuminated the castle behind them and the distracting movements of Gina's body ahead. The terrace ended at a stone balustrade mere yards away.

Gina stopped and looked down. Sangr stood beside her, catching his breath. "It's a long way down," he observed.

"Any ideas?"

"I was following you."

She snorted. "I don't even know why I bothered to bring you."

"You didn't. If you had, we'd have been in and out with the figurine and no one would have been the wiser. Did you really think no one would notice the entire mountain shaking as you tunneled?"

"Look, you over…" Gina cocked her head. "Do you hear something?"

Sangr looked around. "Probably the guards again. Or the priests. I hope it isn't the troll."

"No, no. This is something different, like a tiny voice. It's coming from your tunic."

Sangr listened. Gina was right. He pulled the box containing the idol from the purse he'd been carrying it in and popped it open. The idol, a black stone piece the size of his fist representing some god with way too many arms clambered out and sat on the edge. "Are you people deaf as well as suicidal?" it asked in a tiny voice.

"What?"

"I've been yelling at you to let me out ever since you made it away from the treasure room."

"We were busy," Sangr snapped. "And dammit. Why didn't anyone tell me that you are a magic figurine? Why is it that I can never steal something pretty without it talking to me or giving me the ability to read minds or something?"

The figurine ignored the question. "The treasure room was magically warded to keep me—and the rest of the collection—inanimate. But now, we can talk freely. I am a god." The tiny black statue looked to see if Sangr was impressed. Seeing that he wasn't he turned to Gina and gave her a long look. "If you're planning on sacrificing the wench to my honor, she will do nicely."

Gina took a step forward. "I see you're a male god and as obnoxious as all the rest. Before I toss you off the mountain just for the hell of it, could you answer one question? Which of your arms do you use to—"

"Gina," Sangr interrupted before the god got offended. Though he'd never actually tried it, he imagined that offending gods led to unhealthy interaction with lightning and locusts. "This isn't helping us to think of a way out of here. Someone will be here eventually, and I shudder to think how easy we've made it for them. As you so aptly observed, we've saved them most of the effort. All they really have to do is throw us down the mountain." He turned to the figurine. "What kind of god are you? Do you do lightning at all?"

"No…"

"Demons? Earthquakes? Anything else that can get us out of here and keep them from popping you right back into the treasure room?"

The figurine pulled itself up to its full height. "I am a good of agriculture. I make plants grow."

"Hmm. Disappointing."

"That's because you're just a barbarian who lives by the sword. Civilized people know how to appreciate me."

"It doesn't seem like they were able to do much to keep you from being plundered and stuck into a collection. Maybe you should have hired more barbarians. Isn't there anything you can do to help us out?"

"I can tell you there's a ledge just wide enough to follow around the wall. It starts on that edge of the terrace."

They ran to the place the figurine was pointing and looked over the railing. "It's true. How could you know that?"

The god shrugged. "There are mosses living on it. They told me."

Gina made to climb over the balustrade, but Sangr put a hand on her arm. "I'm going first. If I have to go behind you, I'm not going to be looking where I'm going."

She kept going. "If you can't keep your eyes where they belong, maybe you deserve to fall." She strode gracefully along, dancer's balance making the thin ledge seem like an avenue.

Following behind, Sangr had to use every ounce of his will to keep his eyes trained on the ground in front of him.

Soon enough, the curve of the palace wall took them out of sight of anyone on the terrace. Sangr relaxed and nearly toppled off the ledge. As he windmilled, halfway off balance, the pre-dawn light revealed a tough-looking vine growing along the side of the castle. He managed to grab hold of it mere moments before falling.

"You're welcome," the god figurine said. It didn't seem to be capable of facial expressions—its face was just an artful arrangement of jewels—but he was sure it was smirking at him. He could hear it in the god's tone.

A few steps further ahead, the ledge widened onto a stone roof and Sangr collapsed onto it.

The god spoke. "If my worshippers are still around, they'll pay you handsomely for my safe return."

"Safe return? We're still stuck in a palace on the top of a mountain, and every single way down is crowded with people who want to kill us."

"Have you already forgotten the vine? I can grow a longer one to get you down the wall."

Sangr looked over at Gina. "Please tell me you have a better idea."

She shrugged in response and Sangr sighed. "All right."

It took the god a long time to encourage the vine to grow, and if there hadn't been a terrace just a few levels below them, Sangr was sure they'd have died of old age before being able to get down at all.

The vine held—barely. As he descended, Sangr reasoned that a god like this one could very easily get a civilization killed. It was about as weak a deity as he'd ever heard of.

When they reached the terrace, the god rubbed his hands and spoke. "Now I'll build another to the next level."

"No way. There are steps there. I want to make it down while I'm still young enough to enjoy the money I'm going to get from selling you. And you," he said to Gina. "Take my cloak. I don't want you attracting attention if we happen to run into anyone who isn't already after us."

"So, you're taking me back to my people?" the god said.

"We'll see."

The stairs reached nearly to ground level. These terraces weren't part of the castle's defenses—apparently those were much farther up the mountain on the steepest slopes—but pleasure gardens and exercise yards for the troops.

They soon reached a tree-lined avenue which Sangr recognized as a road leading to the main highway.

"Those guys in the robes don't look happy to see us," Gina noted.

"Yeah," Sangr replied. "I shouldn't have lent you my cloak. Maybe they were expecting you to be naked."

Three magicians, easily recognizable by their dark cloaks and sinister beards, blocked the path ahead. Ten soldiers added muscle to the display.

Gina chuckled. "If those guys find any elementals around here, I'll wrap them around their throat and make them swallow them." She took a step forward.

The god piped up. "Wait. There's no need for an elemental battle. I can deal with these guys. Watch!"

A tree to their right, a medium sized thing with lots of gnarled branches, began to shake. A root lifted itself out of the ground. Then another. The tree, now a huge soldier for their cause advanced on the magicians.

They stood their ground and one of them calmly pulled a large pendant out of his robe.

"Uh, oh," the god said.

"What do you mean, 'uh, oh'?"

The tree turned around, and Sangr could see it had grown a face near the top of its trunk. Dark, evil eyes glowered out at them. It walked purposely towards them.

Ignoring the spluttered protests, Sangr stuffed the god hurriedly back into his box and pulled out his sword.

"You're going to attack a tree with that?" Gina asked. "I suppose I can't fault you for bravery, even if your brains appear to be made of mush."

Thus encouraged, Sangr lunged at the flailing branches with his rapier, trimming one here, another there while attempting to stay out of reach of the bigger boughs. Those were swinging hard enough to break bones.

Everyone—magicians, soldiers, Gina and a group of horses the bad guys had brought with them—watched the strange dance with bemused expressions before Gina finally shouted, "We didn't come all this way so you could do some gardening. Take care of the soldiers. I'll deal with the rest of them."

A sudden gust of wind nearly knocked him off his feet. The tree fared worse. Billowing out like a ship's sail, it briefly took flight and landed among the soldiers, crushing at least two of them. A third man, too slow to get out of the way in time, survived but wailed piteously in a corner.

Sangr took advantage of the confusion to charge into the remaining men. He stabbed one in the stomach and hamstrung another before they reacted. Normally, he would have felt terrible about hurting men who couldn't defend themselves, but when the odds were a bunch of soldiers against one Sangr, his conscience tended to allow him some leeway.

He immediately found himself in a fight for his life. Even with the hours and hours of drilling he'd put in every day of his adult existence, and even though his blade was much lighter and more maneuverable than the ones the guards used, it was all he could do to parry three blades at once. Mounting a counterattack was out of the question, and he also had to keep track of the two uninjured soldiers who weren't actively participating in the fight.

At any moment, he expected the three magicians to finish Gina off and shift their attention to him, but it never happened. At one point, one of the bearded guys unexpectedly caught fire and ran off, screaming.

There seemed to be a lot of wind and flying sparks happening in the magical battle. She was certainly giving them a good fight.

Sangr was happy for Gina's successes, but his arms were beginning to tire. He had to think of something before the three men, unskilled though they might be, finally overran him. His main focus was to keep them occupied and stop them from getting behind him. Three guys spread out, he could deal with, but if they were smart about it…

He decided to use a trick he'd learned from Yella. He let himself fall backwards as if one of his opponents' parries had driven him back and he stumbled onto his rear. But instead of just staying there, he kept going, rolled backwards and somersaulted back to his feet.

Inevitably, upon seeing him fall, one of the three men facing him decided to go in for the kill and stepped out in front of his friends. He found Sangr on his feet, ready for him. The man still lunged, overextended and received a deep gash in the belly for his trouble.

There were still two men left, but the wind seemed to have gone out of their sails and Sangr was able to back them off. He was still concerned about the two men who hadn't joined in, though. What was holding them back?

One of his opponents slipped and Sangr slashed him across the thigh, deep enough that the guy took one look and stumbled out of reach, trying to close the bubbling wound.

Sangr looked his remaining opponent in the eye and smiled. "Looks like it's just you and me, now."

The man ran off towards the stairs.

Now, to help Gina, Sangr thought. He turned towards the bearded men, hoping to catch them by surprise.

He stopped short. The bearded men weren't there. Or rather they were, but they were scattered around the landscape in small pieces. Gina, an expression of concentration on her face, seemed to be straining, moving her arms around in an invisible dance. As he watched, she relaxed and looked like she was about to collapse. Sangr ran forward and caught her.

"Are you all right?"

"Yes, I'm fine. It's just that air elementals don't like to be banished once you call them up. They fight you to the bitter end, you have to assert yourself, especially on the powerful ones. And the ones driving those mountain winds are definitely powerful."

"What happens if you can't control them?"

Gina said nothing, but gave the chunks of raw flesh that had been two magicians a significant look.

"Oh."

"You can leave the small ones like the ones holding your friends over there," she gestured towards the two soldiers that hadn't been part of the fight, "alone for a while, and they won't make trouble. But the big ones…" she shuddered.

"You saved my life," he said. "I would have been killed if you hadn't stopped those two."

"It was self-preservation. I couldn't fight the magicians and the soldiers. I needed to try to even the odds somehow. If they'd gotten past you, I'd have been as good as dead."

"It was a close thing."

Gina sighed. "I know. But we don't have time to talk about it now. We need to leave."

"Can you ride?"

Gina plundered breeches and a pair of boots from one of the dead men and they mounted two of the horses.

"Give me a second," Sangr said. He dismounted and located the pendant the magicians had used to defeat the god. It was under one man's severed leg. He pulled the box containing the indignantly shouting god and gave it a shake. Then he opened it.

"Shut up or I'll shake you again. Good. Tell me something: can you dance?"

"What? Why?"

"Because I can get more money for a dancing figurine than for an annoying talking figurine."

The god was speechless. "How can… you… blasph…" It gathered itself together. "You will take me to my followers and accept any reward they deem fit."

Sangr glared right back. "I will take you to the first jeweler I encounter and sell you as a novelty item for the value of your stones. I could get a better price for you if you danced."

"You will suffer indescribable torments."

Sangr brandished the pendant. "I've seen your power and I'm not scared of it. You almost got us killed. If you don't want a jeweler to pluck out your shiny little rocks, I'd recommend that you start learning a dance routine. It's your choice."

He slammed the god back in the box and mounted again.

"You do realize that half the money we get for him is mine, don't you?"

"Half? If you hadn't blundered in, I would have gotten away without anyone knowing I was there. I'll give you a quarter."

She shrugged. "I can always call the wind back and you can see if your pendant works against an angry elemental."

"All right, maybe I can stretch to a third. But you're robbing me…"

The sound of their bickering echoed back from the surrounding mountains. Sangr settled in for a long ride as he watched the sun come up.

Gustavo Bondoni

In Her Honor

"This should be enough to keep you going for some time," Sangr said, handing Gina a heavy leather purse filled with gold. It was an understatement. With what was in that pouch, she would live comfortably her whole life and leave a decent inheritance to any children unfortunate enough to be born to her.

"That's much more than half."

"I only took what I need. You can have the rest."

She cocked her head at him suspiciously. "What are you up to?"

"Nothing. I want to do something good for somebody before my time comes. Thieves and adventurers don't live particularly long lives, so this might be my last chance."

"You've already done more than enough for me."

Why couldn't she just take the money and leave? They'd only connected on the heist by the sheerest of coincidence, only succeeded by the skin of their teeth. They'd never been lovers. There was nothing tying them together but a few weeks on the road spread over the past few years, and the only time they'd actually traveled alone together was during the past two days.

The silence stretched uncomfortably. What he needed to do next would be unpleasant enough even alone. He didn't know if he could live with himself afterward, but that was something he would think about once it was done. He certainly didn't want witnesses.

"I'm going after a woman," he said flatly.

Gina pouted at him, clearly aware that he was trying to get rid of her and clearly determined to play along. "Is she prettier than I am?"

He studied her. She had hair the color of fire, delicate features and a figure that would have stopped traffic if word hadn't gotten around that she was an elemental mage of considerable—possibly unmatched, no one really knew—power, with a mean streak that was easy to ignite.

"Yes. She is, quite possibly, the most beautiful woman on the plains."

"Oh, yeah?" Gina's eyes sparkled with the game. "What's her name?"

"Maluz." He didn't hesitate because it was true. That *was* her name.

"A likely story. And what are you planning to do once you find her?"

"I'm going to kill her," Sangr said. "I'm going to kill her as slowly as I can."

"I don't believe you. You're not built for that. You're the kind to save damsels in distress, not murder them," Gina replied. But her smile had disappeared. Suddenly, the game had turned deadly serious. "How are you going to live with yourself once the blood dries?"

"I don't know. I'll see how I feel about it then."

She stared at his face for a long time, as though trying to read the inner motivations. He kept all emotion off his face. Finally, she sighed.

"I'm coming with you."

"No, you're not."

"How are you going to stop me?"

"I have the pendant. I'm still immune to magic."

She laughed, a genuine burst of mirth. "That bauble is to protect people against love potions and third-rate spells. Do you really think it can stop me from doing whatever I want with you?"

She was probably right. But he couldn't back down. "Do you want to find out?"

"No. But unless you're willing to kill me as well, I'm coming. You saved me when I was alone and afraid."

"I'm not afraid. And besides, that was a long time ago. I was a different person, then"

Realization hit her. "This is about Yella, isn't it?"

"Yes. This is about Yella. Will you let me do what I have to do?"

"Yes, I will. But I'm coming with you."

He sighed, but said nothing when her horse followed his down the trail.

He wondered what Gina would have said if she'd known about Abren. While the magician might have deserved everything he got and more, it wasn't for what the man had done to Yella. He'd captured her and locked her in some alternate world but, in all honesty, he hadn't harmed her.

At least that was what he said, and Sangr believed him. The problem was that for all practical purposes, she might as well have been dead. She was certainly inaccessible to him.

Sangr had killed Abren in a blind rage. He'd brushed off the magician's offers of help, of trying to find a solution. The look in the man's eyes had told him all he really needed to know. Sangr had been crushed, but had been willing to live and let live, to take his despair with him and leave the magician to continue his wretched mage's existence.

But the man, in a misguided attempt to make it better had said, as a parting comment: "She really will be all right, you know."

Sangr hadn't even thought about it. Thousands, tens of thousands of hours drilling with his rapier had taken over and the sword jumped into his hand, apparently of its own accord.

The wizard was even faster, though. A wave of something washed over him and the pendant hanging from his neck turned hot enough to leave a circular scar.

Whatever the man had hit him with hadn't worked. Abren's eyes opened like two saucers as Sangr's rapier plunged into his chest, up under his sternum and into the magician's heart.

Maybe Gina would have changed her view about Sangr being one of the good guys if she'd seen that. Her belief in his heart of gold would certainly have taken a hit.

And she might also be a little less cavalier about dismissing the pendant if she'd seen how handily it had dealt with Abren's spell.

Of course, Gina was, by all reports a much more powerful mage than Abren on his best day. It was just that control wasn't her strong suit.

Well, as long as she didn't kill them off before they caught Maluz, he could live with it. Besides, as she'd said, there was nothing he could do to keep her from coming along.

"Why are we riding this way?" Gina asked.

"Because Maluz isn't going to stay on the plains. There's nowhere on the Grass Sea she won't be recognized, nowhere she can stay for more than a few days without being trussed up and locked in some potentate's treasure room—or in his Harem. She'll go north."

"But why? There's nothing north but the Ice."

"There's a big city on the Ice. Everyone who's ever lived up north has heard rumors or met travelers who've been there. It's a place of wonders."

Gina rode in silence for some moments, her mount kicking up the dry dust of the plains. "There are plenty of little towns in the jungles behind us where she could live forever, and you'd never find her. Or she could take refuge in one of the mountain fortresses."

She was right. The steamy forests they'd traveled from held dozens of settlements where people had lived since the dawn of time. Only the Ice itself held older villages. He wasn't worried about them, though. "The problem is that you don't know Maluz. She won't lock herself up in some backwater. She wants to be somewhere large, somewhere significant. She wants to be the center of attention."

"So, being born as some kind of magical talisman gave her an overblown sense of her own importance?"

"Maybe. Or maybe being bought and sold like a sack of flour has given her a desire to control things herself for a change."

"You still haven't told me why she'd avoid the mountains. Hell's Gate is supposed to have gotten interesting after I left."

"You might be right about that. But would you risk it in her position? She might be immune to all forms of magic, but I can assure you she doesn't know if demons are actually magic."

"They're elementals. They're magic, Sangr."

"Would you bet your life on it?"

"I do that every single time I work with them."

The landscape of the plains was mainly dusty grassland. They passed the occasional traveler and the odd walled town. It was always easy to tell when a town was about to appear around the next bend or over the next hill because the landscape would suddenly sprout cultivated fields and armed men patrolling the crops to ensure that no one would take them or try to sabotage them; the Tyrants of the plains were engaged in a continual game of subjugation and fealty wherein the loss of a single field might weaken a town sufficiently to create a shift in the pattern.

"Do you think you'll be able to use your magic on Maluz?" Sangr asked. "Is that why you're coming with me?"

She almost looked offended, but Gina wasn't really the kind of person who could pull that off with any real conviction. Anger, fury and even a kind of endearing puppy loyalty, she could do... looking offended, no. "I already told you why I'm coming along. I've got no quarrel with this Maluz of yours." She smirked. "But I have to admit that I'm curious to see this jewel of the plains that has you so hot and bothered."

As he looked north, Sangr thought of Lunk for the first time in years. He wondered what his old friend was up to, and if he'd ever mustered the courage to ask Rita to marry him. He wondered what Lunk would say if Sangr told him of the things he'd seen and done.

He chuckled and shook his head. Knowing Lunk, the infuriating man would simply nod and accept it. He'd probably say something like, "What a wonderful world we live in. It never ceases to amaze me." Lunk wouldn't doubt a single thing Sangr told him; the man would trust Sangr to the ends of the world. He had ample reason to, after all.

And if Sangr told him he was chasing across the continent to kill a beautiful woman, Lunk wouldn't even try to talk him out of it. He'd just nod sadly and offer a drink of seaweed ale warmed at the base of his forge.

He nearly turned east. Getting to the tiny village hugging the coast would mean adding weeks to their journey, but what possible harm could there be in that? They were already months behind their quarry anyway.

There was also the question of how he'd be welcomed. Would people still remember the crime he'd supposedly committed? Would anyone still care? Would Breen still be the same prickly bastard? Or maybe it was all moot, maybe Tianna had figured out who the real murderer was and driven Lunk out of the village, doomed him to die on the Ice.

The sense of homesickness, of wanting to return to a place where he unquestionably belonged, was almost overpowering. But then he remembered the cold nights, being forced to remain inside by the killing winds and reasoned that, just maybe, he could stand to live on the plains a few more years. He could always return when he was older: the village wasn't going anywhere.

The sound of horses tore him from his reverie. A cloud of dust announced at least a half-dozen men riding towards them.

"Can you make them out?" Gina asked. She knew his eyesight was better than hers.

"I'm not really…" Then he caught the colors. "Oh, no."

"Problems?"

"The only way we could be in deeper trouble is if we ran into that demon lord you liberated in the mountains. Those are Favored." He shook his head. "I thought they'd given up on me ages ago."

"Anything I should know about them before they reach us?"

"They can read minds."

"Really?"

"Well, maybe not mine. This pendant should be enough to keep me safe."

"So, they'll just be reading mine, then?"

"Yes."

"Too bad for them." She smirked. It was becoming a habit. "Not that I'm criticizing them or anything, but why are they out to get you?"

"There was a misunderstanding about a large, pink diamond."

"Misunderstanding?"

"They thought it was theirs, and I thought that a diamond lying around where anyone could take it belonged to the first person to come along."

"Lying around? Where?" She sounded suspicious.

"It was in a temple."

"Unguarded?"

"Can we talk about this later? They're nearly here."

"As I said before, too bad for them."

Sangr had no time to ask her what she was planning and no illusions that the Favored were there to talk. He'd faced mind readers back before he'd gotten the pendant, and they were annoying as hell. They always knew exactly what you were going to do next, so even the most mediocre swordsmen in their ranks were nearly impossible to beat.

The good thing about that was that the Favored tended to neglect to train with their blades. The other good thing was that they didn't know his pendant would protect him—and they'd also be cagey because they probably thought he'd still be able to read their minds. It wasn't public knowledge that Abren had removed that particular ability.

On the other hand, there were six of them. He pulled his rapier out of its scabbard as he watched the men rein in.

"Sangr," the leader spat.

"You have me at a disadvantage. I don't think we've been introduced."

"My name is immaterial. I'm a servant of Qalnoth. That is enough."

"Pleased to meet you, Sir Immaterial," Sangr said, raising his hand. "You're not a servant of anything. You're just a foot soldier working for a bunch of petty tyrants in a tiny town who happened to find a magic diamond." He cocked his head at them. "Have you managed to get that back, by the way?"

"That is none of your concern."

"I'd have to disagree with you there. If you have the diamond back, then why would you bother me at all?"

The man ignored the question and glanced towards three men who'd broken off the main group and parked their mounts in front of Gina.

"She's definitely with him," one of them said, "but I don't think she'll be any trouble. I think she's a bit soft in the head."

"What?"

"She's just thinking of how nice it would be if we had a nice breeze. That's it. Over and over again."

Sangr smiled. "So, what are we here for?"

The man facing him turned formal. "Sangr the Thief, you have been tried and condemned to death. We will take you back to Tengut where you will be hanged."

"So, I've finally had a trial?"

"Yes."

"Then all the goons you sent to murder me before were acting outside the law?"

The man sighed. "I assume you're not going to come peacefully?"

"Why would I come with someone who's already told me they intend to kill me? Surely not for the pleasure of your company."

"We're not that bad when you get to know us." He smiled, but he pulled a cavalryman's curved sword from a scabbard on his saddle. It was clear that this was the moment he'd been waiting for. He called back to his men. "Be careful with the little bugger. He's got some way to block the Favor."

The Favor was what they called the ability—given by their magic diamond—to read minds.

Sangr grinned at him and turned to Gina. "Leave the ugly one to me. You can kill the rest if you like."

The Song of Sangr

All six men turned their mounts towards Sangr. They knew better than to listen to anything the enemy might say to confuse them before the battle. They might be indifferent swordsmen, but that didn't mean that they were completely stupid. Well, not all of them, at least. They weren't going to waste their time on a girl who couldn't even think straight.

All six of the horses reached him, but only one of them, the one that belonged to the man who'd spoken to him, still had a rider when it did. The rest ran away, spooked, into an adjacent field.

But Sangr's eyes were on his opponent. This one wasn't an indifferent swordsman; he was actually a reasonable bladesmith that Sangr wouldn't have minded having at his side in a pitched battle. It was evident that he'd even trained to fight from horseback, something Sangr always admired.

But mere competence was not going to help him. Sangr had spent the years since he'd come off the Ice alternatively running from angry magic users and practicing with his sword until his hands blistered— he'd learned early in the process that overdoing it simply meant that he wouldn't be able to practice the following day. A single parry and a quick thrust had the leader of the Favored bleeding from the stomach after their first clash. They both knew the fight was over. The wound itself might not be fatal, but it would weaken him enough that either Sangr would cut him down or he would simply fall off his horse.

Instead of running, trying to save his life, the man spurred his horse forward and charged. The horse, clearly better-trained than Sangr's stable-bought animal, bumped and bit like a thing possessed and the man's blade seemed to work in perfect harmony with it.

Caught, by surprise, Sangr had to fight as hard as he could just to stay alive. He parried desperately, concerned that the heavier blade might knock his own sword aside or, fatally, break the slender metal.

Eventually, though, the inevitable happened. Surprise gone, his opponent began to get careless, and his wound took its toll. He started to falter.

Sangr considered letting him bleed away and drop but felt that would be to unnecessarily prolong the soldier's suffering. After all, this was just a man doing a job. Sangr felt no personal animosity towards him, not even for being an arrogant prick. All of the Favored were arrogant pricks, but at least this guy wasn't a sanctimonious one.

Sangr's rapier flicked once, and a line appeared across his opponent's neck. It was a risky move, not one that he would have attempted had the swordsman not been wounded, but it had the advantage of being immediately fatal. The Favored fell from his horse.

"Thank you," Sangr told Gina.

"For what?"

"For letting me have him."

"Why would you even risk that? I could have dealt with all of them. It's actually harder to pick and choose."

"I need to stay sharp. Maluz has no magic of her own, but she was trained as an assassin. I'm not entirely sure what that entailed, but I assume she has knowledge of numerous sharp metal objects."

"I could have let you have all six, if that was your intention. Would have made it more interesting, don't you think?" Gina said, evidently unimpressed.

"Yeah, except that I need to be alive in order to go through with the rest of the mission."

That elicited a shrug. "We can always get a necromancer. Qalnoth himself knows we've got enough money for it now. Should I have you reanimated if one of these escapades gets you killed?"

Sangr didn't reply and tuned out the rest of what Gina said. He was looking at the bodies on the ground and thinking. His mind wanted to analyze what kind of a breeze could tear five men to pieces that way without harming their horses, but he knew enough about Gina's magic to understand that that was how it functioned: precise, surprising control one moment, unadulterated mayhem the next. He also felt that there was something bigger, something relevant, that he was missing. It was right there, on the tip of consciousness. He turned away in disgust, unable to nail it down amid Gina's incessant chattering.

"Wait," he said, "holding up a finger. What was that last thing you said?"

"Nothing… I just asked how they'd found us."

"That's it…" he whispered. "That *bitch*. These guys might be mad at me, but they haven't been on my case in more than two years. The only explanation is that Maluz knows we're after her, and she knew we'd be around here at around this time. And she went and *told* them so."

Gina looked puzzled. "And how would she have known?"

"I… I'm not sure." He set his jaw. "I guess I'll just have to ask her when we catch up to her." He loosened his death grip on the reins and let his horse amble along the path. He'd need to rub it down well when they stopped for lunch, but now that he knew they were on the right track, he didn't want to waste time tending to his animal.

"Are you just going to leave the rest of them behind?"

"I don't think we'll need them. The roads are perfectly good from here almost to the Ice, and after that, horses will be pretty much useless to us."

"But..." she looked longingly at them. "They're probably worth ten silvers each here on the plains. They like good horses in the walled towns."

He laughed. "Once a thief, always a thief, I guess." He gestured towards the purse tied to her waist. Gina hadn't dared to put it into a saddlebag, she wanted it on her person. "Have you already forgotten that you'll never need money again?"

"Waste not, want not," she replied, matching him ancient saying for ancient saying. "And haven't you ever been hungry before?"

"I've been hungrier than you can imagine. Colder, too. But even if I'd had ten times what you have in that pouch, it wouldn't have made any difference. The Ice doesn't care about the contents of your purse." Maybe this was the opportunity he'd been needing. "But you don't have to subject yourself to that. Why don't you stay here? Round up the horses and sell them somewhere. Just don't sell them in Tengut. Even if they don't recognize their own horses, they really can read your mind there."

"Didn't work for them too well last time."

Sangr nodded his respect. "You caught them by surprise. But you can't spend all your time in the city thinking about the wind."

"You'd be surprised by what I can and can't do," she told him with what was unmistakably a leer. "But stop changing the subject. You won't get rid of me that easily."

Sangr sighed and spurred his horse into a slightly faster walk.

As they rode, Sangr thought of Yella.

They'd never been husband and wife, never even been a formal couple, but in some unspoken way, they'd decided they were together, with all the good and bad that that implied. When he met her, he'd thought she looked beautiful in a slightly dangerous way, but that was the extent of his attraction.

Only when he acquired the curse of telepathy—*when she tricked him into acquiring the curse of telepathy*, he corrected himself—did the wedge that drove them apart from the rest of humanity begin to drive them together.

Things had happened, and they'd gotten through them as a team, and then as more than a team. There had come a time when each, aware that the other was their only hope of being understood by another human being—unless they wanted to throw themselves into the arms of the Favored—had simply accepted it as destiny. Yella had taken longer to accept her fate than Sangr had, and he'd been party to her thoughts as she struggled.

They'd fallen into a comfortable rhythm, and he'd thought it was just that: two logical allies who knew each other so intimately that intimacy became inevitable, walking side-by-side along their allotted path. When the path diverged for them, so would their destinies. They became lovers by necessity more than choice.

He only realized that he'd begun to consider her a part of him, as fundamental to his life as breathing or eating, on the day he realized that she was missing. Abren had been responsible for that, on Maluz's orders. Worse, he'd been waiting for a telepath to come after him and had been waiting with a cure for the curse of the Favor… and a bargain that turned out not to be much of a bargain.

Sangr wasn't sorry to have killed him. The man had deserved to die.

He was only sorry that it hadn't filled the gap left by his failure to recover Yella.

"You did say that she's still the queen of this Summerland place, right?"

Sangr shrugged. "I saw her crowned, and she says she's still the ruler. I see no reason for her to lie to me." *Other than the fact that she's a murderous crazy woman*, he didn't add.

"Then why wouldn't she just go there, raise her army and break us into small pieces? Assuming they don't know about my magic, of course."

"I gather she left her kingdom under a bit of a cloud… and the whole point of her escape was to stop being a slave to those people."

"I thought you said she was the queen."

"Out on the ice, a leader is a slave to his people."

Gina grunted, unconvinced, and Sangr smiled to himself. He knew that the sorceress had always wanted to rule. It was even rumored that the fiasco in Hell's Gate, the overrunning of the city by powerful fire elementals had been her doing, a failed attempt to put herself on the throne in the Tyrant Menthragincar's place.

Initially, Sangr had doubted the whispers. His impression of Gina was one of a slightly scatterbrained beauty with a chip on her shoulder the size of a mountain, but not truly capable of mayhem on a grand scale.

But as he got to know her better, especially since they'd met again in highly informal circumstances in the treasure chamber of a mountain ruler, he realized that she was powerful and irresponsible enough for the rumors to be possible… and probably bad enough at planning more than a single step ahead to make them true.

What he had told her about Maluz, though, was equally true. Shortly after Yella had disappeared, Maluz had, seemingly coincidentally, run into him in a tavern in the southern jungle where he was drinking himself into a stupor.

She'd approached, dressed mostly in perfume, gauze and knives, and pretended to be surprised. She looked like every one of his dreams come to life, wearing an inviting smile which left little room for interpretation.

Her eyes, however, had betrayed her. Even through the haze of drink a single look had sufficed for him to know that Maluz was behind… everything. Suddenly, he wasn't drunk but alert, wasn't looking to forget but to understand.

The change in his demeanor must have been as obvious to her as her own complicity had been to him. Maluz turned to leave, but he'd caught her arm.

"Maluz," he said, forcing a smile. "You must tell me what brings you here."

He'd bought her a drink, and then another and a third. He knew that she would be armed, that she could defend herself, and gave her no chance to do so. Maluz, for her own part knew just how dangerous Sangr could be when angered. She drank.

Eventually, she drank enough. "Forget that skinny wretch," Maluz had said. "Come with me. I'll make you happy."

"What did you do to her?"

"She's all right. I told Abren not to hurt her. I don't want you thinking of her death when you look at me. I want you to know she's alive… but out of your reach forever."

That was all he needed. Now that he had a name, there was no further need to have any contact with this creature. And no further need to drink. He could do something.

But before he left, he looked Maluz in the eye, smiled and told her: "If I ever see you again, I will kill you. I don't have time right now. But I'll do it if I find you again."

They both knew that he had plenty of time… The truth was that he hadn't decided to kill her. Not yet. That would come later, if it came. He never killed people if he could avoid it, especially not young, beautiful girls.

Things changed.

"I wasn't expecting anything like this, that's for certain." After two weeks of doing nothing but growl under her breath about life on the Ice, it was strange to hear wonder in her voice.

Sangr knew exactly how she felt. He'd been hearing stories about the marvelous city of spires and curlicues, carved out of the very ice that surrounded it, since he was old enough to understand. He'd known there was something out there but expected some kind of meagre seaport where people huddled because it was a hub of shipping or fishing or furs. He wasn't expecting the stories to be true.

He most certainly wasn't expecting the wildest of them to be short of the mark.

The city was set within a long valley sporting a narrow natural harbor crammed with wooden ships. Apparently, the warm current that allowed Sangr's village to survive by fishing, reached the sea here, too, as the harbor was ice-free. Behind it stood the smoking caldera of a snow-covered fire mountain.

Other peaks, often too steep-sided even for ice buildup, separated the sky from the white ground around the fumarole.

There, perfectly framed stood the ice spires.

They weren't how Sangr had imagined them as a child. His imagination would never have produced anything so grand. His early experience consisted of small huts made of precious driftwood and of big grey cliffs. The ice city of his mind's eye had been stumpy and white and perhaps two stories tall, if that. Back then, it had seemed full of wonderful constructs.

He simply hadn't been prepared then to imagine the reality. He'd had nothing to build from.

Looking upward, he still didn't. The slender streaks that knifed into the sky seemed to be made from the clearest glass. But they weren't. They were made of frozen water. How or why, they'd been formed was impossible to guess, but they stood there now, defying him to question their existence.

Each was illuminated, shining a different color in the half-light of the northern summer night. Pink. Blue. Green and red. Only one of the spires, among the hundreds before him, was a pure crystal untouched by any of the colors of the rainbow. It was buried towards the middle of the city.

Crowds could be seen milling in the space between the spires, but more impressively, dots of people within each of them could be made out, too. The spires had been hollowed out, made to act as the city's buildings. People reclined on furniture, ate dinner, slept and made love, all in full view of the streets below.

"It makes Hell's Gate look like a collection of huts. How are we going to find anyone in there?"

"I was thinking the same thing." He winced at the surprise in his voice. The world wasn't supposed to wake up the sleeping wonder in his soul. After all, he was here to lose any claim he might have of owning a soul. "It's bigger than I planned for."

"You were expecting to walk in and find her?"

"Maybe not that easily… but essentially, yes. She isn't the kind of person who likes to hide. In most towns, it would be a matter of hours before we ran into someone who could tell us where she was."

"And here?"

He shrugged. "I have no idea. Your guess is as good as mine. All I know is that we won't find out from here. Also, there's no one out here to sell me a drink."

"Now you have my attention."

The distance separating them from the city was more than Sangr expected. His mind had refused to accept just how tall the spires were and to take that into consideration. In fact, as they approached, he began to feel that, at any time, one of the slender towers—or all of them simultaneously—would topple onto them.

"Makes you dizzy to look up at them, doesn't it?" Gina said.

"Yes," Sangr replied, keeping his eyes resolutely fixed on the ground in front of him.

But it was impossible not to look at the people. Their robes were of all colors. He saw traders from the jungle south wrapped in layer upon layer of the colored silks that they normally wore just to cover their modesty. He saw men of the plains. He saw fur traders from the eastern coasts.

And there were men of the west. Men who'd crossed the vast expanse of trackless seas from continents long lost. They spoke amongst themselves in languages he'd never heard, an uncomfortable feeling for a man who was accustomed to hearing the same tongue—with the occasional regional variation—over the course of the wanderings of a lifetime.

They drifted with the crowd, not following a particular path. In the distance the colors shifted. Towers turned from yellow to red to blue without seeming to follow any pre-established pattern or order. Except for one. There always seemed to be a single tower that held no color at all, but Sangr had no way of knowing if it was always the same one or whether colorlessness, like the colors themselves, rotated along the spires.

The tavern they were looking for turned out to be inside one of the spires.

"How come the heat from the people doesn't melt the ice?" Gina asked.

He shrugged. "Maybe it's magic ice. Maybe the freezing cold outside keeps everything solid. Maybe I don't care because that man is selling drinks."

Hot drinks, as it turned out. The concoction kicked like an angry mule but was served warm and sweetened with some kind of berry juice. Sangr thought that after a dozen or so, he might actually begin to feel like he wouldn't freeze solid at any moment, which was a relief after a few days out on the Ice.

He smiled but when he found himself wishing Yella was there to share this marvel with him, he ordered two more drinks. Warmth might come eventually, but he wanted forgetfulness now.

The tavern had rooms in the upper levels and a man led them up an ice staircase so long it made Sangr dizzy.

All he remembered was that the bed was made of ice, with some kind of huge animal-skin rug laid over it. Then oblivion, welcome as only sleep and death were to a man with nothing left to live for, overcame him.

The next day, he woke naked, covered by the skin. The warmth of Gina's equally bare flesh was a welcome presence beside him, and he only pushed her away reluctantly. He knew that nothing had happened in the night. He could always remember sleeping with a woman, no matter how drunk he was.

Gina had been soft and tempting, and the bed was a colder and less pleasant place when she wasn't touching him.

But he wouldn't, he couldn't, defile Yella's memory that way. Not while the woman who'd taken her was still alive.

Gina raised an eyebrow but didn't protest. She might be a bit rough around the edges, but she wasn't stupid. She understood him better than he normally gave her credit for. She got out of bed and dressed quickly. "I suppose you want to get started as soon as possible."

"Whatever gave you that idea?"

She laughed, not dignifying the question with an answer.

The throngs intimidated him. How to ask questions that would lead him to Maluz? *Who* to ask? He shrugged and did what he'd do in any tiny hamlet. He asked the big ugly man behind the bar, trying to ignore that the bar was a huge wall of completely clear ice and that the crowd seemed to consist of the entire population of the plains.

"I'm looking for a woman," he told the man.

"It looks to me like you have one."

"A different one."

"That might get you into trouble."

Sangr sighed to himself. At least some things never changed. There were two types of people behind bars in his experience: the ones who would grunt and let you talk until your money or your capacity to hold your drink was exhausted, and the kind who considered themselves the local wit. It was not too hard to guess which kind this guy was.

"Her name is Maluz. She probably has a lot of money."

"Then you aren't likely to find her in this part of town."

Sangr looked around. Even from within the building he could see the city. The walls were so clear that it was almost as if they weren't really there. But even with those advantages, he couldn't see what the man was talking about. The people around him looked perfectly tame, no real sign of the rough elements one would associate with a bad part of a city. Likewise, the distance revealed nothing that could be interpreted as being grander or more important than the structure they were in; the other spires were beautiful, but not noticeably more so.

He stood for a few moments drinking in the soft pinks and yellows and pale blues. As always, he spotted a spire with no color and reminded himself to go have a look at it if they had time. It seemed to call to him, plain and transparent as it was among its colorful peers.

"Which way is a better part of town?" Sangr said.

The man shrugged. "North. In general, the closer you get to the fire mountain, the better the people. But be careful up there. They don't like visitors."

They thanked the man and descended back to street level. The roads were of snow, packed to the consistency of black ice and scarred by the passage of thousands of cramponed feet.

The crowds thinned as they moved north and, despite how it had looked from afar, Sangr did notice a subtle change in the way people looked. Of course, they were all still bundled in voluminous furs—

anything else would have been utterly impractical in the freezing weather—but something about them seemed off.

When he finally realized what it was, he almost laughed out loud.

It was the way they walked.

Most people in every town he'd ever been to shifted imperceptibly to one side when you approached, allowing just enough room for you to pass, as long as you performed the same shift.

The people in the northern reaches of the Ice City—he still didn't know what the inhabitants called it—didn't. They assumed you would get out of their way. It was a natural enough thing to want, of course: a slight correction in the direction of travel on the ice could easily be enough to send you sprawling, so the upper classes had evolved into straight-line walkers, expecting everyone else to acknowledge their superiority by scrambling out of the way.

He wondered what would happen if two of them met head on, but he supposed they had some way of determining precedence. Probably the same method by which they infallibly detected invaders in their realm.

Sangr and Gina's furs were the best that money could buy, yet every one of the inhabitants of the richer quarter that they crossed managed to give them a look that spoke to just how far out of their natural element they had wandered. It was disconcerting; out on the plains, everyone gave you the benefit of the doubt until they could ascertain where you stood on the social scale. Here, they seemed to know instinctively—or just to assume that all visitors were the social equivalent of pond scum.

Gina had been completely—uncharacteristically—silent. That was fine by Sangr; he was lost in his own brooding thoughts anyway. When she spoke, he jumped.

"Can we get a drink?"

Sangr shrugged. "Sure. Any particular reason why?"

"Yeah. We're not going to find her by walking around in circles the way we've been doing. And if anyone else bumps into me, I'll call up a fire elemental from that volcano over there and tear them all to pieces."

"That would get their attention, I guess, but it might also give us away. All right, let's find a tavern."

The silence that thundered at them as they crossed the icy floor of the common room was different from the typical silencing of a tavern when a stranger walked in. For one thing, it lasted longer.

Instead of returning to their conversations every head followed their progress to the transparent bar.

In Sangr's experience, the men behind the bar were usually neutrals, serving the drink with only minor cautionary words when justified, but otherwise attempting invisibility. They, after all, were the ones who had to clean up if trouble struck, so they tended to strive for prevention rather than provocation.

"Get out," the barman told them. "Now."

Sangr paused, surprised.

"No," Gina said. "You're going to serve me a drink. In fact, I'm taking this bottle." She took a bottle of clear liquid, smelled the contents and poured them into two mugs already lined up on the counter.

The man's eyes goggled. "I think you'll probably regret that. Hino owns this place, you know. Only his friends can drink here."

"Tell this Hino guy that he'd better make friends with me very quickly or I'll uproot this whole building and shove it up his ass," Gina growled.

Sangr had to stifle a laugh at the man's expression. Surely no one had ever spoken to him like that before, certainly not while he was under the protection of the great Hino. He wondered idly if Gina could make good on her threat. He wouldn't have put it past her, especially not with a large volcano to siphon power from.

But he also knew the story of what had happened in Hell's Gate. There were limits to how well Gina could control her elementals… and people were still paying the price for her hubris.

A man stood up and walked over to them. His hair was nearly as white as his skin and his eyes were of the watery blue that Sangr had come to associate with the natives of the city.

He smiled, more amused than concerned, and looked Gina up and down. The smile turned to a laugh. "You know, I think you actually would, at that. You'd definitely try, at least. I suppose you're some kind of powerful witch?"

"You suppose right, except I'm a sorceress, not a witch. Witches play around with weeds and try to cure people. I break people who make me angry, and then I break their buildings." She returned his look and allowed her expression to convey precisely how unimpressed she was. "And who are you?"

"I'm Hino," he said. "And I'd really prefer to have you as a friend than… well, let's just say that this is a big building." He didn't seem particularly worried about the threats—more curious as to who the visitors were than anything else. "So, your drinks are on me… with one condition."

Gina tensed. "What might that be?"

"I want to know what you're up to. My one major weakness is that I'm incurably curious."

"No," Gina said, sipping the drink. "Your major defect is that you surround yourself with idiots." She nodded towards the guy behind the bar. "The curiosity is just a dangerous secondary problem."

Hino laughed. "Come on. Let's get you to a table before my staff decides to poison you."

They sat and Sangr tasted the drink. Whatever it was, it burned as it went down. He poured himself another cup. "We're looking for a woman," he said. "Her name is Maluz."

"Yes. She's here," Hino nodded.

"Where?" Sangr's languidity vanished. The faith that had brought them across a continent, into the very frozen reaches of the Ice, was vindicated. There was no real reason for his quarry to actually be in that city… except that he was certain of it. Sangr felt a sense of relief, the knowledge that his quest was nearing its end and that rest would soon be at hand.

Hino peered at him. To that point, he'd been addressing Gina, probably in the belief that the person making threats would likely be the leader of any groups, or at least the spokesperson. "She's north of here. In the labyrinth."

"Of course, she is," Sangr said. "It couldn't be any other way, could it?"

Their host looked puzzled. "What does that mean?"

It meant, Sangr thought, that there was always a labyrinth. Or a cave, or a dungeon or a castle with a million halls. And there was always a monster, or a fabulous treasure, or the world's most alluring woman at the end of it. Just once, he wished the object would walk up to him and tell him to do his worst, preferably in a room with a fireplace somewhere. Maybe they could have a drink and talk about it.

He sighed. "Nothing. I'm just tired, that's all. What can you tell us about this labyrinth?"

"It's north of us. And that means that your girl is hobnobbing with royalty. If you're serious about going after her, be careful. People up there aren't as friendly as we are."

"You must be joking. Do they spit on you as soon as they see you?" Gina asked. She gave the impression of being immersed in her drink, but it was evident that she was following along. "Nah. It would probably freeze before they could hit you." She went back to staring into her cup without waiting for a reply.

Hino sighed. "I guess we do come across as cold, don't we?"

Sangr chuckled. "Friend, the weather is cold. You people are downright unfriendly."

"I guess it might look that way, but we're not, really. It's just that the people in this part of town actually live here all year long. We know about the long nights. We understand that if the buildings weren't illuminated from within, we'd all kill ourselves. Most people are just passing through, looking for the nearest place to drink. And a lot of them take a proprietary view of both anything that isn't nailed down and any woman who doesn't cut them dead. They're mostly sailors."

"But well-to-do sailors. I've never seen such a prosperous town," Sangr noted.

"It's a hard place to get to, albeit a profitable one. The captains know that sailors who are too unruly tend to fail to return, and they crew their ships accordingly."

He let the implications of that pronouncement hang in the air. Sangr knew the place was too good to be true. He'd been to dozens of ports, all rife with sailors drunk, dirty and diseased. The men who peopled the southern reaches of this city, while clearly not nobility, were an incredibly well-behaved bunch. "I suppose you have one hell of a city watch."

"They're not as bloodthirsty as they used to be. They no longer need to kill people as often as they used to, Word gets around. And word about demons with swords gets around even faster."

Suddenly, illumination hit Sangr. "Let me guess. When the demon guardians aren't in use, do they live in the labyrinth by any chance?"

Hino looked surprised. "Why, yes. But I didn't think anyone who knew about that would tell it to a stranger in our city."

"No one told me anything," Sangr said. "But with the way my luck has been going lately, I just knew that would be the answer. They're demons, then?"

"Yes. Red ones. They tend to leave very ugly corpses behind when they get done with people who break the law."

"All right. What else do I need to know about the maze?"

"The labyrinth connects all the buildings in the northern end of the city and there's no other way into the Royal Towers. The guardians can tell at a glance if you belong there or not. If you do, they ignore you. If you don't, they tear you to shreds."

"Of course."

"So, you'll turn back?"

"No. I've come too far to turn back. How did Maluz get in there if it's so damned hard?"

"I have no idea. Do you think the rich and powerful talk to the likes of me?"

"I thought you were rich and powerful."

Hino smiled sadly. "Everything is relative, my friend."

The labyrinth looked almost exactly how Sangr had imagined it. Even in a city of ice, he'd suspected that the thing would be made of stone. It just fit better: a maze of ice just didn't set the right tone of grim inevitability that a trap for unwanted visitors needed. Also, what fun would it be if intruders could see the guardians—whatever those turned out to be—coming towards them? Stone, unlike the strangely crystalline ice of this city, would conceal the horrors nicely.

Sangr sighed and strapped his rapier on more tightly. He decided to get it over with… something told him that, though he wouldn't come back alive from this quest, it would be Maluz who ended him, not some doorman.

"Wait," Gina said. "Do you know what's in there?"

"The man said demons, so I guess it's demons."

"Are you seriously planning to go after them all alone?"

"I was hoping you'd come with me. You've dealt with demons before."

"That didn't go so well."

"You're still in one piece and walking around. I'd say it went much better than you had any right to expect."

"I sold an entire city into demonic slavery and barely made it out alive."

"As I said, you did fine. Most people get eaten. And from what I hear, that was a demon lord… there won't be any of those in here."

"I'll do my best. What most people call demons are just elementals under some kind of compulsion to serve. I can control them. If there are any real demons in there, though, we're probably dead."

"I can live with… wait." Sangr held up a hand. "You know what? I don't want to play by these stupid rules anymore. Yella was always telling me that I would come to my senses someday, and I think that day might have finally come." His expression darkened. "I'm just sad it came too late to do me… to do *her*… any good."

"Er… What?" She looked confused.

"We're not going into the labyrinth. It's what Maluz wants us to do. Even if she thinks we'll make it out the other end, navigating the maze will give her all the warning she needs to get the hell out again and disappear onto a ship or something. I don't want that. I want to catch her with her breeches around her ankles."

"That only works on men," Gina said.

"You don't know Maluz, then. She has the morals of an alley cat. It's not her fault, but I no longer care. She has to die."

"So, what's your plan to find her? There have to be at least three dozen buildings over there, and the only way in is through the dungeon. We'll need to go through and check each one, even if you don't want to."

"No. We won't. In the first place, those buildings are made of ice. How much power do you think a fire elemental would need to burn us a hole in the wall?"

She studied the nearest spire. "Not much, unless they're held up by some kind of really strong magic."

"They're not. I can guarantee that," Sangr said.

"Except you're not an expert on these sorts of things. It would even take me a long time to find any evidence, and I actually know what I'm looking for."

"All I know is that if those towers are held up by magic, they'd fall down as soon as Maluz set foot in one."

Gina looked up at the spires. "That actually makes sense. It's a pity they didn't fall on her. It would have saved us a lot of trouble."

"I want to kill her myself. I'm just glad no one else has decided to slit her throat before now."

"She doesn't sound like she's easy to kill. To start with, she made it through that labyrinth."

"Maluz is no more difficult to kill than anyone else with her training. The only problem is that most people who have to deal with people like her tend to rely on magic. After all, it's much easier to burn an assassin to a crisp with a well-placed magical fireball than it is to fight her with a sword. But I don't have that problem. I am better with a blade than she is."

"We still have to find her, and I'm pretty sure that whoever lives inside these buildings is going to send out the army as soon as we start burning holes in their walls. She isn't going to be easy to find, even if we get the building right on one of the first tries."

"On the contrary. I know exactly where she is, and if we hurry, we won't even need to look for her." He pointed at a building. It happened to be the one building in sight with no color. It was only about two hundred paces away, one of the nearest spires connected to the labyrinth.

"How do you know it's that one?"

"How do you think these buildings get their pretty lights?"

"How should I… you think they're magical?"

"Of course, they are," Sangr said. "How else would you light a tower of ice without melting it? And that one just went out, which means that she just walked in. If we hurry, she won't be able to lose herself too far inside."

The stone walls of the maze were rough-hewn and as jagged as the ice walls were smooth. They had very little difficulty in climbing on top of them and heading towards the unilluminated spire. In fact, the major hurdle facing them seemed to be to avoid sliding off the top once they were up. The snow above the labyrinth was powdery, but hid patches of slippery ice just below the surface. In other places, the snow had accumulated in drifts higher than their chest. They tumbled more than once, but avoided falling back to ground.

"Call up a fire elemental and burn a hole in this wall," Sangr said. "Then get the hell out of here."

They were already starting to attract attention. People were beginning to cluster around the transparent partition, pointing towards the strangers that had appeared outside their tower. The men and women inside weren't dressed in the ubiquitous furs but in blue and purple robes.

"I'm going with you," Gina replied.

"Look. I know you want to come, and I thank you for all your help. I really couldn't have made it this far without you. But I'm not planning on coming back."

Saying it out loud made him understand that death had been his objective from the beginning. He would kill Maluz in here and then he would succumb to the tender mercies of the Royal Guard. Death by palace troops was a fate that he almost considered natural causes. It was the way he was sure he'd go. But it had always seemed to him that the day of death was always a little further away, that no matter how bleak things looked, there would be a way to escape the closing jaws of doom.

But then he'd always wanted to. Not today. Today, he would welcome the blade of the guardsman that managed to get through his defenses. He would watch his own blood flow and freeze on the icy floor and sense the stopping of his heart. He would watch his breath, visible since they'd walked onto the ice, slowly disappear again.

Of course, he'd take as many of them with him as he possibly could. He had a reputation to maintain after all. But if a chance for escape presented itself, he wouldn't take it.

"I know," Gina said. "I've known since you told me you were coming after her."

"Do you want to die with me? I don't want you to die for me."

"I'm pretty hard to kill. But if you do happen to die, I will be there to watch. The very least I can do is to take your story back to civilization with me. That way, people won't have to wonder what happened to the great Sangr."

She didn't give him an opportunity to protest. Evidently, she'd been busy while they were talking, and she had an elemental under her control. The wall hissed and bubbled and, with a minimum of fuss, a round hole appeared in the ice in front of them. The people who'd hitherto been observing with interest suddenly began to shout in alarm and, Sangr imagined, to call for the nearest troops.

He jumped into the building with rapier drawn and the crowd scattered, men and women alike screeching for deliverance. He gave Gina a wry look. "I don't think they really want to fight."

"Yeah, until their reinforcements arrive. We need to find this girl and do something about her. Which way is she?"

Sangr checked. The walls of the building were still uncolored. He looked up, but there was a crowd on the floor directly above them, and he didn't know

Maluz well enough to recognize her by the soles of her shoes. "We'll have to go have a look."

He ran to the central stairs, slipping all over the ice. He wondered why the royals didn't use carpeting on their floors. Yes, it would become wet with time, but surely there was some way to avoid that? The only place where any concessions to the fact that people were using the city were made seemed to be in the bed chambers. And there, only the beds themselves had any kind of covering on them. Was the transparency of the city really that important? Or was there another reason for the unhealthy fascination with seeing everything that went on inside?

Still, he reasoned, this time, the strangeness of the terrain actually worked in their favor. Sangr took the steps two at a time; if he fell, he would get back up.

His rapier, visible to all, opened up a corridor among the people on the next floor up, but Maluz was nowhere to be seen. The nice thing about looking for this particular woman was that she couldn't disguise herself with magic. She could wear a hood, or a mask, or elaborate makeup, but doing so would only call attention to her: no one else was thus concealed.

He took to the stairs again. She had to be in the building.

The next floor was nearly empty. A large, cleared expanse with a raised dais at one end was the very picture of a ballroom, but the empty floor was devoid of revelers. The few people crossing it to get to the next flight were not his quarry.

The next two floors also proved fruitless, but the third was more promising. A banquet hall dominated by four long tables—made of wood, probably to keep the food from growing immediately cold—at which dozens of people were taking a meal. Half of them were women, and many had the long dark hair that could easily belong to Maluz.

Sangr began to check each in turn when he felt Gina tugging his arm. "Look at that," she said.

At first, he couldn't tell what she might be referring to. She appeared to be pointing at the transparent wall. Then he realized that the ice that stood between the banquet hall and the frigid air outside had turned a lovely shade of salmon.

"Damn," Sangr spat. "She must have seen us and left." He turned back in the direction of the stairs. "Check to see which of the other buildings loses its color!"

They slid down three flights but before they could make the level where they'd left their exit hole, they encountered a group of spearmen.

"We'll need to leave through the wall," Sangr said.

"Way ahead of you," Gina responded with a smirk. The wall beside the stairs was already beginning to seethe.

As soon as the hole was big enough to admit him, Sangr jumped through, yanking his companion along with him.

"Wait—" Gina began, but then they landed on the snow below. A big drift cushioned most of the fall and he yanked her to her feet. She seemed to want to say something.

"Not now. Spears can be thrown, and downwards just makes it easier for them." He tugged her around the side of the spire, out of range of the men peering through the hole they'd just tumbled from.

"All right," Sangr said. "Now we need to try to spot the next building to go out."

"She'll just run from us again."

He shrugged. "I don't have any better ideas."

"I do. Look."

A single line of footprints, clearly visible in the fresh snow, led away from the hole that Sangr and Gina had made to enter the tower. Someone had left that way. About three hundred paces away, a dark figure could be seen hurrying northwards.

Sangr didn't even bother to wonder if it really was Maluz. He ground his teeth and set off after her as fast as the treacherous footing permitted.

Gina, beside him kept up a running commentary. "She's heading towards the mountain. I wonder why she would do that?"

And a few moments later. "If she's immune to magic, maybe she thinks that a place full of elementals will be more dangerous to you than to her. She's a smart one, this Maluz of yours, isn't she?"

"Utterly brilliant. If her mind hadn't been warped by her upbringing, she would be the subject of admiration all across the plains: smart, beautiful and impervious to magic. She'd probably be the supreme tyrant of everything by now."

"Well, you have to admit that her upbringing was messed up."

He actually stopped. "Yes. I admit that. But wasn't yours?"

"I didn't turn out that well."

"How many of your friends have you killed."

"I've killed a lot of people, Sangr."

"I know that. I asked how many of your friends? How many people who showed you kindness and loyalty have you butchered in cold blood?"

"I never felt the need to do so, that's all."

Sangr chuckled. "Yeah, I can imagine. You have a heart of stone. That's why you followed me all the way up here even though you know I'm determined to die in the process."

"It just seems like a waste," Gina replied, but Sangr noticed that she looked away when she said it.

"Sure. Well in her case, it's not a question. Maluz has killed—or tried to kill—everyone who ever did anything for her."

"Except for you."

"She thinks I'm the key to her freedom. She hasn't realized that her prison is inside her own mind."

"And you won't give her that chance. Because she killed Yella."

Sangr set off again. "Yella isn't dead. If all she'd done was to kill her, I might have let this go. But Yella is out there somewhere." He gestured at the space around them. "I don't know if she can see what I'm doing. I don't even really know if she'd approve of it. But the one thing I do know is that, if she can see me, she will know that I still remember her, and that, approve or not, I fought for her to the last breath."

Gina mumbled something too softly for Sangr to hear and they trudged through the snow.

The first elemental hit them at the base of the volcano. The warmth coming up through the earth itself had melted most of the snow to reveal a dusty slope covered in broken bits of flat rock. The footing was even more treacherous than it had been on the ice.

A screaming, screeching fireball approached from the upslope direction, flinging sparks behind it.

Sangr dropped to the ground, but Gina just stopped and sighed. She held up a hand and the flame-colored creature halted its advance. The fireball became a red shadow in which the vague shape of a tiny creature could be seen. Gina snapped her fingers at it impatiently and it disappeared with a tiny wail.

"Did you destroy it?"

"Nah, just banished it to the bottom of the caldera. It will take ages to fight its way back up… assuming one of the bigger elementals doesn't have it for lunch. The others should leave us alone now. Well, unless there's a really big one around here."

"What do we do if there's a really big one?"

"I'll try to stop it, but I'd advise you to run like hell."

They trudged up the loose grey rock, some kind of dust-colored stone. Vapor drifted up from the edge of the crater.

"Where's she going?" he grunted.

"How should I know? She's your obsession."

They reached the edge. Down, perhaps fifty paces below a flat dust-covered plain greeted them. Occasional fumaroles spewed noxious steam into the air, but those seemed to be concentrated towards the center of the crater.

"Where's the lava?"

"Under that rock. This volcano is not about to erupt any time soon," Gina said with a certainty that Sangr had to admire. If it did go, they would be torn to dust.

A quarter of the way across the crater the dark figure stood facing them. Even at this distance, Sangr could see that she'd drawn her sword. He smiled; what better place could there possibly be for a desperate fight to the death?

He advanced slowly, savoring the moment. The end of months of chase, of more than a year's hopeless desperation, came down to these few moments. Swordplay often seemed eternal when you were struggling for your life, but he knew that few fights ever lasted more than a few minutes—if that.

He stood before her, no more than four or five steps separating him from the object of his rage. "Hello, Maluz," he said. "I've come to kill you."

She sighed. "I knew you would. I knew you'd regret letting me go that day. I saw it in your eyes. Only habit, the habit of helping people like me and not hurting women if you could help it kept you back, didn't it?"

"Maybe. But I also heard what you did to Hemery. And to the people they sent after you. Abren talked quite a bit before I ended his suffering."

"I had no choice. They wanted to lock me up again."

"You could have left at any time. There was no need to kill anyone."

"I wanted to. But Hemery caught me packing. It was easier that way."

"Easier."

Color touched her cheeks, a sneer marred her perfect, delicate features. "Do you know what your problem is, Sangr? You were born free, so you've never understood what it's like to belong to someone, to know that every single second of your life is available in service to the pleasure of some sweating pig of a king who hasn't bathed in six months."

"Hemery wasn't like that. He was a good man who married you because you asked him to."

"What difference does that make? Being a queen, even his queen, was just another cage. I was a slave to the whims of everyone in Summerland. I almost preferred life in the Harem."

"And afterwards? A bunch of maids and retainers murdered horribly. Were they really a threat?"

"They had soldiers with them. I couldn't kill just the soldiers. The magic I had with me wouldn't allow that." She gave him a pleading look, all big wet eyes and pouty lips. It was a look that would have worked on any man but Sangr. "Can't you see? They wanted to take me back. They wanted to put me in the cage again."

"They were your friends."

"I thought you were my friend, too."

"I was. And I would have helped you if you'd come to me. But you had to take Yella."

"She would never have let me near you again. She hated me."

"Maybe she just saw the truth before I did. Pity she didn't know you were coming. She'd have spotted your intentions miles away. Probably have had your liver on a spike." He shook his head. "You know the worst part about it, the very worst? I would have been angry at her if she'd hurt you. Angry. I wouldn't have been able to see that you're just a snake in the grass and I would have tried to stop her. But I think that, just this once, she wouldn't have listened to me."

Sangr shrugged out of the voluminous fur he wore and drew his rapier. "So, I'm going to finish what she never got a chance to start."

Maluz raised her own blade, dropping her overcoat to the ground. "I'm not going to roll over and die easily, Sangr."

He smiled. "I'm glad to hear it."

It was like a sparring session. She'd been taught well, all the formal tricks and parries and ripostes. She would have given an indifferent swordsman— one of the Favored, for example—fits.

But Sangr was not an indifferent swordsman. As soon as the first few blows were exchanged, he knew that she was a dead woman. He let her fight desperately, not doing anything that any of a thousand sparring partners before him wouldn't have done. He let her think that they were evenly matched, observing but not exploiting a dozen small mistakes that would have allowed him to gut her like a fish.

He didn't want to kill her quickly. He wanted her to realize that she was overmatched. Wanted her to feel the dread of oncoming death, to know that he was toying with her as her arm tired.

Lazily, almost casually, he bent in closer and turned a straight thrust into a slash at the last moment. A cut appeared in her white tunic and blood soaked the cloth. He'd cut the bottom of her right breast. He knew how proud of them Maluz was.

He parried a little more, letting her realize that perfect beauty was no longer hers. Even if she lived, a cut that deep would leave a nasty scar—a scar that no magician would be able to remove.

He targeted her face next. The first cut marred her cheek, the next removed the tip of her nose. He chuckled at that one.

But Maluz was beyond caring about her looks. Her eyes were wide, scared, showing too much white. She knew.

So Sangr stopped cutting things off. He didn't want new pain to distract her from the fact that, right here, right now, she was breathing her last. The metallic sound of blade against blade and the labored breathing of the combatants was the only sound to be heard.

"Enough," Sangr said. He took a step forward and took her blade hand in a firm grip. He squeezed savagely and the sword fell to the floor. Then he dragged her to the edge and looked her straight in the eye. "Goodbye Maluz. This should set you free. It will set us both free."

"No, please…"

Sangr didn't listen. He took the last step and they both fell from the precipice in a shower of loose rock. Maluz screamed and pushed him away, tumbling out of his reach. He'd expected them to fall together. The ground would powder their bones, burst their soft organs like so much overripe fruit. Their blood would pool together.

But even in this, Maluz seemed determined to foil him. She tumbled into the distance and somehow managed to gain ground on him, falling much faster. She hit the ground long before him. Her body bounced as she hit, and then fell back to the rock, broken, bloody and deflated. In death there was no sign of her otherworldly beauty. She was just so much meat.

Sangr closed his eyes and waited for the impact. It seemed to be taking much too long. He had time to wonder if Yella was watching from wherever she was. He wondered if she was all right.

Then peace came over him. Of course, she would be all right. She was Yella…. Everyone else in the strange universe where Abren had exiled her needed to worry: Yella was a force of nature. She would be perfectly fine.

And now he'd avenged her.

The ground hit him hard, and his thoughts stopped.

Pain. Disorientation and pain.

Those sensations warred with the certainty that he shouldn't be feeling any pain. He was dead. Pain was a thing for the living.

"Oh, thank the spirits. You're all right."

He thought he should recognize the voice. It was a woman's voice. Yella?

No. Not Yella. Yella was gone.

"Gina?" he whispered hoarsely. "Did you die as well?"

"You're not dead. You just took a nasty bump to the head, that's all."

"But Maluz…"

"Yeah, she got crushed good. Wish I'd been able to see her before. The way she looks now, I can't really say what all the fuss was about."

"If… then how…" It was getting easier to speak, but his thoughts were still proving difficult to marshal.

"When a sorceress decides you're not going to die, it's better to believe her. Although I'd forgotten about that damned amulet of yours. I had to put everything I had and call in every air elemental for leagues around to keep you from hitting the ground too hard. And even then, I thought I'd failed. You took a good wallop."

"Yeah, I can tell."

There was a long silence. Sangr tried to open his eyes, but it hurt too much. He simply settled down and waited for Gina to continue talking as he tried to take stock of how he felt. Nothing broken, he thought, although everything seemed bruised and scraped. He flexed his left leg and was rewarded with searing pain… but the leg moved.

"It's customary to thank someone who just saved your life."

"You know I wanted to die," he replied.

"Well, if that's the way you feel about it, just roll into the nearest fumarole. The gases will kill you even if the heat doesn't."

He heard footsteps moving away.

"No. Wait." The stomping stopped and he heard her coming back. "Thank you."

He opened his eyes and found Gina kneeling beside him. Her eyes, so often guarded and unreadable, were moist. A tear tracked down the dust caked on her face.

"I'm glad you're here. I'm glad I'm alive," he said. Then, with an effort, he raised his hand to her neck and pulled her face close. He kissed her, not long, not with any passion—he hurt too much to give her the kiss she deserved, the one he now realized he'd wanted to give her since he'd run into her in the treasure room—but it was a lingering, warm kiss that, he hoped, promised her more when the time came.

She returned it with enough heat to let him know what she felt, but soon pulled back. She was still crying. "What about Yella?"

He smiled. "She's gone, and she can take care of herself. I won't worry about her anymore."

"Promise?"

"I'll try."

She thought about it. "I guess that will have to do for now. So, what next?"

"I've always wanted to see the western continent. A long sea journey is just what I need for my body to mend, and I don't think the royal family will let us stay in their city very long." He smiled at her. "Do you think we'll have favorable winds?"

She returned his smile. "Yes, I think I can manage that… if you lose that stupid amulet."

He rested his head on the rock again. Maluz had been right about one thing, at least: freedom was worth paying almost any price for.